青詩明理思千載
古今抒情詩三百首
漢英對照

llel Reading of 300 Ancient and Modern Chinese Lyrical Poems：
Qing Dynasty （Chinese-English）

著者：林明理　Author：Dr. Lin Ming-Li
譯者：張智中　Translator：Prof. Zhang Zhizhong

著者簡介
About the Author & Poet

學者詩人林明理博士〈1961-〉,臺灣雲林縣人,法學碩士、榮譽文學博士。她曾任教於大學,是位詩人評論家,擅長繪畫及攝影,著有詩集,散文、詩歌評論等文學專著35本書,包括在義大利合著的譯詩集4本。其詩作被翻譯成法語、西班牙語、義大利語、俄語及英文等多種,作品發表於報刊及學術期刊等已達兩千四百餘篇。中國學刊物包括《南京師範大學文學院學報》等多篇。

Dr. Lin Mingli (1961-), poet and scholar, born in Yunlin County, Taiwan, Master of Law, honorary Ph. D. in literature. She once taught at a university and is a poetry critic, and she is good at painting and photography. She is the author of 35 literary books, including poetry collections, prose, and poetry reviews, as well as a collection of translated poems co-authored and published in Italy. Her poems have been translated into French, Spanish, Italian, Russian and English, etc., and over 2,400 poems and articles have been published in newspapers and academic journals.

清詩明理思千載
古今抒情詩三百首
漢英對照

©林明理專書 monograph、義大利出版的中英譯詩合著
Chinese-English Poetry Co-author published in Italy
© Lin Ming-Li's monographs and co-authored Chinese-English Poetry collections published in Italy

1. 《秋收的黃昏》*The evening of autumn*。高雄市：春暉出版社，2008。ISBN 978-986-695-045-2
2. 《夜櫻－林明理詩畫集》*Cherry Blossoms at Night* 高雄市：春暉出版社，2009。ISBN 978-986-695-068-9
3. 《新詩的意象與內涵－當代詩家作品賞析》*The Imagery and Connetation of New Poetry －A Collection of Critical Poetry Analysis*。臺北市：文津出版社，2010。ISBN 978-957-688-913-0
4. 《藝術與自然的融合－當代詩文評論集》*The Fusion Of Art and Nature*。臺北市：文史哲出版社，2011。ISBN 978-957-549-966-2
5. 《山楂樹》*Hawthorn Poems* by Lin Mingli（林明理詩集）。臺北市：文史哲出版社，2011。ISBN 978-957-549-975-4
6. 《回憶的沙漏》*Sandglass Of Memory*（中英對照譯詩集）英譯：吳鈞。臺北市：秀威出版社，2012。ISBN 978-986-221-900-3
7. 《湧動著一泓清泉—現代詩文評論》*A Gushing Spring-A Collection Of Comments On Modern Literary Works*。臺北市：文史哲出版社，2012。ISBN 978-986-314-024-5
8. 《清雨塘》*Clear Rain Pond*（中英對照譯詩集）英譯：吳鈞。臺北市：文史哲出版社，2012。ISBN 978-986-314-076-4
9. 《用詩藝開拓美—林明理讀詩》*Developing Beauty Though The Art Of Poetry－Lin Mingli On Poetry*。臺北市：秀威出版社，2013。ISBN 978-986-326-059-2
10. 《海頌－林明理詩文集》*Hymn To the Ocean*（poems and Essays）。臺北市：文史哲出版社，2013。ISBN 978-986-314-119-8

著者簡介

11. 《林明理報刊評論 1990-2000》Published Commentaries 1990-2000。文史哲出版社，2013。ISBN 978-986-314-155-6
12. 《行走中的歌者－林明理談詩》The Walking singer －Ming-Li Lin On Poetry。臺北市：文史哲出版社，2013。ISBN 978-986-314-156-3
13. 《山居歲月》Days in the Mountains（中英對照譯詩集）英譯：吳鈞。臺北市：文史哲出版社，2015。ISBN 978-986-314-252-2
14. 《夏之吟》Summer Songs（中英法譯詩集）。英譯：馬為義（筆名：非馬）(Dr. William Marr)。法譯：阿薩納斯・薩拉西（Athanase Vantchev de Thracy）。法國巴黎：索倫紮拉文化學院（The Cultural Institute of Solenzara），2015。ISBN 978-2-37356-020-6
15. 《默喚》Silent Call（中英法譯詩集）。英譯：諾頓・霍奇斯（Norton Hodges）。法譯：阿薩納斯・薩拉西（Athanase Vantchev de Thracy）。法國巴黎：索倫紮拉文化學院（The Cultural Institute of Solenzara），2016。ISBN 978-2-37356-022-0
16. 《林明理散文集》Lin Ming Li's Collected essays。臺北市：文史哲出版社，2016。ISBN 978-986-314-291-1
17. 《名家現代詩賞析》Appreciation of the work of Famous Modern Poets。臺北市：文史哲出版社，2016。ISBN 978-986-314-302-4
18. 《我的歌 My Song》，法譯：Athanase Vantchev de Thracy 中法譯詩集。臺北市：文史哲出版社，2017。ISBN 978-986-314-359-8
19. 《諦聽 Listen》，中英對照詩集，英譯：馬為義（筆名：非馬）(Dr. William Marr)，臺北市：文史哲出版社，2018。ISBN 978-986-314-401-4
20. 《現代詩賞析》，Appreciation of the work of Modern Poets，臺北市：文史哲出版社，2018。ISBN 978-986-314-412-0

21. 《原野之聲》Voice of the Wilderness，英譯：馬為義（筆名：非馬）（Dr. William Marr），臺北市：文史哲出版社，2019。ISBN 978-986-314-453-3
22. 《思念在彼方　散文暨新詩》，Longing over the other side（prose and poetry），臺北市：文史哲出版社，2020。ISBN 978-986-314-505-9
23. 《甜蜜的記憶（散文暨新詩)》，Sweet memories（prose and poetry），臺北市：文史哲出版社，2021。ISBN 978-986-314-555-4
24. 《詩河（詩評、散文暨新詩)》，The Poetic River（Poetry review, prose and poetry），臺北市：文史哲出版社，2022。ISBN 978-986-314-603-2
25. 《庫爾特·F·斯瓦泰克，林明理，喬凡尼·坎皮西詩選》（中英對照）Carmina Selecta (Selected Poems) by Kurt F. Svatek, Lin Mingli, Giovanni Campisi，義大利：Edizioni Universum（埃迪采恩尼大學），宇宙出版社，2023.01。
26. 《紀念達夫尼斯和克洛伊》（中英對照）詩選 In memory of Daphnis and Chloe，作者：Renza Agnelli，Sara Ciampi，Lin Mingli 林明理，義大利：Edizioni Universum（埃迪采恩尼大學），宇宙出版社，書封面，林明理畫作（聖母大殿），2023.02。
27. 《詩林明理古今抒情詩一六〇首》（漢英對照）Parallel Reading of 160 Classical and New Chinese Lyrical Poems (Chinese-English)，英譯：張智中，臺北市：文史哲出版社，2023.04。ISBN 978-986-314-637-5
28. 《愛的讚歌》（詩評、散文暨新詩》Hymn Of Love（Poetry review, prose and poetry），臺北市：文史哲出版社，2023.05。ISBN 978-986-314-638-4
29. 《埃內斯托·卡漢，薩拉·錢皮，林明理和平詩選》（義英對照）（Italian-English），Carmina Selecta (Selected Poems) by Ernesto Kahan, Sara Ciampi, Lin Mingli Peace-Pace，義大利：Edizioni Universum（埃迪采恩尼大學），宇宙出版社，2023.11。ISBN 978-889-980-379-7

6

30. 《祈禱與工作》，中英義詩集，Ora Et Labora Trilogia di Autori Trilingue: Italiano, Cinese, Inglese 作者的三語三部曲：義大利語、中文、英語 Trilingual Trilogy of Authors: Italian, Chinese, English，作者：奧內拉・卡布奇尼 Ornella Cappuccini，非馬 William Marr，林明理 Lin Mingli，義大利，宇宙出版社，2024.06。
31. 《名家抒情詩評賞》（漢英對照）Appraisal of Lyric Poems by Famous Artists，張智中教授英譯，臺北市：文史哲出版社，2024.06。ISBN 978-986-314-675-9
32. 《山的沉默》Silence of the Mountains，散文集，臺北市：文史哲出版社，2024.09。ISBN 978-986-314-685-8
33. 《宋詩明理接千載——古今抒情詩三百首》（漢英對照）Parallel Reading of 300 Ancient and Modern Chinese Lyrical Poems (Chinese-English)，臺中市：天空數位圖書出版，2024.10，ISBN 978-626-7576-00-7
34. 《元詩明理接千載——古今抒情詩三百首》（漢英對照）Parallel Reading of 300 Ancient and Modern Chinese Lyrical Poems (Chinese-English) :Jin, Yuan, and Ming Dynasties，臺中市：天空數位圖書出版，2024.11，ISBN 978-626-7576-02-1，ISBN 978-626-7576-03-8（彩圖版）
35. 《清詩明理思千載——古今抒情詩三百首》（漢英對照）Parallel Reading of 300 Ancient and Modern Chinese Lyrical Poems: Qing Dynasty (Chinese-English)，臺中市：天空數位圖書出版，2025.01，ISBN 978-626-7576-08-3
36. 《清詩明理思千載——古今抒情詩三百首》（漢英對照）Parallel Reading of 300 Ancient and Modern Chinese Lyrical Poems: Qing Dynasty (Chinese-English)，臺中市：天空數位圖書出版，2025.01，ISBN 978-626-7576-09-0（彩圖版）

清詩明理思千載
古今抒情詩三百首
漢英對照

由理是畫家詩人,有敏銳的藝術洞察力并深知藝術創作的內蘊,因而從事詩論寫作便游刃有余,初中肯綮,祝賀她又一部詩論集出版以饗廣大讀者。
山東大學 吳開晉
二〇一六.元月

©山東大學中文系吳開晉教授(1934-2019)於 2016 年元月贈予著者林明理墨寶。

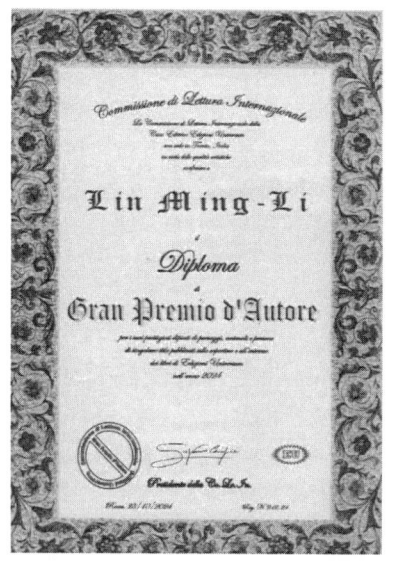

©2024.10.23 獲頒義大利國際閱讀委員會獎狀兩張,林明理著作《名家抒情詩評賞》Appreciation of Lyrical Poems by famous Poems,以及繪畫文憑 Diploma。

譯者簡介
About the Author & Translator

　　張智中，天津市南開大學外國語學院教授、博士研究生導師、翻譯系主任，中國翻譯協會理事，中國英漢語比較研究會典籍英譯專業委員會副會長，天津師範大學跨文化與世界文學研究院兼職教授，世界漢學·文學中國研究會理事兼英文秘書長，天津市比較文學學會理事，第五屆天津市人民政府學位委員會評議組成員、專業學位教育指導委員會委員，國家社科基金專案通訊評審專家和結項鑒定專家，天津外國語大學中央文獻翻譯研究基地兼職研究員，《國際詩歌翻譯》季刊客座總編，《世界漢學》英文主編，《中國當代詩歌導讀》編委會成員，中國當代詩歌獎評委等。已出版編、譯、著120餘部，發表學術論文130餘篇，曾獲翻譯與科研多種獎項。漢詩英譯多走向國外，獲國際著名詩人和翻譯家的廣泛好評。譯詩觀：但為傳神，不拘其形，散文筆法，詩意內容；將漢詩英譯提高到英詩的高度。

Zhang Zhizhong is professor, doctoral supervisor and dean of the Translation Department of the School of Foreign Studies, Nankai University which is located in Tianjin; meanwhile, he is director of Translators' Association of China, vice chairman of the Committee for English Translation of Chinese Classics of the Association for Comparative Studies of English and Chinese, part-time professor of Cross-Culture & World Literature Academy of Tianjin Normal University, director and English secretary-general of World Sinology Literary China Seminar, director of Tianjin Comparative Literature Society, member of Tianjin Municipal Government Academic Degree Committee, member of Tianjin Municipal Government Professional Degree Education Guiding Committee, expert for the approval and evaluation of projects funded by the National Social Science Foundation of China, part-time researcher at the Central Literature Translation Research Base of Tianjin Foreign Studies University, guest editor of *Rendition of International Poetry*, English editor-in-chief of *World Sinology*, member of the editing board of *Guided Reading Series in Contemporary Chinese Poetry*, and member of the Board for Contemporary Chinese Poetry Prizes. He has published more than 120 books and 130 academic papers, and he has won a host of prizes in translation and academic research. His English translation of Chinese poetry is widely acclaimed throughout the world, and is favorably reviewed by international poets and translators. His view on poetry translation: spirit over form, prose enjambment to rewrite Chinese poetry into sterling English poetry.

著者暨編譯者導言
Introduction by the Compiler-Translator

　　學者詩人林明理從她自己所感覺到的與對清詩閱讀的經驗回憶裡進行篩選、組合，欲使其創作的詩歌加在編譯的清詩之後，以期望讀者更貼近地感覺和瞭解詩美的世界。而我認為，若能讓清詩和現代詩研究同步相輔相成，讓翻譯詩歌的涵義變得更生動活潑，以趨使學生對欣賞詩歌與研讀上產生了更大的興趣，這是此書最重要的價值，也可以加深閱讀時的感性和體悟，這也是我的期許。

張智中教授
於 2025 年 01 月於南開大學外國語學院翻譯系

　　Lin Ming-Li, as a scholar-poet of Taiwan, is a great lover of poetry, and she selects her own poems to be paired up with the quatrains by Chinese poets of Jin, Yuan, and Ming dynasties, which have similar themes or sentiments, in order for readers to appreciate more thoroughly the beauty of poetry. It is my belief that, if the reading and translation of both ancient Chinese poems and modern Chinese poems can be undertaken simultaneously, the understanding of poetry will be deepened, and poetry translation will be more flexible through enlivening — and the readers' interest in poetry, hopefully, will be greatly heightened.

Zhang Zhizhong
January, 2025
Translation Department of the School of Foreign Studies,
Nankai University

藝術之藝術，詞藻之神采，以及文學之光華皆寓於純樸之中。

──美國詩人沃爾特・惠特曼
（Walt Whitman，1819 年-1892 年）

The art of art, the glory of expression and the sunshine of the light of letters, is simplicity.

— By Walt Whitman (1819-1892), American poet

清詩明理思千載
古今抒情詩三百首
漢英對照

目錄
Table of Contents

1. 留題秦淮丁家水閣二首（其二）（錢謙益）Inscriptions on the Water Pavilion of the Ding Family (No. 2) (Qian Qianyi)
永安溪，我的愛（林明理）Yong'an Stream, My Love (Lin Ming-Li)·················· 28
2. 詠同心蘭四絕句（其三）（錢謙益）Ode to the Orchid Flower (No. 3) (Qian Qianyi)
在風中，寫你的名字（林明理）To Write Your Name in the Wind (Lin Ming-Li) ·················· 29
3. 西湖（柳如是）The West Lake (Liu Rushi)
在醉月湖的寧靜中（林明理）In the Quietude of the Drunken Moon Lake (Lin Ming-Li) ·················· 30
4. 與兒子雍（金聖歎）To My Son Upon My Death (Jin Shengtan)
寫給小女莫莉（林明理）To My Little Daughter Molly (Lin Ming-Li)·················· 32
5. 臨別口號遍謝彌天大人謬知我者（金聖歎）To My Readers Upon My Death (Jin Shengtan)
在福爾摩沙島嶼之間——緬懷曹永和院士（林明理）Between the Islands of Formosa: In Memory of Academician Cao Yonghe (Lin Ming-Li) ·················· 34
6. 阻雪（吳偉業）Snowed In (Wu Weiye)
張家界之夢（林明理）The Dream of Zhangjiajie (Lin Ming-Li)·················· 36
7. 塞下曲（顧炎武）A Border Song (Gu Yanwu)
我怎能停止為你而歌（林明理）How Can I Stop Singing for You (Lin Ming-Li) ·················· 40
8. 舟中見獵犬有感（宋琬）Inspired at the Sight of a Hound in the Boat (Song Wan)
冥想——致詩人穆旦（林明理）Meditation: to Mu Dan as a Poet (Lin Ming-Li) ·················· 42

14

目錄

9. 上巳將過金陵（龔鼎孳）Passing by the Ancient Town of Jinling (Gong Dingzi)
你的影跡在每一次思潮之上（林明理）Your Shadow Is Over Every Thought (Lin Ming-Li) ································ 44
10. 自題桃花楊柳圖（顧媚）Self-Inscription on a Painting of Peach Flowers & Willow Trees (Gu Mei)
夜思（林明理）Night Thoughts (Lin Ming-Li) ················ 46
11. 雪中閣望（施閏章）Snowy Landscape Seen from a Pavilion (Shi Runzhang)
冬季的旅行（林明理）Winter Journey (Lin Ming-Li) ·········· 48
12. 悼亡四首（其一）（王夫之）Lament for My Deceased Wife (No. 1) (Wang Fuzhi)
憶（林明理）Recollection (Lin Ming-Li) ························ 50
13. 客發苕溪（葉燮）Homeward Sailing on Shaoxi River (Ye Xie)
我的波斯菊（林明理）My Mexican Aster (Lin Ming-Li) ······ 52
14. 來青軒雪（朱彝尊）Snowing Over the Green Pavilion (Zhu Yizun)
每當黃昏飄進窗口（林明理）Whenever the Evening Drifts Into the Window (Lin Ming-Li) ································ 54
15. 花前（屈大均）Before the Flowers (Qu Dajun)
松林中的風聲（林明理）The Wind in the Pines (Lin Ming-Li)·· 57
16. 再過露筋祠（王士禎）Once More Passing by the Virgin's Temple (Wang Shizhen)
你是一株半開的青蓮（林明理）You Are a Half-Blossoming Green Lotus (Lin Ming-Li) ·· 58
17. 秦淮雜詩（王士禎）On Qinhuai River (Wang Shizhen)
自由（林明理）Freedom (Lin Ming-Li) ·························· 61
18. 次韻答王司寇阮亭先生見贈（蒲松齡）Reply to Wang Shizhen (Pu Songling)
吾友張智中教授（林明理）To Professor Zhang Zhizhong as My Friend (Lin Ming-Li) ·· 62
19. 客愁（洪昇）Homesickness (Hong Sheng)
佳節又重陽（林明理）The Double Ninth Festival (Lin Ming-Li)· 63

20. 北固山看大江（孔尚任）The Great River Seen from the Northern Mountain (Kong Shangren)
    秋在白沙屯（林明理）Autumn in Baishatun (Lin Ming-Li) … 65
21. 《桃花扇傳奇》題辭（陳宇王）Inscription On *Legend of Peach Blossom Fan* (Chen Yuwang)
    勇氣──祝賀川普總統（Donald Trump）Courage: Congratulations to President Donald Trump (Lin Ming-Li) … 67
22. 青溪口號（查慎行）Improvised on the Blue River (Zha Shenxing)
    二層坪水橋之歌（林明理）Song of the Two-Floor Flat Water Bridge (Lin Ming-Li) … 69
23. 秣陵懷古（納蘭性德）Cherishing the Past in the Old Capital (Nalan Xingde)
    華夏龍脈雕塑群（林明理）Chinese Dragon Vein Sculpture Group (Lin Ming-Li) … 71
24. 過許州（沈德潛）Passing by Xuzhou (Shen Deqian)
    獻給青龍峽的歌（林明理）A Song Dedicated to Qinglong Gorge (Lin Ming-Li) … 73
25. 柳（金農）The Drooping Willow (Jin Nong)
    在四月桐的夢幻邊緣（林明理）On the Edge of the Fond Dream of April Parasol Tree (Lin Ming-Li) … 76
26. 湖樓題壁（厲鶚）Inscription on the Wall of a Lakeside Pavilion (Li E)
    七星潭之戀（林明理）Love of the Seven-Star Pool (Lin Ming-Li) … 78
27. 竹石（鄭燮）A Bamboo Biting in the Rock (Zheng Xie)
    通海秀山行（林明理）Journey to the Fair Mountain in Tonghai County (Lin Ming-Li) … 79
28. 濰縣署中畫竹（鄭燮）Written on a Painting of Bamboo (Zheng Xie)
    敘利亞內戰悲歌（林明理）Dirge for the Syrian Civil War (Lin Ming-Li) … 83
29. 聞蛙（倪瑞璿）Croaking Frogs (Ni Ruixuan)
    夜裡聽到礁脈（林明理）The Reef Is Heard at Night (Lin Ming-Li) … 85

目錄

30. 馬嵬（袁枚）Concubine Yang (Yuan Mei)
    昨夜下了一場雨（林明理）It Has Rained Last Night
    (Lin Ming-Li) ··· 87
31. 遣興（袁枚）Inspired on Poetry Composition (Yuan Mei)
    感謝在我身邊（林明理）Thanks for Being Here With Me
    (Lin Ming-Li) ··· 88
32. 雞（袁枚）The Chicken (Yuan Mei)
    哈特曼山斑馬（林明理）Equus Zebra Hartmannae (Lin Ming-Li) · 90
33. 推窗（袁枚）Upon Opening the Window (Yuan Mei)
    無論是過去或現在（林明理）In the Past or at the Present
    (Lin Ming-Li) ··· 92
34. 富春至嚴陵山水甚佳（其一）（紀昀）Journeying Along the
    River Fair with Hills (No. 1) (Ji Yun)
    昨夜，在五岩山醉人的夢幻裡（林明理）Last Night, in the
    Fond Dream of Wuyan Mountain (Lin Ming-Li) ···················· 94
35. 富春至嚴陵山水甚佳（其二）（紀昀）Journeying Along the
    River Fair with Hills (No. 2) (Ji Yun)
    在彼淇河（林明理）By the Qi River (Lin Ming-Li) ············· 96
36. 題畫（蔣士銓）Inscription on a Painting (Jiang Shiquan)
    重遊石門水庫（林明理）Once More to Shimen Reservoi
    (Lin Ming-Li) ··· 99
37. 論詩（趙翼）On Poetry Writing (Zhao Yi)
    清雨塘（林明理）Limpid Rain Pond (Lin Ming-Li) ············ 101
38. 野步（趙翼）Ambling in the Wilderness (Zhao Yi)
    獻給湯顯祖之歌（林明理）A Song Dedicated to Tang Xianzu,
    Shakespeare in China (Lin Ming-Li)································· 102
39. 江上竹枝詞（其四）（姚鼐）Bamboo Branch Song on the
    River (No. 4) (Yao Nai)
    書寫王功漁港（林明理）On Wanggong Fishing Port
    (Lin Ming-Li) ·· 105
40. 別老母（黃景仁）Parting With My Old Mother
    (Huang Jingren)
    蘿蔔糕（林明理）Turnip Pudding (Lin Ming-Li) ·············· 107
41. 新雷（張維屏）The First Thunder of Spring (Zhang Wei-ping)
    春之歌（林明理）The Song of Spring (Lin Ming-Li) ········· 110

17

清詩明理思千載
● 古今抒情詩三百首
漢英對照

42. 己亥雜詩（之五）（龔自珍）Miscellanies Composed in 1839 (No. 5) (Gong Zizhen)
    湖畔冥想（林明理）Lakeside Meditation (Lin Ming-Li) ……112
43. 己亥雜詩（之一二五）（龔自珍）Miscellanies Composed in 1839 (No. 125) (Gong Zizhen)
    寫給屈原之歌（林明理）A Song for Qu Yuan (Lin Ming-Li) ‥114
44. 日本雜事詩（黃遵憲）Mount Fuji of Japan (Huang Zunxian)
    嵩山之夢（林明理）The Dream of Songshan Mountain (Lin Ming-Li)……………………………………116
45. 山村夜雨（祁寯藻）Night Rain in a Mountain Village (Qi Junzao)
    當愛情靠近時（林明理）When Love Approaches (Lin Ming-Li)……………………………………120
46. 邯鄲旅店（王星誠）The Inn of Handan (Wang Xingxian)
    冬日神山部落（林明理）Sacred Mountain Tribe in Winter (Lin Ming-Li)……………………………………122
47. 新霽（郭慶藩）Letup of a Snowfall (Guo Qingfan)
    憶阿里山（林明理）Memory of Ali Mountain (Lin Ming-Li) ‥124
48. 暮春（席佩蘭）Late Spring (Xi Peilan)
    龍田桐花季之歌（林明理）The Song of Tong Flower Festival (Lin Ming-Li)……………………………………125
49. 夏夜示外（席佩蘭）The Summer Night (Xi Peilan)
    在真實世界裡（林明理）In the Real World (Lin Ming-Li)……128
50. 聽鶯（孫蓀意）The Oriole (Sun Sunyi)
    安義的春天（林明理）The Spring of Anyi (Lin Ming-Li)……130
51. 書懷（周寶生）Inspired in an Instant (Zhou Baosheng)
    我原鄉的欖仁樹（林明理）An Olive Tree of My Hometown (Lin Ming-Li)……………………………………134
52. 對月（徐韋）Facing the Moon (Xu Wei)
    秋夜（林明理）Autumn Night (Lin Ming-Li) ……………136
53. 鄉思（胡友蘭）Homesickness (Hu Youlan)
    回憶（林明理）Memory (Lin Ming-Li) ……………………137
54. 桐江夜泊（彭孫貽）Tongjiang River at Night (Peng Sunyi)
    七股潟湖夕照（林明理）Evening Glow Over the Seven Lagoon Lake (Lin Ming-Li)……………………………139

18

55. 山行詠紅葉（其一）（蔣超）Red Leaves in the Mountain (No. 1) (Jiang Chao)
    關山遊（林明理）Visiting Guanshan Town (Lin Ming-Li) ···· 141
56. 舟中戲題（徐倬）On the Boat (Xu Zhuo)
    富岡海堤小吟（林明理）Ode to the Tomioka Seawall
    (Lin Ming-Li) ··· 143
57. 偶成（沈守正）An Impromptu (Shen Shouzheng)
    野地（林明理）The Wild Field (Lin Ming-Li) ················ 145
58. 鉛山河口即目（其一）（王奐曾）A Glimpse of Hekou Town
    in Yanshan County (No. 1) (Wang Huanzeng)
    致雙溪（林明理）To Shuangxi (Lin Ming-Li) ················ 148
59. 鉛山河口即目（其二）（王奐曾）A Glimpse of Hekou Town
    in Yanshan County (No. 2) (Wang Huanzeng)
    淡水黃昏（林明理）Tamsui Dusk (Lin Ming-Li) ·············· 150
60. 西池（曹寅）The West Pool (Cao Yin)
    竹子湖之戀（林明理）Love of Zhuzihu (Lin Ming-Li) ········ 152
61. 題畫三首（其一）（曹寅）Three Poems on Paintings (No. 1)
    (Cao Yin)
    水沙連之戀（林明理）Love of Shuishalian Pool (Lin Ming-Li) ·· 154
62. 漫興（魏基）An Impromptu (Wei Ji)
    驀然回首（林明理）Looking Back Suddenly (Lin Ming-Li) ·· 157
63. 下堯峰（閔華）The Lower Yao Peak (Min Hua)
    修路工人（林明理）Road Workers (Lin Ming-Li) ············ 158
64. 黃昏（黃任）Dusk (Huang Ren)
    回眸恆春夕照（林明理）Backward Glancing at the Sunset
    of Hengchun (Lin Ming-Li) ·································· 160
65. 獨遊上帶溪二絕句（其一）（黃任）Two Quatrains Composed
    During Solitary Touring Shangdai Creek (No. 1) (Huang Ren)
    牡丹水庫即景（林明理）View of Mudan Reservoir
    (Lin Ming-Li) ··· 162
66. 夜過夢溪（張如炯）Night Passing by Mengxi, or Dreamy
    Creek (Zhang Ruxia)
    相見居延海（林明理）Meeting in Juyan Lake Basin
    (Lin Ming-Li) ··· 165

清詩明理思千載
古今抒情詩三百首
漢英對照

67. 舟望（黃家鳳）Gazing From the Boat (Huang Jiafeng)
    你繫著落日的漁光（林明理）You Are Tied to the Fishing
    Light of the Setting Sun (Lin Ming-Li) ·······························167
68. 題方邵鶴琴鶴送秋圖（馬曰琯）Inscription on a Painting of
    Autumn (Ma Yueguan)
    劍門蜀道遺址（林明理）Ruins of Jianmen Shu Road
    (Lin Ming-Li)···169
69. 杭州半山看桃花（馬曰琯）Admiring Peach Flowers in
    Banshan Mountain of Hangzhou (Ma Yueguan)
    大好河山張家口（林明理）The Great Rivers & Mountains in
    Zhangjiakou (Lin Ming-Li)··171
70. 蟋蟀（李四維）Crickets (Li Siwei)
    遠方傳來的樂音（林明理）The Sound of Music From Afar
    (Lin Ming-Li)···174
71. 山中雪後（鄭燮）In the Mountain After Snowing (Zheng Xie)
    二月春雪（林明理）Spring Snow (Lin Ming-Li) ·············175
72. 芭蕉（鄭燮）Plantain Trees (Zheng Xie)
    曇花的故事（林明理）The Story of Night-blooming Cereus
    (Lin Ming-Li)···177
73. 小廊（鄭燮）The Small Corridor (Zheng Xie)
    秋暮（林明理）An Autumn Dusk (Lin Ming-Li)···············180
74. 登長溪嶺（葉元坊）Climbing the Changxi Ridge (Ye Yuanfang)
    踏青詠春（林明理）Ode to Spring and Spring Outing
    (Lin Ming-Li)···181
75. 顴鵲樓（喬光烈）The Stork Tower (Qiao Guanglie)
    緬懷億載金城（林明理）Cherishing Memory of the
    Erkunshen Turret (Lin Ming-Li) ··183
76. 盤豆驛（楊鸞）Pandou Post (Yang Luan)
    等著你，岱根塔拉（林明理）Waiting for You, Dagentara
    (Lin Ming-Li)···186
77. 偶成（朱一蜚）An Impromptu Poem (Zhu Yifui)
    睡吧，青灣情人海（林明理）Fall Asleep, Green Bay
    Lovers' Sea (Lin Ming-Li)···188

20

78. 山行（姚範）A Mountain Trip (Yao Fan)
南庄油桐花開時（林明理）When Tung Tree Flowers Are
Flowering in Nanzhuang (Lin Ming-Li)·················· 190
79. 即景（其一）（慶蘭）Inspired by the Sight (No. 1) (Qing Lan)
東勢林場（林明理）Dongshi Forest Farm (Lin Ming-Li) ····· 193
80. 即景（其二）（慶蘭）Inspired by the Sight(No. 2) (Qing Lan)
米故鄉──池上（林明理）The Land of Rice: Chishang
(Lin Ming-Li) ·· 196
81. 嘉禾寓中聞秋蟲（謝垣）Katydids in Autumn (Xie Yuan)
寄霍童古鎮（林明理）To Ancient Huotong Town (Lin Ming-Li) ·· 198
82. 漁父（蔣浩）An Old Fisherman (Jiang Hao)
噶瑪蘭之歌（林明理）Song of Kebalan (Lin Ming-Li) ······· 199
83. 中秋無月（德普）Mid-autumn Moon Festival Without Moon
(De Pu)
坐在秋陽下（林明理）Sitting in the Autumn Sun (Lin Ming-Li)·· 203
84. 觀水（旺都特納木濟勒）Watching the Water
(Wangdu Tena Muzil)
布拉格之秋（林明理）Autumn in Prague (Lin Ming-Li)······ 205
85. 桐廬道中雜詩（其一）（程同義）Miscellaneous Poems
Along the Tonglu Road (No. 1) (Cheng Tongyi)
聽泉（林明理）Listening to the Spring (Lin Ming-Li) ········· 206
86. 桐廬道中雜詩（其二）（程同義）Miscellaneous Poems
Along the Tonglu Road (No. 2) (Cheng Tongyi)
聽海（林明理）Listening to the Sea (Lin Ming-Li)············ 207
87. 聞雁（徐志源）The Honking of Wild Geese (Xu Zhiyuan)
大冠鷲的天空（林明理）The Sky of the Crested Serpent
Eagle (Lin Ming-Li)·· 209
88. 嘲燕（金和）Jeering at the Sea Swallows (Jin He)
重生的棕熊（林明理）A Reborn Brown Bear (Lin Ming-Li) ·· 212
89. 十一日夜坐（易順鼎）Night Sitting (Yi Shunding)
歲暮（林明理）The Close of the Year (Lin Ming-Li)··········· 214
90. 天童山中月夜獨坐（其一）（易順鼎）Moonlit Night, Solitary
Sitting in Tiantong Mountain (No. 1) (Yi Shunding)
四草湖中（林明理）In Sicao Lake (Lin Ming-Li)·············· 217

清詩明理思千載
古今抒情詩三百首
漢英對照

91. 天童山中月夜獨坐（其二）（易順鼎）Moonlit Night, Solitary Sitting in Tiantong Mountain (No. 2) (Yi Shunding)
新埔柿農（林明理）Farmers of Persimmons in Xinpu Town (Lin Ming-Li)··········219

92. 丙戌十二月二十四日雪中游鄧尉三十二絕句（其二十三）（易順鼎）A Trip to the Snowy Dengwei Mountain (No. 23) (Yi Shunding)
海煙（林明理）The Sea Mist (Lin Ming-Li)··········221

93. 邠州七絕（譚嗣同）A Quatrain Composed in Binzhou (Tan Sitong)
時光裡的和平島（林明理）Heping Island in Time (Lin Ming-Li)··········224

94. 獄中題壁（譚嗣同）Inscription on the Wall of the Prison (Tan Sitong)
鵝鑾鼻燈塔（林明理）The Eluanbi Lighthouse (Lin Ming-Li)··········228

95. 偶題（姚永概）An Impromptu Poem (Yao Yonggai)
美在大安森林公園（林明理）Ode to Da'an Forest Park (Lin Ming-Li)··········230

96. 西樓（黃節）The West Tower (Huang Jie)
小野柳漫步（林明理）Promenade in Xiaoyeliu Scenic Area (Lin Ming-Li)··········232

97. 詠梅十首（其九）（秋瑾）Ode to Plum Blossoms (No. 9) (Qiu Jin)
一顆瑩潔的燦星——悼葉嘉瑩教授（林明理）A Bright, Brilliant Star: Mourning Professor Chiaying Yeh (Lin Ming-Li)··234

98. 詠梅十首（其十）（秋瑾）Ode to Plum Blossoms (No. 10) (Qiu Jin)
朱鸝（林明理）The Crested Ibis (Lin Ming-Li)··········236

99. 登山六首（其一）（周實）Mountaineering (No.1) (Zhou Shi)
在下龍灣島上（林明理）On Ha Long Bay Island (Lin Ming-Li)··········239

100. 詠紙鳶（方芳佩）Ode to the Paper Kite (Fang Fangpei)
二林舊社田龜夢（林明理）The Field Turtle Dream of Erlin Old Society (Lin Ming-Li)··········241

目錄

101. 樂府體（馮班）A Folk Song (Feng Ban)
    給岩上的信（林明理）A Letter to Yan Shang (Lin Ming-Li)⋯ 243
102. 春感（王崇簡）Spring Inspiration (Wang Chongjian)
    北極熊（林明理）The Polar Bear (Lin Ming-Li) ⋯⋯⋯⋯⋯ 245
103. 絕句（林古度）A Quatrain (Lin Gudu)
    給 Bulgarian poet Radko Radkov（1940-2009）（林明理）
    To Bulgarian poet Radko Radkov (1940-2009) (Lin Ming-Li)⋯ 246
104. 池上（張光啟）Over the Pool (Zhang Guangqi)
    秋收的黃昏（林明理）Dusk of the Autumn Harvest
    (Lin Ming-Li) ⋯⋯⋯⋯⋯⋯⋯⋯⋯⋯⋯⋯⋯⋯⋯⋯⋯⋯ 248
105. 早起（宗渭）Early Rising (Zong Wei)
    愛的禮讚（林明理）In Praise of Love (Lin Ming-Li)⋯⋯⋯ 250
106. 曉雨（王庭）Morning Rain (Wang Ting)
    細密的雨聲（林明理）The Thick Sound of the Rain
    (Lin Ming-Li) ⋯⋯⋯⋯⋯⋯⋯⋯⋯⋯⋯⋯⋯⋯⋯⋯⋯⋯ 252
107. 宿山中（張履祥）Lodging in the Mountain (Zhang Lüxiang)
    致摯友非馬（林明理）To My Best Friend Dr. William Marr
    (Lin Ming-Li) ⋯⋯⋯⋯⋯⋯⋯⋯⋯⋯⋯⋯⋯⋯⋯⋯⋯⋯ 253
108. 五夜（陳一策）The Fifth Watch of Night (Chen Yice)
    今夜，我走入一星燈火（林明理）Tonight, I Walk Into
    a Star of Light (Lin Ming-Li) ⋯⋯⋯⋯⋯⋯⋯⋯⋯⋯⋯⋯ 255
109. 山行（施閏章）A Mountain Trip (Shi Runzhang)
    當陽光照耀達娜伊谷（林明理）When the Sun Shines Into
    Tanayiku (Lin Ming-Li) ⋯⋯⋯⋯⋯⋯⋯⋯⋯⋯⋯⋯⋯⋯ 256
110. 夜坐天遊峰得月（施閏章）Night Sitting in Heavenly
    Mountain to Admire the Moon (Shi Runzhang)
    光之湖（林明理）The Lake of Light (Lin Ming-Li)⋯⋯⋯⋯ 259
111. 題畫（吳綺）Inscription on a Painting (Wu Qi)
    在沙巴東岸的谷地（林明理）In the Valley of the East Coast
    of Sabah (Lin Ming-Li) ⋯⋯⋯⋯⋯⋯⋯⋯⋯⋯⋯⋯⋯⋯ 260
112. 夜坐（孫枝蔚）Night Sitting (Sun Zhiwei)
    螢光與飛蟲（林明理）Fluorescence and Fireflies (Lin Ming-Li) · 262

23

清詩明理思千載
古今抒情詩三百首
漢英對照

113. 微雲移時月出（王士禧）The Moon Peeps Through Thin Clouds (Wang Shixi)
追悼——出版家劉振強前輩（林明理）In Memoriam of Liu Zhenqiang as a Famous Publisher (Lin Ming-Li)⋯⋯263
114. 題畫（湯貽汾）Inscription on a Painting (Tang Yifen)
致巴爾札克（Honoré de Balzac, 1799-1850）（林明理）To Balzac (Honoré de Balzac, 1799-1850) (Lin Ming-Li) ⋯⋯265
115. 題畫（湯斌）Inscription on a Painting (Tang Bin)
寂靜無聲的深夜（林明理）The Silent Night (Lin Ming-Li) ⋯267
116. 閨情（夏宗沂）Boudoir Repinings (Xia Zongyi)
月桃記憶（林明理）Shell-flower Memory (Lin Ming-Li) ⋯⋯269
117. 讀曲歌（朱彝尊）A Song (Zhu Yizun)
丁香花開（林明理）Flowering Lilacs (Lin Ming-Li)⋯⋯272
118. 惜花（其二）（李經垓）Cherishing Flowers (No. 2) (Li Jinggai)
我的歌（林明理）My Song (Lin Ming-Li)⋯⋯274
119. 曉起（葛元福）Getting Up in the Morning (Ge Yuanfu)
青煙（林明理）Blue Smoke (Lin Ming-Li) ⋯⋯275
120. 宿山園（謝芳連）Lodging in a Mountain Yard (Xie Fanglian)
剪影（林明理）Sketch (Lin Ming-Li)⋯⋯277
121. 密雲望行人（謝芳連）Watching Wanderers in Miyun (Xie Fanglian)
銀背大猩猩（林明理）Silverback Gorilla (Lin Ming-Li)⋯⋯279
122. 落花（宋犖）Falling Flowers (Song Luo)
約克郡的春天（林明理）Spring in Yorkshire (Lin Ming-Li) ⋯280
123. 待友（王敔）Waiting for a Friend (Wang Yu)
寄語哥哥（林明理）A Message to My Brother (Lin Ming-Li) ⋯282
124. 黃竹子歌（申涵盼）Song of Yellow Bamboos (Shen Hanpan)
極端氣候下（林明理）In Extreme Weather (Lin Ming-Li)⋯⋯284
125. 溪上（張增慶）Over the Creek (Zhang Zengqing)
卑南溪（林明理）The Pinan River (Lin Ming-Li)⋯⋯286
126. 渡江（文點）Crossing the River (Wen Dian)
詩與白冷圳的間奏曲（林明理）Intermezzo Between Poems and Bailengzhun (Lin Ming-Li)⋯⋯288

127. 桃花谷（張實居）The Valley of Peach Flowers (Zhang Shiju)
 觀霧—雲的故鄉（林明理）Watching Clouds: the Hometown
 of Clouds (Lin Ming-Li)··································· 290
128. 山居（洪昇）Mountain Life (Hong Sheng)
 詩河（林明理）The Poetic River (Lin Ming-Li) ················ 292
129. 採蓮歌（王鴻緒）Lotus-Picking Song (Wang Hongxu)
 岩川之夜（林明理）The Night of Iwakawa (Lin Ming-Li)···· 293
130. 別後作（劉獻廷）Composed Upon Departure (Liu Xianting)
 致友人李浩（林明理）To My Friend Li Hao (Lin Ming-Li)·· 295
131. 夜宿養素堂東偏（查慎行）Lodging for the Night
 (Zha Shengxing)
 集集站遐想（林明理）Reverie of the Jiji Station (Lin Ming-Li)·· 298
132. 舟中書所見（查慎行）Night Sight from the Boat
 (Zha Shengxing)
 日出新蘭漁港（林明理）Sunrise Over Xinlan Fishing Port
 (Lin Ming-Li) ·· 300
133. 梅花（蔣錫震）Plum Blossoms (Jiang Xizhen)
 春雪飛紅（林明理）Spring Snow Flying with Red
 (Lin Ming-Li) ·· 302
134. 月橋行秋（陳仁）The Moon Bridge in Autumn (Chen Ren)
 夢橋（林明理）The Dream Bridge (Lin Ming-Li) ·············· 304
135. 白髮（翁志琦）Gray Hairs (Weng Zhiqi)
 夜思（林明理）Night Missing & Pining (Lin Ming-Li)········ 306
136. 邦均野寺（慎郡王）A Wild Temple in Bangjun (Shen Junwang)
 暮秋裡的春花——讀瓦西里基·德拉古尼詩集《越過夏季》
 （林明理）Spring Flowers in Late Autumn: Reading the poetry
 collection *Through the Season of Summer* by Vasiliki Dragouni
 (Lin Ming-Li)··· 307
137. 長橋（顧於觀）A Long Bridge (Gu Yuguan)
 CT273，仲夏寶島號（林明理）CT273, Summer Formosa
 (Lin Ming-Li) ·· 309
138. 雜詠（大寧）A Random Poem(Da Ning)
 末日地窖（林明理）The Doomsday Vault (Lin Ming-Li)····· 311
139. 暮春（翁格）Late Spring (Weng Ge)
 等候黎明（林明理）Waiting for the Dawn (Lin Ming-Li)····· 314

140. 山中暮歸（張廷玉）Late Return in the Mountain (Zhang Tingyu)
　　　阿德湖森林（林明理）Ade Lake Forest (Lin Ming-Li)·······315
141. 偶見（王文清）An Occasional View (Wang Wenqing)
　　　燈下讀《田裏爬行的滋味》（林明理）Reading *The Taste of Crawling in the Field* Under the Lamp (Lin Ming-Li)··········317
142. 梅花塢坐月（翁照）Admiring the Moon in Plum Blossoms Dock (Weng Zhao)
　　　梅花鹿（林明理）The Sika Deer (Lin Ming-Li)·············319
143. 太白樓（馬翮飛）The Tower of Li Bai (Ma Hefei)
　　　緬懷億載金城（林明理）In Memory of the Eternal Golden Fort (Lin Ming-Li)················320
144. 題畫（鄭燮）Inscription on a Painting of Bamboos (Zheng Xie)
　　　鯨之舞（林明理）The Dance of Whales (Lin Ming-Li)········323
145. 田家（任瑗）The Farmer (Ren Yuan)
　　　北門潟湖夕照（林明理）Evening Glow Over the Lagoon in the Beimen (Lin Ming-Li)················324
146. 金山寺晚望（郭楷）An Evening View of the Gold Hill Temple (Guo Kai)
　　　東隆宮街景（林明理）The Streetscape of Donglong Temple (Lin Ming-Li)················327
147. 苔（袁枚）The Moss (Yuan Mei)
　　　向科爾沁草原的防護林英雄致敬（林明理）Homage to the Heroes of Horqin Grassland Shelterbelt (Lin Ming-Li)··········329
148. 十二月十五夜（袁枚）On the Night of December 15th (Yuan Mei)
　　　沉浸在此刻（林明理）Immersed in the Moment (Lin Ming-Li)··331
149. 吳中竹枝詞（徐士鉉）A Bamboo Song (Xu Shixuan)
　　　雨，落在愛河的冬夜（林明理）Raindrops, Dropping on the Winter Night of Love (Lin Ming-Li)················334
150. 雨過（袁枚）After a Rain (Yuan Mei)
　　　雨中的綠意（林明理）Green in the Rain (Lin Ming-Li)·······336

附錄：細讀張智中的一本書（林明理）
Appendix：Close Reading of a Book by Zhang Zhizhong (Lin Ming-Li)················339

清詩明理思千載

古今抒情詩三百首

漢英對照

清詩明理思千載
古今抒情詩三百首
漢英對照

1.

留題秦淮丁家水閣二首（其二）   錢謙益

苑外楊花待暮潮，隔溪桃葉限紅橋。
夕陽凝望春如水，丁字簾前是六朝。

Inscriptions on the Water Pavilion of the Ding Family (No. 2)   Qian Qianyi

Beyond the garden the willow down
is wafting over the surging evening

tide; beyond the stream, the Peach-
Leaf-Lover Ferry keeps watch over

the Red Bridge. The setting sun is
gazing through water-like spring; before

T-shaped Curtain, the splendors of
the Six Dynasties are called to mind.

永安溪，我的愛   林明理

野花，白鷺，蘆葦，溪灘
天藍如鏡，誰能知曉你的奧秘
風依舊吟詠——送來你的名字
帆影點點，泛過閃耀的南峰

而你
聲音幽柔甜蜜，如戀人一般
我真想遠離一切空虛的迷惘
讓燃燒的夢想飛向月光下的故鄉

Yong'an Stream, My Love Lin Ming-Li

Wild flowers, egrets, reeds, creeks and beaches
The sky is blue like a mirror; who knows your mystery
The wind is still singing — to bring your name
Dots after dots sails, flashing over the shining South Peak

And you
With a soft and sweet voice, like a lover
How I want to get away from all the empty confusion
And let my burning dream fly to my moonlit hometown

詠同心蘭四絕句（其三）　　　　　錢謙益

並頭容易共心難，香草真當日以蘭。
不似西陵凡草木，漫將啼眼引郎看。

Ode to the Orchid Flower (No. 3)
Qian Qianyi

Easy: head to head; difficult:
the same heart. The scented

grass may be viewed as the
orchid flower, which is different

from the commonly seen grass
in a common garden, whose

清詩明理思千載
● 古今抒情詩三百首
　　漢英對照．

dewy eyes gladden easily
at the glad eye of anybody.

在風中，寫你的名字　　　　　　　　　林明理

在風中，寫你的名字，像新月一樣
當它升到山巔同白晝擦身而過，
四周是歌聲，鳥語與花香的喜悅
而你是永恆，抹不掉燈火輝煌的故鄉。

To Write Your Name in the Wind

Lin Ming-Li

To write your name in the wind, like a new moon
When it rises atop the hill and brushes past the day,
All about are the songs, the joy of birds' twitters and flowery scent
And you are eternal, never able to blot out the home of brilliant lamps.

♈ ♈ ♈

3 ·

西湖　　　　　　　　　　　　　　　柳如是

垂楊小院繡簾東，鶯閣殘枝蝶趁風。
大抵西泠寒食路，桃花得氣美人中。

The West Lake

Liu Rushi

The small yard green with weeping willows,
to the east of the embroidered curtain, the

30

pavilion of orioles is spotty and flecky with
dead twigs and faded flowers, over and among

which butterflies are flitting and flying in the
wind. On the Cold Food Day, along Xiling Road,

the peach flowers, immersed in the breath of
famous beauties, are beautiful by themselves.

在醉月湖的寧靜中 林明理

正月冬陽
在醉月湖的寧靜中
呼吸著綠蔭

瞧，白鵝藍鴨　拍綠了水岸
把亭臺變得更加華美
那鐘聲依舊
杜鵑依舊
鳥聲聚集在
高傲的樹端彌留
而我們行進著

在緩緩而落的黃昏下
我又回憶起那段金色時光
是多麼歡愉

台大校園「醉月湖」
By the Drunken Moon Lake
of Taiwan University

In the Quietude of the Drunken Moon Lake
Lin Ming-Li

The winter sun of the first lunar month
In the quietude of the Drunken Moon Lake
Is breathing the green shade

Look, white geese and blue ducks   paddling the water green
The pavilions are more attractive
The bell is still ringing
The cuckoos still remain
The birds' twitters gather
And linger atop lofty trees
And we are moving on

In the slowly descending dusk
Again I recall the golden time
The boundless happiness

4 ·

與兒子雍   金聖歎

與汝為親妙在疏，如形隨影只於書。
今朝疏到無疏地，無著天親果宴如。

To My Son Upon My Death   Jin Shengtan

As father-and-son, the wonder
of our relationship lies in the

seeming distance; concerning
scholarship, you are a follower

of me like my shadow. Now
our distance is as distant as

寫給小女莫莉   林明理

「嗨,甜心寶貝。妳又變瘦了嗎?
讓我將一片片紅楓葉繫在星空上
在妳窗口飄盪微響。」
「妳聽到夢裡娘親的呼喚嗎?北風又臨
東岸,月兒倚著夜鷹盯梢的眼打呵欠。
而妳依然獨自走在回家的路上。」

「嗨,我的甜心。妳看起來美極了。
讓我將所有記憶,擲向彩虹頂端
在妳睡前逐漸清晰。」
「風在吹……一秒秒地逝去了,
而妳令人無法置信的勇氣,依然
像展翅的鷹,喜歡翱翔在澄淨的天藍。」

To My Little Daughter Molly   Lin Ming-Li

"Hi, baby. Have you lost your weight again?
Let me tie some red maple leaves to the starry sky
For your window to be slightly noisy with wafting."
"Did you hear your mom's calling in your dream? The north wind
Again comes to the east coast, the moon yawning by leaning to the nighthawk's eye.
And you are still walking home alone."

"Hi, baby. You look stunning.
Let me throw all my memories atop the rainbow
To be gradually clear before you go to bed."
"The wind is blowing... passing by one second after another,
And your incredible courage remains

清詩明理思千載
古今抒情詩三百首
漢英對照

Like an eagle with outspread wings who likes soaring in the clear blue sky."

☙ ☙ ☙

5．

臨別口號遍謝彌天大人謬知我者　　金聖歎

東西南北海天疏，萬裡來尋聖歎書。
聖歎只留書種在，累君青眼看何如？

To My Readers Upon My Death　Jin Shengtan

North and south, west and
east, as far as poles apart;

in spite of the great distance,
readers come in search of my

books. Upon my death I leave
behind my son as an erudite

scholar, who is to be taken
care of, would you please?

在福爾摩沙島嶼之間——緬懷曹永和院士[1]

　　　　　　　　　　　　　　　林明理

都說
在崇山峻嶺中

---

[1] 曹永和（1920-2014）是臺灣的中央研究院院士，以研究臺灣荷西統治時期與提出「臺灣島史觀」著名，享壽 94 歲。

總會見到輝映出弧線的虹彩,
而我眼中的他
在福爾摩沙島嶼之間
　所留下的足印,
就是臺灣島史上
　這樣的一條虹彩。

都說
所有歷史隱痛
在時空的軌道上
總會飄浮,
　離開疆界,——
此刻,我默讀他的故事,
　太平洋濤聲不絕,
山脈全然甦醒過來,齊聲讚美。

—2024.9.28

Between the Islands of Formosa: In Memory of Academician Cao Yonghe[2]

Lin Ming-Li

It is universally said
That in the high mountains and lofty hills
There will always be a brilliant arc of rainbow
And in my eyes
Between the islands of Formosa
The footprints left behind
Are such a rainbow
In the history of Taiwan Island.

---

[2] Cao Yonghe (1920-2014) was an academician of the Academia Sinica in Taiwan, famous for his research on the Dutch rule of Taiwan and his views on the history of the island of Taiwan. He has lived for 94 years.

清詩明理思千載
古今抒情詩三百首
漢英對照

It is universally said
That all the hidden pains of history,
In the orbit of time and space,
Are to be floating
To leave the boundary —
Now, I silently read his story;
The Pacific is constantly noisy with waves;
All the mountains are awake, a chorus of praise.

— September 28, 2024

❀ ❀ ❀

6 ·

阻雪　　　　　　　　　　　吳偉業

關山雖勝路難堪，才上征鞍又解驂。
十丈黃塵千尺雪，可知俱不似江南。

Snowed In　　　　　　Wu Weiye

In spite of fair hills and rills,
hard is the road; the moment I

mount the horse, I have to dismount
owing to the difficult advancing.

Yellow dust rising and rolling heavenward, or snow snowing for so long

—a bleak scene which is different
from that of the Southern Shore.

張家界之夢   林明理

1.
我是雲,我曾走向你
那一座座拔地而起的石崖
塗染太陽的顏色

啊,這比世上什麼夢還要逼真
也許要走過許多彎路
也許也不那麼勇敢過
但為了能飄搖著
尋找歇息的帳篷
我停下,是為了飛騰的激情
我歌著,是為了古老的龍王洞
如何去裝扮那蒼涼的天穹
如何想起你深深的一吻
輕輕地,我攀著砂岩峰林
飛繞月宮
讓周圍的一切都變得無關緊要

有誰知
我飄搖著,感到自在消遙
還把你的形象寫在我的日記之中

2.
用衝越天子山的峰牆
跨過千丈寒風的肆虐
用不老的禦筆之奇
畫開一匹匹武士馴馬

你這峰林之王
正指揮著百鳥的合鳴

清詩明理思千載
● 古今抒情詩三百首
　　漢英對照,

盼仙女漫步而來
橋上神兵聚會
橋下唯一的語言
是綠色

3.
夜晚的沱江
努力向前,靜靜地流
河畔燈光閃爍,歌聲迷濛
啊,你是中國南方最美麗的
鳳凰古城
那青石板街,新砌的城牆
還有吊腳樓
阿拉營趕場的叫賣聲
民族風味濃厚
萬名塔上的風,掠過虹橋
在歷經三百多年滄桑後
燦然地笑了

The Dream of Zhangjiajie   Lin Ming-Li

1.
I am the cloud, who have ever approached you
One after another rocky cliff rising abruptly out of the ground
Painted with the color of the sun

Ah, this is more vivid than any dream in the world
Perhaps a host of detours are to be taken
Perhaps it has not been so brave
Yet in order to sway and swing
In search of a tent to rest
I stop, for the seething passion
I sing, for the old Dragon King's Cave
How to decorate the cold, bleak sky

How to think of your profound kiss
Gently, I climb the mountains of sandstone
Flying around the moon
To make everything around me seem insignificant

Who knows
I float, feeling at ease
And to write your image in my diary

2.
With the peak walls of Tianzi Mountain
To tame the ravages of thousands of feet of chilly wind
With the magic of the immortal imperial pen
To draw one after another warrior-horse

You, king of the mountains
Are directing the chorus of hundreds of birds
Expecting the fairies to walk here
On the bridge a gathering of gods
The only language under the bridge
Is green color

3.
At night, the Tuojiang River
Makes efforts to move forward, quietly flowing;
The river is flashing with lights, dreamy with singing;
Oh, you are the most beautiful ancient city of Phoenix
In southern China.
The blue stone street, the new walls,
And the stilted buildings,
Ala camp hawking and marketing,
Rich with national flavor.
The wind on the tower blows by the Rainbow Bridge,
After over three hundred years of vicissitudes,
Beaming with brilliant smiles.

✿ ✿ ✿

清詩明理思千載
● 古今抒情詩三百首
　　漢英對照

7.

塞下曲 　　　　　　　　　　　　　　　　　顧炎武

趙信城邊雪化塵，紇幹山下雀呼春。
即今三月鶯花滿，長作江南夢裡人。

A Border Song 　　　　　　　　　　　Gu Yanwu

The accumulated snow in the outskirts
of Zhaoxin Town begins to thaw;

beneath Hegan Mountain the swallows
are twittering through spring. The third

moon sees grass growing and warblers
flying, when the frontier soldier, a ghost

now, is still alive in the fond dream
of his lover in the Southern Shore.

我怎能停止為你而歌 　　　　　　　　　林明理

你說
每條巷弄都存著一種記憶
每個鄉親那麼溫暖樸真
瞧！這櫻花讓世上所有的星子
都跟我在瞬間靜默下來了
我怎能停止為你而歌

你那凝視的目光
從北方沿著黃河走來
喚醒了我的靈魂
在花的沉默面前

古老的琴弦
仍悠悠訴說著老城的舊事

而我從海上帶來
所懷的誠摯和鋪展的
夢,帶著夏日羚羊般的歡愉
我的心中,有你的驕傲
在你清美的水波裡
一切都變成了詩句

你說
我來了只是因為老城的等候
即使那山峰的水影遮住了我的視線
我也能看得見河上有船
我已遠行
在飛向一條詩河的地圖上

How Can I Stop Singing for You Lin Ming-Li

You say
There is a memory in each lane
Every villager is so warm and innocent
Look! The cherry blossoms let all the stars in the world
With me in an instant silence down
How can I stop singing for you

Your gaze
From the north along the Yellow River
To awaken my soul
Before the silence of flowers
The ancient strings
Are still telling the past events of the old city

And I have brought from the sea
My sincere and spreading

Dream, with summer antelope-like joy
In my heart, with pride of you
In your clear, beautiful waves
All have turned into poetry

You say
I come only because of the old city's waiting
Though the water shadow of the mountain has obscured my vision
I can see the boat on the river
I am on a long journey
On a map flying to a river of poetry

8 ·

舟中見獵犬有感 　　　　　　　　宋琬

秋水蘆花一片明，難同鷹隼共功名。
檣邊飯飽垂頭睡，也似英雄髀肉生。

Inspired at the Sight of a Hound in the Boat
Song Wan

A stretch of autumn water
is bright with reedy blossoms;

a hound in the boat fails
to prey as the falcon does.

Well-fed, it sleeps so lazily
by the mast, no scope for

displaying his abilities
like tethered heroes.

冥想——致詩人穆旦 　　　　　　　　林明理

直到你能步入繆斯的殿堂
我才相信
你已生氣勃勃
歌詠著神妙的詩句
才能預感
你如大熊星清晰浮現
躺在海面細品島嶼四季的流轉
驅走我心中的激蕩

而你行了一個奇蹟——
恰似一棵不凋的樹
當我走近　想畫你微笑的
姿態,自信,謙虛,還有
堅定的眼神。
在我眼睛深處,你的微笑如歌
不可思議卻令人開懷

Meditation: to Mu Dan as a Poet

　　　　　　　　　　　　　　Lin Ming-Li

It isn't until you step into the palace of the Muse
That I come to believe
You are full of vigor and vitality
Singing with your divine poetic lines
I can foresee
You emerge clearly like the bear star
Lying on the sea to savor the turning of four seasons
To drive away all the agitation in my heart

清詩明理恩千載
● 古今抒情詩三百首
　　漢英對照，

And you have performed a miracle —
Like an immortal tree
As I approach to paint your smiling
Posture, confidence, modesty, and
Determined eyes.
In the depths of my eyes, your song-like smile
Inconceivable, yet joyful

❦ ❦ ❦

9．

上巳將過金陵　　　　　　　　　龔鼎孳

倚檻春愁玉樹飄，空江鐵鎖野煙銷。
興懷何限蘭亭感，流水青山送六朝。

Passing by the Ancient Town of Jinling
　　　　　　　　　　　　　　　Gong Dingzi

Leaning against the balustrade, laden
with spring grief, wafting in the air

is the lingering tune presaging a fallen
state. Looking at the great expanse of

the Long River, I cannot help recalling
the river-blocking iron chain, which

has disappeared like smoke dispersing
in the wilderness. I feel inspired at the

sight of the Orchid Pavilion, the object
of a famous literary piece through the

ages, when the running water & blue
hills bid farewell to the Six Dynasties.

你的影跡在每一次思潮之上[3] 　　　　林明理

啊，讓我奮起翅膀
如鷹之姿，瞰整片海洋
歌聲中五嶽和天堂也似的故鄉
長城和黃河同蘭亭的愛
一向是我最深的顧盼
入秋了，留下來的那輪月
是多少遊子的凝注
是多少墨客的讚嘆

我欣然，讀你騰躍而矯健的詩
從這裡，對遠洋與高山
對著全部華夏兒女，握緊那手
讓文明之花馨香萬里
讓大地的淚變得聖潔而美麗
讓永恆的黃土芬芳綿長
啊，東方已曉——
你的影跡在每一次思潮之上

Your Shadow Is Over Every Thought[4]

Lin Ming-Li

Ah, let me flutter my wings
In the posture of an eagle, overlooking the whole ocean
In the singing the five mountains and the heaven-like hometown

---

[3] 緬懷王羲之千古之誦〈蘭亭序〉，是書法史上的豐碑，有感而文。

[4] In memory of Wang Xizhi through the ages for his *Preface of the Orchid Pavilion*, which is a monument in the history of calligraphy, hence inspired.

清詩明理思千載
古今抒情詩三百首
漢英對照

The Great Wall and the Yellow River with the love of the Orchid Pavilion
Have always been my deepest expectation
It is autumn, the moon which remains
Is the gaze of how many wanderers
And the sigh of how many literary men

I am glad to read your poems filled with vigor and vitality
From here, to the distant ocean and mountains
To all Chinese daughters and sons, hold hands firmly
For the flowers of civilization to be fragrant through thousands of miles
For the tears of the earth to be sacred and beautiful
For the eternal loess to be lingeringly fragrant
Oh, the morning breaks in the East
Your shadow is over every thought

❀ ❀ ❀

10 ·

自題桃花楊柳圖　　　　　　　　　　顧媚

郎道花紅如妾面，妾言柳綠似郎衣。
何時化得鶼鶼鳥，拂葉穿花一處飛。

Self-Inscription on a Painting of Peach Flowers & Willow Trees　　Gu Mei

You say the red flowers are
suggestive of my fair face; I say

the green willows are evocative
of your clothes. When can we

be transformed into a pair of
lovebirds, flying and flitting,

through tufts of leaves and
among masses of flowers.

夜思   林明理

是的,我想的,是你
　　——褐色眼睛
　使我無力地,像隻雷鳥
在覆雪中靜止不動

　何處有悠揚的風
　　夜何以如此深重
只有雪花會來親吻
　　滾燙的胸中
　分解
　　　這愛情的激動

Night Thoughts   Lin Ming-Li

Yes, I miss you, it is you
　— Brown eyes
Which make me powerless, like a thunderbird
Sitting still in the accumulated snow

Where comes the melodious wind
　　Why the night is so profound
Only the snowflakes come to kiss
In the passionate bosom
To resolve
　　The excitement of love

清詩明理思千載
古今抒情詩三百首
漢英對照

11 ·

雪中閣望 　　　　　　　　　　　　　　施閏章

江城草閣俯漁磯，雪滿千山失翠微。
笑指白雲來樹杪，不知卻是片帆飛。

Snowy Landscape Seen from a Pavilion
Shi Runzhang

A riverside pavilion overlooks
the fishing rock; thousands

of hills are white with snow —
green is concealed. Smilingly,

the watcher points afar at the
white clouds fleeting over tree-

tops, without knowing that they
are white sails sailing fast.

冬季的旅行 　　　　　　　　　　　　林明理

在密西西比河上空
第一場雪和寂靜
　把我迷住了。

高地的大角羊
像個永不退避的勇士，
莊嚴地面對現實。

一群雪雁
　齊力
趕跑偷偷潛入的敵人。

三兩隻鱷魚寶寶
　用乳齒咬住了魚。
驚動了我的目光。

一隻脫困的水獺
　穿過冰水和初露的陽光，
在雪地上打滾，抖一抖，
乍現在他臉上的幸福。

　　　　　　　　　　　　－2024.10.12

Winter Journey 　　　　　Lin Ming-Li

Over the Mississippi River
The first snow and its silence
Has captivated me

The highland bighorn sheep
Like a warrior who never beats a retreat
Solemnly faces the reality

A flock of snow geese
Together
Drive away the stealthily intruding enemy

Two or three baby crocodiles
Grab the fish with their teeth
Which surprises my eyes

An escaped bank beaver
Through the ice water and the first glimmer of sunshine

清詩明理思千載
● 古今抒情詩三百首
　漢英對照，

Is rolling in the snowy ground, shaking
With happiness appearing on its face

－October 12, 2024

🌷 🌷 🌷

12 ·

悼亡四首（其一） 　　　王夫之

十年前此曉霜天，驚破晨鐘夢亦仙。
一斷藕絲無續處，寒風落葉灑新阡。

Lament for My Deceased Wife (No. 1)

Wang Fuzhi

In this very frostily chilly morning
ten years ago, the toll, like a bolt

from the blue, breaks my dream
when my wife departs from the mortal

world. Severed, yet still connected,
still entangled; withered leaves,

against the cold wind, are wafting
and whirling over her new grave.

憶 　　　林明理

輕輕地揮別
因為愛會惹人淚
如果再有輪迴
會不會又回到了原點

如果沒有距離
會不會讓思念減滅
我就這樣想著
不覺又過了數千年

你是雲霧裡的月光
若隱若現，航入我視界
你是繆斯的王子，是詩的泉源
到哪裡
才能揮去那盤旋不離的身影
到哪裡
才能尋回那年相遇的瞬間

啊，夢裡的詩人
讓我由衷地呼喚
我願是藍山雀
在溪谷，在雲天
痴迷於你的神奇
飛入你沉思的窗前
雀躍地哼歌
——讓愛長遠

－2017.4.1

Recollection　　　　　　　　　　　Lin Ming-Li

Gently waving goodbye
For love brings tears
If there is a reincarnation
Will it be back to the original place
If without distance
Will the longing be diminished or not
Thus thinking and pondering
Thousands of years are slipping by

清詩明理思千載
古今抒情詩三百首
漢英對照

You are the moonlight through clouds
Disappearing and appearing in my vision
You are the prince of the muse, the fountain of poetry
Where can I go
To get rid of the lingering form
Where can I go
To find the moment of encounter in that year

Ah, the poet in my dream
For me to call you sincerely
I wish I were a blue tit
Over the creek, in the cloudy sky
Infatuated with your magic
Flying before your contemplative window
To sing joyfully
—Long live our love

—April 1, 2017

🌷 🌷 🌷

13 ·

客發苕溪　　　　　　　　　　葉燮

客心如水水如愁，容易歸舟趁疾流。
忽訝船窗送吳語，故山月已掛船頭。

Homeward Sailing on Shaoxi River
Ye Xie

The roamer's heart is like
water which is suggestive

of sorrow; the smooth sailing
is smoother with the swift

current. The boat window is
surprised to hear native dialect,

when the moon of native
hill is bright over the prow.

我的波斯菊[5]　　　　　　　　　　　林明理

我的波斯菊
美麗的仙子
你的白色花瓣
高雅純潔
在我心頭開放
自由又暢快
在休耕的原野上
隨風搖晃相吻

是做夢嗎
我聽見了你的花語
來自何方
欲往何處
你什麼也不回答
像隻白文鳥
只留下短短一行字
朋友，珍重吧，心

---

[5] 臺灣雲林縣莿桐花海，連續三年結合當地休耕所種植的向日葵、波斯菊等綠肥作物，不僅增進土地肥力，又讓故鄉成為過年期間賞花的旅遊景點，因而為詩。

清詩明理思千載
● 古今抒情詩三百首
　　漢英對照，

My Mexican Aster[6]　　　　　　　　Lin Ming-Li

My Mexican aster
The beautiful fairy
Your white petals
Pure and elegant
Blossoming in my heart
Free and joyful
In the fallow field
Shaking and kissing in the wind

Is it a dream
I have heard your flowery words
From where
Where to go
You answer nothing
Like a white-rumped munia
Leaving only a short line
Take care, my friend, O heart

✿ ✿ ✿

14 ·

來青軒雪　　　　　　　　　　　　朱彝尊

天書稠疊此山亭，往事猶傳翠輦經。
莫倚危欄頻北望，十三陵樹幾曾青？

---

[6] The sea of tung flowers in Yunlin County, Taiwan, combined with green fertilizer crops such as sunflowers and Mexican asters planted in the local fallow for three consecutive years, not only improve the fertility of the land, but also make my hometown a tourist spot for appreciating flowers during the Chinese New Year, hence the poem.

Snowing Over the Green Pavilion

Zhu Yizun

The mountain pavilion is alive
with imperial calligraphies, and

imperial carriages used to come to
visit. No, please don't lean against

the balustrade to look northward,
where trees in the Ming Dynasty

Tombs have lost their green under a
blanket of snow which is still snowing.

每當黃昏飄進窗口

林明理

常青藤種子開始酣睡
松針的氣味總是
穿牆破隙
刺亂我的衫袖……
尤其在夜裡與融雪之後

儘管它們就在屋外的彎路
離我只有咫尺之隔
我還是喜歡偷偷地眺望
恣意的松鼠到處採擷
遺落的球果

當我腳底裹上驚奇並浸染
枝頭的木香
四野的生物彷彿重新敞開
一種香甜而富饒的感覺
如同被石壁的回音所彈奏

清詩明理思千載
古今抒情詩三百首
漢英對照

它像崖邊的流雲般孤獨
也像古老的豎琴那樣沉碧
每當黃昏飄進我的窗口……
我將松針藏在那
苦澀的地土之中

Whenever the Evening Drifts Into the Window
Lin Ming-Li

The ivy seeds begin to slumber
The smell of pine needles always
Penetrates the walls through cracks
To puncture my sleeves...
Particularly at night and when snow begins to melt

Though they are just on a bend outside my house
Only within a foot from me
Still I like to steal a glance
At the free-wheeling squirrels picking up
The lost cones

When my feet are wrapped in wonder and soaked
With the wooden scent from the branches
The creatures in the field seem to open
A sweet and rich feeling
As if played by the echoes of the stone walls

It is as lonely as a cloud on the cliff
And as deep-green as the old harp
When dusk comes to my window
I hide the pine needles
In the bitter earth

❀ ❀ ❀

15．

花前　　　　　　　　　　　　　　屈大均

花前小立影徘徊，風解吹裙百摺開。
已有淚光同白露，不須明月上衣來。

Before the Flowers　　　　　　　Qu Dajun

Before the flowers she
stands and stares, the shadow

lengthening and lingering;
the wind gently blows to

ruffle her skirt. Her teardrops
are like white dewdrops,

no need for the moon to
shine bright on her dress.

松林中的風聲　　　　　　　　　　林明理

約好松林見的
在隆冬之晨
雨滴漠漠飄灑
野風吼著失眠的夜
時間停在松膠的氣味

這林中　已然青蒼老結
半闔窗前
而我簾幃高捲，細數
歎息與凋謝的海棠落葉
方未覺　曉鐘在霜天

清詩明理思千載
● 古今抒情詩三百首
　　漢英對照

不變的天風
過路的吹動
那地土已踩遍
夜霧卻又隱消

The Wind in the Pines　　　　　Lin Ming-Li

Appointment to meet in the pine forest
In the middle of winter morning
Raindrops are dropping, dripping, and drifting
The wild wind is roaring through the insomnia night
Time stops in the smell of pine gum

In the woods　it is aged and green
Before the half closed window
I roll up the curtain, counting
Sighs and the withering begonia leaves
Before coming to know the clock in the frosty sky

The unchanging heavenly wind
Passes across the land
The earth has been trodden through
The night fog fades away

☙ ☙ ☙

16 ·

再過露筋祠　　　　　　　　　　王士禎

翠羽明璫尚儼然，湖雲祠樹碧於煙。
行人繫纜月初墜，門外野風開白蓮。

Once More Passing by the Virgin's Temple
Wang Shizhen

With headwear, and with earrings,
the virgin is with a tidy posture;

clouds wafting over lake, trees in
the temple are green through the

pervading mist. The traveler tethers
the boat when the moon is on the sinking;

the wild wind from without the door
blows open the white lotus flowers.

你是一株半開的青蓮
林明理

你是一株半開的青蓮
在倒影的水中
如夢初醒的明媚
花朵上的朝露是
音樂，飄在空中
融入了岳麓山的無邊狂野

你的憂傷是西下的斜陽
藍色是記憶
紅色是思念
當山風拂過，四季流轉
你似喜似悲
用僅有的芬芳把大地擁抱

你的微笑是曲澗的飛瀑
在寺廟與潭水之間

清詩明理思千載
● 古今抒情詩三百首
　　漢英對照，

庸容自在　充滿暖意
你聽風，聽雨呢喃
歌咏著偉大與渺小
聲調時疾時徐，真誠而美好

You Are a Half-Blossoming Green Lotus
Lin Ming-Li

You are a half-blossoming green lotus
In the reflected water
The beauty as if waking up from a dream
Morning dew in the beautiful flowers
Is music floating in the air
Blending into the boundless wildness of the Yuelu Mountain

Your sadness is the sun setting in the west
Blue is the memory
Red is the yearning
When the mountain wind blows, turning of the four seasons
You seem to be joyful and sorrowful
With the only fragrance to embrace the earth

Your smile is a winding waterfall
Between the temple and the pool of water
At great ease　full of warmth
You listen to the wind, to the whispering rain
Singing the great and the small
The voice now fast and then slow, genuine and beautiful

⚘ ⚘ ⚘

17 ·

秦淮雜詩   王士禎

年來腸斷秣陵舟,夢繞秦淮水上樓。
十日雨絲風片裡,濃春煙景似殘秋。

On Qinhuai River   Wang Shizhen

From year to year I am heartbroken
on the boat along Qinhuai River

by Nanjing; I'm haunted with
dreamy thoughts about the river-

side mansions. For ten days the
height of spring is a picture of

threads of rain & sheets of wind,
which is suggestive of late autumn.

自由   林明理

自由
   既非戰利品或奢侈品
它應像空氣或花香般自然
而不該讓大地為它
——流血流汗

Freedom   Lin Ming-Li

Freedom
Is neither a trophy nor an article of luxury

清詩明理思千載
● 古今抒情詩三百首
　　漢英對照

It should be natural, like air or flowery scent
The last thing is for the great earth
— To sweat and shed blood for it

☙ ☙ ☙

18 ·

次韻答王司寇阮亭先生見贈　　　　　　　　蒲松齡

志異書成共笑之，布袍蕭索鬢如絲。
十年頗得黃州夢，冷雨寒燈夜話時。

Reply to Wang Shizhen　　　　Pu Songling

My freshly written Stories of Ghosts is a
delightful reader, when I am plain-clothed

and silver-haired from the labor of it.
Through ten years I am privy to the mind

of Su Shi, an exiled poet who is an attentive
listener of ghost stories, and I, under a cold

lamp soaked in cold rainy nights, write and
rewrite to relieve the grievances in my heart.

吾友張智中教授　　　　　　　　　　　　林明理

在充滿學術氣氛的黃昏，
你的校園四周印著
　柳條兒搖擺的腳跡，

62

而你獨自諦聽
　　把鳥聲還有
風聲捎來的
　　一些古詩的音韻
　　納入了你的思想之海。

－2024.10.10 收到吾友智中傳來一張新照，有感而作。

To Professor Zhang Zhizhong as My Friend
Lin Ming-Li

In the evening filled with academic atmosphere
Your campus is fair and alive
With swinging willows twigs
When you are listening by yourself
To the birds' songs and
The rhymes of ancient Chinese poems
Brought by the wind
—All into the sea of your thoughts

—October 10, 2024, inspired upon receiving a freshly-taken photo from Professor Zhang Zhizhong.

✿ ✿ ✿

19．

客愁
洪昇

夜夜賈舡裡，思鄉愁奈何。
醒聽北人語，夢聽南人歌。

清詩明理思千載
● 古今抒情詩三百首
　　漢英對照,

Homesickness
Hong Sheng

From night to night in
a trading boat; my home-

sickness is helpless.
Awake, I hear northern

dialects; dreamy, audible
are southern tongues.

佳節又重陽
林明理

當我老了真好,像茱萸
在初夏綻放而在秋天成熟
從花兒變成紫果
從歡顏變成孤傲
隨著遍處菊花,風箏
在孩童嘻笑聲中飄搖
我登高遠眺
讓心回歸自然
耳中飄蕩的是大雁歌聲
還有那悠揚多情的風
滔不盡萬里長江的秋色
朋友,萬物都讓我想起你
有酒
今夜你在這兒也許會聽到
月光盈滿老城的歡笑

The Double Ninth Festival
Lin Ming-Li

How nice when I am old, like the dogwood
Blooming in early summer and ripening in autumn
From flowers to purple fruits

From joyful visage to solitary pride
Along with the rambling chrysanthemums, kites
Are fluttering amid the laughter of children
I climb the heights to look afar
For my heart to be back to nature
Aloud in my ears are the songs of wild geese
And the melodious, passionate wind
The autumn tints of the Yangtze River spread endless
My dear friend, everything is suggestive of you
With wine
Here tonight you may hear
The laughter of the old city brimming with moonlight.

☙ ☙ ☙

20 ·

北固山看大江 孔尚任

孤城鐵甕四山圍，絕頂高秋坐落暉。
眼見長江趨大海，青天卻似向西飛。

The Great River Seen from the Northern Mountain
Kong Shangren

The solitary iron-clad town is
enclosed all about with mountains；

atop the peak of peaks of the Northern
Mountain, the high autumn sees

me sitting and watching the setting
sun. The great river is seen speedily

running toward the sea, when the blue
sky seems to be flying westward.

秋在白沙屯[7]

林明理

一根根巨大的
　　白色風車轉啊轉，
秋天的大海更加湛藍，
這是風和沙的故鄉，
　　山丘一片綠意。
我怎能錯過
　　相遇的悸動？
店仔街古厝的溫情，
　　多年不曾變樣，

金色的浪花翻滾跳躍，
　　陣陣秋風捲起潮浪，
年復一年的世代兒女
守望著這最後的古老。
啊讓我再一次發現──
　　那不可錯過的落日，
彷若天地間
　　只剩下我
和獨自吟唱的風。

Autumn in Baishatun[8]

Lin Ming-Li

A huge white windmill
　　Is turning and turning;
The autumnal sea is more blue.

---

[7] 白沙屯位於臺灣苗栗縣通霄鎮，是指白沙堆積如山丘的意思。
[8] Baishatun, located in Tongxiao Township, Miaoli County, means that the white sand is piled up like a hill.

This is the hometown of wind and sand,
    The hills veiled in green.
How can I miss it:
    The palpitation of encounter?
The warmth of the old shop in the street,
    Have not changed for many years.

The golden waves are frothing and leaping,
    The autumn winds rolling up the tide.
Generations after generations of children from year to year
Keep watch of the last old age.
Oh let me discover it again —
    The sunset which cannot be missed,
As if between Heaven and Earth
        Only I myself remain
    As well as the wind which is singing solitarily.

⚘ ⚘ ⚘

21 ·

《桃花扇傳奇》題辭　　　　　　　　陳宇王

玉樹歌殘跡已陳，南朝宮殿柳條新。
福王少小風流慣，不愛江山愛美人。

Inscription On *Legend of Peach Blossom Fan*　　　Chen Yuwang

Gone is the voluptuous life
filled with *The Jade Tree Song*;

the palaces of the Southern
dynasty are fair with fresh willows.

清詩明理思千載
古今抒情詩三百首
漢英對照

The prince has formed
a dissolute habit since his

childhood, and he loves
beauty instead of landscape.

勇氣——祝賀川普總統（Donald Trump）[9]

林明理

勇氣，親民，直言不諱
以及未受驚駭的選民
這些令你成了獲勝者
而多數人在經歷了同樣的震撼後
只能宣稱　覺得有句話還是
挺妙的！那就是讓人傳頌的：
「Make America great again！」

林明理畫作：
〈眾人的祝福〉

－寫於台灣 2024 年 11 月 6 日傍晚

Courage: Congratulations to President Donald Trump[10]

Lin Ming-Li

Courage, popularity, straight-talking
And the unfrightened voters
All make you the winner
When the majority who have experienced similar shock

---

[9] 八年前，我曾在美國《亞特蘭大新聞》發表過此詩。今天再次祝賀川普，他在 2024 年 11 月 6 日，再度當選為美國總統，並在發表勝選感言中表示：「讓美國再度偉大！」。

[10] I have published this poem in the American *The Atlanta News* eight years ago. Congratulations again today to Donald Trump, who was re-elected President of the United States on November 6, 2024. He said in his victory speech: "Make America Great Again!"

Can claim that a slogan
Is wonderful! Which is on everybody's lips
"Make America great again!"
　　　－Written on the evening of November 6, 2024, Taiwan

⚘ ⚘ ⚘

22·

青溪口號　　　　　　　　　　　　　　查慎行

來船桅杆高，去船櫓聲好。
上水厭灘多，下水惜灘少。

Improvised on the Blue River Zha Shenxing

The to-ships are tall with
masts, and the fro-ships are

pleasantly voiced with oars.
Upstream, beaches are

not favored; downstream,
beaches are very welcome.

二層坪水橋之歌[11]　　　　　　　　　林明理

我歡呼當白鷺掠過
畫一道美麗弧線

---

[11] 這座水橋位於臺灣臺東縣鹿野鄉瑞隆村坪頂路旁。據說，五十年前建造時，當地農民憑著鋤頭、扁擔、畚箕，用人力挑土墊高水路，艱鉅地完成了圳水輸送任務。在這片田野上，常能見到普悠瑪火車奔馳、白鷺冉冉而過的身姿……迴首水橋，盡興踏影而歸。

清詩明理思千載
● 古今抒情詩三百首
　漢英對照

我暢飲在鹿野
二層坪水橋的陽光
我凝視如海的稻浪
泛起一圈圈金色波紋
我知道溪流在舞蹈
天邊那片雲絮
已伴隨著一小抹晚霞消融了

當朦朧月在山頂上神秘地笑
我知道世界在寬廣的目光中
會變得更好，而我
竟忘記了年華的流逝
半個世紀過去了嗎
我將帶著這片活風景
再次找到希望的風帆
搖晃在航向故鄉的海面上

Song of the Two-Floor Flat Water Bridge[12]

Lin Ming-Li

I hail at the sight of the egrets flying
In a beautiful arc
I drink unrestrainedly in the field of deer
The sunshine of the Two-Floor Flat Water Bridge
I gaze at the sea of rice waves

---

[12] The water bridge is located next to Pingding Road in Ruilong Village, Luye Township, Taitung County, Taiwan. It is said that when it was built 50 years ago, local farmers, with hoes, poles and dustpans, used human labor to lift soil and cushion the waterway, and arduously completed the task of irrigation water transportation. In this field, you can often see the Puyuma train running, egrets slowly flying and passing by……Looking back on the water bridge, returning to the heart's content.

Circles of golden ripples
I know the stream is on the dancing
The fleecy clouds in the horizon
Have melted with a little touch of sunset

When the hazy moon is smiling mysteriously atop the mountain
I know in the broad vision the world
Will be better, and I
Have forgotten the lapse of time
Half a century has passed?
With this living landscape I will
Find the sail of hope again
Shaking on the sea bound for home

❀ ❀ ❀

23 •

秣陵懷古 　　　　　　　　　　　納蘭性德

山色江聲共寂寥，十三陵樹晚蕭蕭。
中原事業如江左，芳草何須怨六朝？

Cherishing the Past in the Old Capital
　　　　　　　　　　　Nalan Xingde

The mountain colors & the river
sounds are so drear; the trees on

the Thirteen Imperial Tombs are
soughing & rustling against the even-

tide. The kingly powers and royal
pomps are on the waning and declining;

清詩明理思千載
● 古今抒情詩三百首
　　漢英對照

no need for the fragrant grass to
complain about the past six dynasties.

華夏龍脈雕塑群　　　　　　　　　林明理

沒有到華夏龍脈
等於沒有看盡了風光

這些雕塑群
果是陝西的鎮寶
我在秦嶺深處散步
時空彷彿回到遠古
春秋、秦漢到三國
或從唐宋到明清

車在飛奔
向未來繼續前進

噢，我無法想像
那是怎樣的年代
又是怎樣的沙場
但這有何關係
眼前一切
已然變了許多模樣
人民在前進，甚至走得更穩當

沒有流盡了血汗
就沒有今日蜀道的輝煌

Chinese Dragon Vein Sculpture Group
Lin Ming-Li

Without visiting the Chinese Dragon Vein
The fair view has not been fully appreciated

These sculptures
Are the rare treasures of Shaanxi province
I walk in the depths of the Qinling Mountains
Time & space seems to return to the remote past
The Spring and Autumn Period, Qin and Han Dynasties, the Three Kingdoms
Or from the Tang & Song dynasties to the Ming and Qing dynasties

The car is speeding
Ahead into the future

Oh, it is hard for me to imagine
What kind of time it is
And what kind of battlefield
But what does it matter
Everything before the eye
Has changed a lot
People are moving forward, even walking more steadily

Without exhausting sweat and blood
Without the glory of today's Sichuan Road

♣ ♣ ♣

24 •

過許州   沈德潛

到處陂塘決決流,垂楊百里罨平疇。
行人便覺鬚眉綠,一路蟬聲過許州。

Passing by Xuzhou   Shen Deqian

Rivers here and ponds there are
overflowing with water; willows

清詩明理思千載
● 古今抒情詩三百首
　　漢英對照，

drooping through hundreds of miles
to screen the field. The traveler

feels to be invaded in the brows
by the suffusing green, when he

passes by Xuzhou, constantly
accompanied by the songs of cicadas.

獻給青龍峽[13]的歌　　　　　　　　　林明理

誰打開了神秘的魔盒
靜謐
靜謐的煙波浩渺
浩渺於山峽的雲臺山──
光影裡一幅幅山水畫卷
畫出中原第一峽
畫出七彩潭和倒流泉
畫出瀑溪和雄峰
畫出溶洞和植物群落
但畫不出
看谷不見谷，聞水不見水的模樣

瞧瞧千年的榔樹
還有古牌坊和樓閣
似等待依序而來的日子
在蟲鳥唧唧的奏鳴中
靜聽
我在遙遠的遠方獻上一束詩
向長谷的頂巔呼喊
這裡看起來的確像天堂

---

[13] 青龍峽風景名勝區位於河南省焦作市修武縣，是河南雲臺山世界地質公園主要遊覽區之一，被譽為「中原第一峽」。

把世界帶進青龍峽吧
啊我願再次與你相擁，像隻蒼鷹
在望龍瀑的肩膀上長吻

A Song Dedicated to Qinglong Gorge[14]

Lin Ming-Li

Who has opened the mysterious magic box
Quiet itself
The quiet wide expanse of mist-covered waters
The Yuntai Mountain vast and misty in the gorge —
Through light & shadow one after another roll of landscape painting
The first gorge in the Central Plain
The pool of seven colors and the spring of backflow
The waterfalls and the spectacular peak
The karst caves and plant communities
But fail to paint
The appearance of dim valleys and invisible waters

Look at the thousand-year-old nut trees
And ancient archways and pavilions
As if waiting for the days to come in sequence
In the chirps of insects and birds
Listen carefully
I offer a bunch of poems in the far distance
And shout to the top of the long valley
Here it really looks like heaven
Bring the world into the Qinglong Gorge
Oh let me embrace you again, like an eagle
Kissing and kissing on the shoulders of the Dragon Waterfall

---

[14] Qinglongxia Scenic Area is located in Xiuwu County, Jiaozuo City, Henan Province. It is one of the main tourist spots of Yuntai Mountain Global Geopark in Henan Province and is known as "the first Gorge in the Central Plain".

清詩明理思千載
古今抒情詩三百首
漢英對照

❀ ❀ ❀

25 ·

柳 金農

銷魂橋外綠匆匆,樹亦銷魂客送空。
萬縷千絲生便好,剪刀誰說勝春風?

The Drooping Willow Jin Nong

Beyond the Heart-Broken Bridge
lush and luxuriant are the green

willows; seeing the guests off,
the trees are also heart-broken.

Myriads of drooping willows
are fair by themselves —

who says a pair of scissors
cut sharper than spring breeze?

在四月桐的夢幻邊緣 林明理

多麼美麗的初夏
我不停地尋思
像隻藍蝶找到了小瀑布
你彈著遙遠的琴音
在四月桐的夢幻邊緣
如鳴泉飛雨

輕輕
漫過林野,穿繞溪間
等待一個相約
在螢舞季節
懸在我耳畔,依呀作響

要是我能穿越時空
浸沉於台三線山谷的夜色
只有蟲鳴和水聲
從高處越嶺而來
啊,所有話語都無法描繪
你是獨奏的驚雪

On the Edge of the Fond Dream of April Parasol Tree
Lin Ming-Li

What a beautiful early summer
I keep thinking
Like a blue butterfly who has found a small waterfall
You play the distant music
On the edge of the fond dream of April parasol tree
Like the fountain noisy with flying rain

Gently
Through the woods, across the stream
Waiting for an appointment
In the season of dancing fireflies
Hovering in my ears, with a noise

If I can travel through time & space
To be immersed in the night of Taisanxian Valley
With only the sound of insects and water
Coming from the high mountains
Ah, no words can describe
You as a solo of surprising snow

清詩明理思千載
古今抒情詩三百首
漢英對照

❀ ❀ ❀

26·

湖樓題壁   厲鶚

水落山寒處,盈盈記踏春。
朱欄今已朽,何況倚欄人。

Inscription on the Wall of a Lakeside Pavilion   Li E

The rivers and creeks are still
running in the cold mountain,

where we have ever gone on
spring outing from year to year

—my love and me. The red
balustrade is red no more; my

fair lady is fair no more — yet she
lingers and stays in my memory.

七星潭之戀   林明理

我喜歡聆聽大海,看慢舞的雲彩
一灣澄碧的水,浪花輕吻堤岸
在靜謐的月牙灣低迴

誰要是沒有領略過
旭日、沙灘和輕風
就無法理解歡樂或痛苦或漂泊的憂傷

我茫茫然回首,多少年後
會響起什麼樣的聲音
就像這風兒把愛輕輕寫在沙上

林明理攝於臺灣花蓮縣
七星潭
Photo taken by Lin Ming-Li by the Seven-Star Pool, Hualien County, Taiwan

Love of the Seven-Star Pool   Lin Ming-Li

I like to listen to the sea, to see the slow-dancing clouds
A bay of clear water, waves gently kissing the bank
Lowly back in the quiet crescent bay

Those who have not experienced
The rising sun, sand and gentle wind
Fail to understand joy or pain or the wandering sorrow

Blankly I look back, years later
What sound will be aloud
Like the wind which is writing love gently in the sand

❁ ❁ ❁

27 ·

竹石   鄭燮

咬定青山不放鬆,立根原在破岩中。
千磨萬擊還堅勁,任爾東西南北風。

清詩明理思千載
● 古今抒情詩三百首
　　漢英對照,

A Bamboo Biting in the Rock   Zheng Xie

of the green mountain
is deeply rooted in the

crevice. Windswept,
weathered, weather-beaten,

weather-worn, it is still
strong and sturdy, in spite

of winds from the north
or south or east or west.

通海秀山[15]行   林明理

仰臥海峽
反覆想起你的面容
那墨綠的森林睡得多香甜
從雲嶺江南間透出了
一輪明月，映照千古的詩
多光燦的穹天

是什麼樹
把你遮得如此茂密
訴說這座雄城的蒼茫
像一首沉思的船歌

是什麼雨
和詩人一樣多情
擁有同一片天空
俯視滇中的大地

---

[15] 秀山位於中國雲南省玉溪市通海縣縣城南隅。

是什麼花
沿著石砌的山道
開在三元宮內
如此高雅，未曾衰老

是什麼碑刻
遍懸著歌頌你
秀甲南滇的美譽
在古柏閣的迴廊間

是什麼聲音
試圖喚起我
在純淨的光波裡
閱盡這亭臺楹聯的美妙

我泅過通海的陽光
還有古木和安詳的河流
我看見自己站在
百里杞湖，彷若隔世
而你在陽光下成長
目光炯炯，微笑如風

Journey to the Fair Mountain[16] in Tonghai County
Lin Ming-Li

Lying over the straits
To repeatedly think of your face
The dark green forest sleeps so sweetly
From the cloudy ranges of the Southern Shore

---

[16] The Fair Mountain is located in the south of Tonghai County, Yuxi City, Yunnan Province, China.

清詩明理思千載
古今抒情詩三百首
漢英對照,

A wheel of moon peeps, to shine over the poems of thousands of years
How brilliant is the sky

What kind of tree
Covers you so thickly
Speaking of the vastness of this mighty city
Like a contemplative boat song

What kind of rain
Sentimental like a poet
Under the same sky
Overlooking the land of central Yunnan province

What kind of flowers
Along the stony mountain path
Blooming in the Ternary Palace
So elegantly, never aging

What kind of inscriptions
Hanging to sing praises of you
Renowned beauty of Southern Yunnan province
In the cloisters of the pavilion of ancient pines

What kind of sound
Trying to arouse me
In the pure light wave
To read and admire the wonder of the pavilion couplets

I swim through the sunshine of Tonghai County
As well as the ancient trees and the peaceful river
I see myself standing by
The Qi Lake spreading for a hundred miles, as if in the previous existence
You are growing up in the sunshine
Your eyes are bright, and your smile like a gentle wind

♆ ♆ ♆

28.

濰縣署中畫竹   鄭燮

衙齋臥聽蕭蕭竹，疑是民間疾苦聲。
些小吾曹州縣吏，一枝一葉總關情。

Written on a Painting of Bamboo
Zheng Xie

The bamboo leaves are rustling
and whispering without the

window of my office, which
seem to be the complaints

of the people. A petty official
I am, yet all the bamboo

leaves, all the people's hard-
ships, are my close concern.

敘利亞內戰悲歌   林明理

風起了
　　環視這片焦土——
八年苦戰之夜
每道光，都令人抖顫！
每次襲擊，
　　都是哀嚎。

這場戰爭，——
令三十七萬餘人
　　數千名兒童死於戰火。

清詩明理思千載
● 古今抒情詩三百首
　　漢英對照，

千萬個敘利亞人
　到異國他鄉
　艱難地討生活。

啊，難民危機仍在，——
　失學的
　　乞討的兒童…
天空哭泣了！
　返鄉之路——
　　路迢迢。

—2019.08.06

Dirge for the Syrian Civil War Lin Ming-Li

The wind rises
　Looking about the scorched land —
Eight years of bitter war in the night
Each beam of light is shocking!
Each attack,
　　It is a sad cry.

The war —
Has killed more than 370,000 people
　And thousands of children.
Tens of millions of Syrians
　Are struggling to make
　A living in a foreign land.

Ah, the refugee crisis is still there —
　　Those who are drop out of school
　　And the begging children……
The sky is weeping!
　The homeward road —
　　Is so long, so lengthy.

—August 6, 2019

🌷 🌷 🌷

29 ·

閒蛙   倪瑞璿

草綠清池水面寬,終朝閣閣叫平安。
無人能脫征賦累,只有青蛙不屬官。

Croaking Frogs   Ni Ruixuan

Grass growing green by a
pool wide with limpid water,

where frogs are croaking
freely from morning to

night. No, nobody can be
free from official levy &

tax, except the frogs, who
are governed by nobody.

夜裡聽到礁脈   林明理

那一定源自海的髮梢
　飄遊著,
白的夜,比它更稠密的水
顫顫地　在冰天裡迴旋。

湖面是一岬山影相疊,
映著斑嘴環企鵝的儀隊

清詩明理思千載
● 古今抒情詩三百首
　　漢英對照,

在甜眠，一隻白鯊縱情
遊弋於未經探險的深礁。

我不禁循著灣邊和老樹叢
諦聽
這模糊中的藍灰的綠
瞧，星星也已連動；

各處的風，滿地的葉
　彷彿一起呼號，
只有人類錯誤的迷失，
　不驚不響。

而我的追尋
執著與愛的力量，
　緊跟著風
許會在未來，端視海洋！

The Reef Is Heard at Night   Lin Ming-Li

It must be from the hair ends of the sea
　Floating,
The white night, the water denser than it
Trembling and whirling in the icy sky.

The surface of the lake is a shadow of mountains,
Reflecting the spotted-bill penguin guard
Sweet sleeping, a white shark is letting loose
Swimming in the deep reef which remains unexplored.

I cannot help but follow the bay and the old trees
To hear
The blue & grey green in the blur
Look, the stars are on the moving;

The wind from all directions, the leaves all over the ground
    Seem to cry and wail together,
Only human beings are lost in error,
    Without any trembling sound.

And my pursuit
The power of love and perseverance,
    Closely following the wind
Perhaps in the future, examining the sea!

✿ ✿ ✿

30 ·

馬嵬   袁枚

莫唱當年長恨歌，人間亦自有銀河。
石壕村裡夫妻別，淚比長生殿上多。

Concubine Yang   Yuan Mei

Sing no more songs about the love
between the emperor & Concubine Yang;

the Silver River severs a mortal
couple after another couple. In *The*

Stone Moat Village, a famous poem
by Bai Juyi, the connubial love is

greater than the imperial love depicted
in *The Song of Everlasting Sorrow*.

87

清詩明理思千載
古今抒情詩三百首
漢英對照

昨天下了一場雨　　　　　　　　　　林明理

你坐在開滿艾菊的岸邊
孤伶伶地佇候
也許你未曾注意
在你焦慮的目光裡，我已悄悄成長
當春天來臨
我就是那朵隱藏在飛燕草款冬裡的花
聽你神秘的詩思
在我耳畔輕聲細語

It Has Rained Last Night　　　　Lin Ming-Li

You are sitting alone by the shore fair with bitter buttons
Waiting solitarily
Perhaps you fail to notice
In your anxious sight, I have grown up quietly
With the advent of spring
I am the flower hidden in the delphinium
To listen to your mysterious poetic thoughts
Whispering in my ears

♈ ♈ ♈

31．

遣興　　　　　　　　　　　　　　袁枚

愛好由來下筆難，一詩千改始心安。
阿婆還似初笄女，頭未梳成不許看。

Inspired on Poetry Composition

Yuan Mei

Striving for poetic beauty, it is
hard to compose a perfect poem,

though it is polished, revised,
and improved — still with little

satisfaction. A veteran poet is like
a naïve girl, who refuses to show

herself up in the public before she
finishes her prinking & primping.

感謝在我身邊

林明理

這是 2024 年秋天,
飛燕掠過山脈與藍色的海洋
　以及轉黃的稻穗;
我在東岸的水聲與塵灰中,
　想像命運之輪
把我們帶向何其相似的路。

縱然不知路的盡頭在哪兒,
　但我仍會回首瞧瞧:
感謝你,讓我滿懷欣喜
把生命中
　甜蜜的回憶
和那些詩歌,緊緊相繫。

－2024.9.19

清詩明理思千載
古今抒情詩三百首
漢英對照

Thanks for Being Here With Me

Lin Ming-Li

It is the autumn of 2024,
When the flying swallows sweep over the mountains and the blue sea
   And the yellowing ears of rice;
Amid the sound of water and dust on the east coast,
   I imagine the wheel of fate
Taking us along the similar path.

Even if I don't know where the end of the road is,
   I will look back to see:
Thank you, and I'm filled with joys
To connect the sweet
   Memories of life
With those poems closely.

—September 19, 2024

❀ ❀ ❀

32 ·

雞
袁枚

養雞縱雞食，雞肥乃烹之。
主人計自佳，不可使雞知。

The Chicken
Yuan Mei

The chicken is fattened
through free eating,

until it is killed for food.
This is privy to the feeder,

instead of the chicken,
who is kept in the dark.

哈特曼山斑馬[17]　　　　　　　　　林明理

天亮了，我充滿希望
　在世界變動的人群中
我仍喜歡在陡峭的山邊
　站崗著。
聽那些風聲和花鳥
　——察看敵情的預兆！

Equus Zebra Hartmannae[18]　　Lin Ming-Li

The day breaks, and I am full of hope
　In the changing world
Still I like to stand guard
　At the steep hillside
Listen to the wind and flowers & birds
　— To detect the movement of the enemy!

♣ ♣ ♣

---

[17] 哈特曼山斑馬（學名：*Equus zebra hartmannae*），又名哈氏山斑馬或山斑馬哈氏亞種，是棲息在安哥拉西南部及納米比亞西部的山斑馬亞種，是一種較為珍貴的斑馬群種，被國際自然保護聯盟（IUCN）列為易危物種。

[18] Southwestern Angola and western Namibia are major habitats of Hartmann mountain zebra (scientific name: Equus zebra hartmannae), also known as Hastelloy zebra or mountain Zebra's subspecies. These zebras have become vulnerable species according to the International Union for the Conservation of Nature (IUCN).

清詩明理思千載
● 古今抒情詩三百首
漢英對照

33．

推窗　　　　　　　　　　　　　　　　　　袁枚

連宵風雨惡，蓬戶不輕開。
山似相思久，推窗撲面來。

Upon Opening the Window　　　　　Yuan Mei

Day & night and night &
day: a nonstop violent storm;

doors and windows closely
closed up. A letup of the stormy

weather, the mountains, upon
opening the window, invade

and intrude within through
languishing longing & pining.

無論是過去或現在　　　　　　　　　　　　林明理

無論是過去或現在：湛藍和青草、
巨石與白浪、燈塔與鷗鳥，
當我喜愛這一切，
喜愛玻璃船和俏皮的梅花鹿，
而自以為是在天涯海角；

當我移動腳步，直想靠近
這綠島[19]與沙灘，岩洞與山丘，

---

[19] 綠島是一座位於臺灣臺東縣外海、太平洋中的海島，原是關政治犯的監獄，如今已改為「綠島人權文化園區」的「綠洲山莊」。

人權紀念碑前的往事和滄桑歷史，
已然隨著時間慢慢蒸散了；

當我仰天獨自遐想，
就像永久地等待——
允諾我的時間老人，
我們才剛剛相遇，甚至不願離開。

In the Past or at the Present　　　Lin Ming-Li

In the past or at the present: blue and grass,
Boulders and white waves, lighthouses and hagdons,
When I love all these,
Love glass boats and lovely sika deer,
And think I am in the ends of the earth;

When I move steps, intending to approach
The green island[20] and the beach, the cave and the hill,
The past and the historical vicissitudes before the monument of Human rights
Have slowly evaporated with the passage of time;

When I look up to the sky to daydream alone,
It is like waiting forever —
To allow my time as an old man,
We have just met, and we hate to depart from each other.

☙ ☙ ☙

---

[20] The Green Island is an island in the Pacific Ocean off Taitung County, Taiwan, which used to be a prison for political prisoners, and now it is transformed into an "Oasis Villa" of "the Green Island Human Rights and Culture Park".

清詩明理思千載
古今抒情詩三百首
漢英對照

34.

富春至嚴陵山水甚佳（其一） 紀昀

沿江無數好山迎，才出杭州眼便明。
兩岸濛濛空翠合，琉璃鏡裡一帆行。

Journeying Along the River Fair with Hills (No. 1) Ji Yun

Along the river countless fair
hills are greeting, hating to say

goodbye; out of Hangzhou, the
eye is brightened by the bright

sight: the banks are misty with
emerald green in the air, dim

and distant, and a sail is sailing
in, or through, a mirror so bright.

昨夜，在五岩山醉人的夢幻裡 林明理

昨夜，在五岩山[21]醉人的夢幻裡，
我但願，是隻不眠的白鳥！
遊到石窟上，目睹它的榮耀。

這裡已是春天，
那顆星子卻牽引著我……

---

[21] 五岩山，又名蘇門山，古有兩觀一寺，南為五岩寺，北為棲霞觀，下為葆光觀，是宗教聖地。它位於河南省鶴壁市老市區八公里處太行山北麓，因山有五谷，突起五峰，故曰五岩。

飛到高深的樹叢裡，
看佛頭山氣勢巍峨，
一種充滿梵唱的和諧，
在夜裡更感親切。

看窟龕和造像的鬼斧神工，
看護法獅子，閃著光燦的顏色！
看大氣之中，何等欣欣向榮，
看南北朝晚期藝術如此美妙！
你聽，還有各種合奏——
原來不離去的，還有沉思的蘆葦。

啊，那豈不是繆斯的腳？
讓我悄悄跟著走過去吧！
去石梯子和天池
還有
孫登洞的頂峰，
好似在一個光明的國度。

噢，只要我是隻不眠的白鳥，
親愛的，
多渴望出沒在如夢的山腰！

Last Night, in the Fond Dream of Wuyan Mountain Lin Ming-Li

Last night, in the fond dream of Wuyan Mountain[22],
I hope that I were a white bird that does not sleep!

---

[22] The Wuyan Mountain, also known as Sumen Mountain, boasts two pavilions and a temple in ancient times; to the south is Wuyan Temple, and to the north is Qixia Pavilion, below which is the Baoguang Pavilion as a religious holy place. It is located at the northern foot of Taihang Mountain, eight kilometers away from the old urban area of Hebi, Henan Province. Owing to its five valleys with five protruding peaks, the mountain is called Wuyan, or five rocks.

Swimming to the grotto, to witness its glory.

It is spring here,
Yet the star is drawing me....
Flying to the massive tall trees,
To see the Buddha Head Mountain towering and spectacular,
A kind of harmony filling Brahma singing,
More endearing at night.

Look at the extraordinary workmanship of the cave niche and the statue,
Look at the law-protecting lion, shining with a bright color!
Look at the atmosphere, which is so prosperous,
Look at the wonderful art of the late Northern and Southern dynasties!
Listen, there are ensembles —
And he who refuses to depart, the brooding reeds.

Ah, isn't that the Muse's foot?
Let me follow it quietly!
To the top of the Stone Ladder and the Heavenly Pool
As well as
The peak with Sunden Cave,
As if in a kingdom of light.

Oh, if only I were a sleepless white bird,
My dear,
How I long to haunt the mountainside of dreams!

♆ ♆ ♆

35 ·

富春至嚴陵山水甚佳（其二） 紀昀

濃似春雲淡似煙，參差綠到大江邊。
斜陽流水推篷坐，翠色隨人欲上船。

Journeying Along the River Fair with Hills (No. 2)
Ji Yun

Massy like spring clouds, pale
like lingering mist; a motley

of green is greening the bankside. The awning uplifted, to

see water running & rippling
through the slanting sunshine,

when the emerald green is
invading the manned boat.

在彼淇河[23]
林明理

看哪，這蕩蕩淇水，
像鑲滿寶石，閃閃耀耀，
你看它威然在山林
如何化為太極圖騰！
它的光線伸向穹頂，
隨時間來回飛旋……
一旦觸到豫北
就釋出燦燦的微笑。

哦，即使我無法明白，
你是如此純淨；
不知是本著創世主安排

---

[23] 淇河是豫北地區唯一一條未被污染的河流，被稱為「北方灘江」，因主要流經河南鶴壁市，因而被稱為「鶴壁市母河」。

還是為給這世界帶來異彩！……
但遠方森森古柏與
晨鐘暮鼓
似乎也在聆聽
你的琅琅之聲，好似白鶴輕躍。

By the Qi River[24] Lin Ming-Li

Look, the rippling Qi River water,
As if studded with gems, shining and glittering,
You see how spectacular it is in the mountain forest
To be transformed into Tai Ji totem!
Its light reaches into the heavenly dome,
Swirling back and forth through time……
Once it touches the north of Henan,
It gives a brilliant smile.

Oh, even though I cannot understand,
You are so pure;
Not knowing if it is arranged by the Creator
Or to bring splendor to this world! ……
But the distant massive pine trees
And the morning bell & evening drum
Seem to be listening
To your clear sound, like a white crane which is leaping.

※ ※ ※

---

[24] The Qi River is the only unpolluted river in northern Henan Province, known as "the Fair Lijiang River in the North"; since it mainly flows through the city of Hebi, Henan Province, it is called the "Mother River of He."

36 ·

題畫 　　　　　　　　　　　　　　　蔣士銓

不寫晴山寫雨山,似呵明鏡照煙鬟。
人間萬象模糊好,風馬雲車便往還。

Inscription on a Painting 　　　Jiang Shiquan

The mountain veiled in rain, instead
of a sunlit mountain, is painted —

seemingly, a bright mirror is mirroring
a peak wreathed in suffusing fog.

It is ideal for myriads of things in
the world to be vague and obscure,

through which carriages, like winds
& clouds, come and go at great ease.

重遊石門水庫[25] 　　　　　　　　　林明理

那年,夏風走過
大壩淼淼波光
林道上不見楓紅
卻喚起了我親切的情感與詩篇

百花開遍公園
綠潭與白鷺

---

[25] 石門水庫啟用於 1964 年,耗資約 32 億台幣,位於桃園市大溪區、龍潭區、復興區,是臺灣第一座多功能水庫。每年秋末冬初,槭林公園及楓林步道,是最佳賞遊之處。

清詩明理思千載
古今抒情詩三百首
漢英對照

唱出我最純粹的感動
山巒越發明晰，蟲鳴繞繚寂靜

啊，我願是飛遠的那隻灰鳥
重尋記憶裡青澀的童年
呼吸在遊艇上如此飄然
往事、歡悅還有歌聲──
沸騰了我的血

作者於 2012 年 7 月 13 日與臺師大胡其德教授、蔣教授同遊石門水庫留影。
On July 13, 2012, the author took a photo with Professor Hu Qide and Professor Jiang from Taiwan Normal University at Shimen Reservoir.

Once More to Shimen Reservoir[26]

Lin Ming-Li

That year, the summer wind blows across
The dam is brilliant with waves
The forest road is bare of any maple-red
Yet it arouses my endearing feelings and poems

A variety of flowers bloom in the park
Green pools and white egrets
Sing out my purest touch
The mountains are clearer, insects chirping through lingering silence

---

[26] Shimen Reservoir is put into use in 1964 at the cost of about 3.2 billion Taiwan dollars. It is located in Daxi District, Longtan District, and Fuxing District of Taoyuan City as the first multifunctional reservoir in Taiwan. Each year in late autumn and early winter, Maple Forest Park and Maple Forest Trail are the best scenic spots to visit.

Oh, I wish I were the gray bird flying far away
In search of the green childhood in memory
So ethereal is the breath on the yacht
The past events, joys, and songs—
Which boil my blood

🌷 🌷 🌷

37 ·

論詩　　　　　　　　　　　　　　　趙翼

李杜詩篇萬口傳，至今已覺不新鮮。
江山代有才人出，各領風騷數百年。

On Poetry Writing　　　　　　　Zhao Yi

The poems by twin-poets of
Li Bai and Du Fu are read from

lips to lips, from generation to
generation, but now they fail

to cater to public taste. Gifted
poets are born and reborn in the

land of fair hills and rills, each
leading the way for hundreds of years.

清雨塘　　　　　　　　　　　　　林明理

野花飛落，雨繞樹輕舞
池面，像綠蔭的春野
在纏路的水草底下
映出永不退縮的天邊

清詩明理思千載
古今抒情詩三百首
漢英對照

遊魚笑語低昂
月意是久別重逢的杳然
夜啊，一片雪花消融的哀音
讓天地互相傳看

Limpid Rain Pond Lin Ming-Li

Wild flowers flying, raindrops gently dancing about the trees
The surface of the pond is like the spring field alive with green shadows
Under the entwining floating grass
The never-retreating horizon is reflected

The swimming fishes are gurgling
The moon is distant, a reunion after long separation
Oh, night, the dirge of a melting snowflake
For the heaven and earth to see by turns

❦ ❦ ❦

38 ·

野步 趙翼

峭寒催換木棉裘，倚仗郊原作近遊。
最是秋風管閒事，紅他楓葉白人頭。

Ambling in the Wilderness Zhao Yi

A faint chill, and I change myself into a cotton-padded coat;

a cane in hand, I am ambling
in the wilderness within my

physical strength. The autumn wind is meddling and busy-

bodied — to redden maple leaves and to whiten people's heads.

獻給湯顯祖之歌　　　　　　　　　林明理

風在演奏你的樂曲
那柳影沉垂靜謐
那小湖碧波的三生樓
那一段水袖流連的摺子戲
還是和往昔一樣
時光未曾衰老
而你的愛已生長成故鄉的星子
聚在牡丹亭上呢喃溫存
瞧，山茶花
在你的身旁唱起了歌
多少歲月過去了
又承載了多少悲歡離合的故事
重演這舞臺上的多少舊夢
以及那深深淺淺的離愁
多少次目光彌留在南城
你閃亮了東方的靈魂
就如雪松和大地輝耀

我好似一隻蝶兒
在秋日裡迷了路
在銀杏和紅楓林中漫舞
輕吻蘆葦旁的燈芯草
忽兒吹來了園中桂花的芳香
忽而又送來了樹林的舞蹈
在我心中撫河靜臥成銀色

清詩明理思千載
* 古今抒情詩三百首
  漢英對照,

而你的身影朝霞般絢爛
一切是那麼熟悉
又那麼神奇
在波光的倒影中傲然屹立
溢滿鷗鳥的鳴啼
可我在風中
在遠方的綠野中穿行
啊,請同我乾一杯貢酒
你鮮活的碑表上
在臨川之鄉,刻著中國的莎士比亞之名

A Song Dedicated to Tang Xianzu, Shakespeare in China
Lin Ming-Li

The wind is playing your tune
The willowy shadows are sinking in silence
The Three-Life-Tower which boasts a small lake rippling with wave
The folding opera filled with water sleeves
Still the same as in the past
Time has not grown old
When your love has grown into the stars of your hometown
Gathering and whispering warmly over the Peony Pavilion
Look, camellia
Sings beside you
How many years have gone by
With how many stories of joys and sorrows
Restaged are how many old dreams
And how many deep and shallow departing sorrows
How many times the eyes are fixed in the South City
You have brightened the soul of the east
Like cedars and the brilliant earth

I am like a butterfly
Who has lost his way in autumn

Dancing in the ginkgo and red maple forest
Gently kissing the rushes next to the reeds
Suddenly wafting is the sweet-scented osmanthus in the garden
And then the dance of the woods
In my heart the river is lying quietly into silver
When your figure is gorgeous like the morning glow
Everything is so familiar
And so magical
Standing proud in the reflection of the waves of light
Overflowing with the music of seagulls
But I am caught in the wind
Walking in the distant green field
Ah, please toast with me a cup of wine
On your vivid monument
In your native place of Linchuan, carved is your name as Shakespeare in China

❦ ❦ ❦

39．

江上竹枝詞（其四）　　　　　　　姚鼐

東風送客上江船，西風催客下江船。
天公若肯如儂願，便作西風吹一年。

Bamboo Branch Song on the River (No. 4)
Yao Nai

The east wind arising,
the boat leaves my home;

the west wind arising,
the boat returns home.

清詩明理思千載
古今抒情詩三百首
漢英對照

O Heaven, please grant
my fond wish: blow, blow

—keep the west wind
blowing through the year.

書寫王功漁港　　　　　　　　　　　林明理

風車在漁港中歌唱
漁港也在潮間中激響
望海寮上一艘艘竹筏搖擺
如整齊一致的黑武士

水鳥說話——紅樹林說話
招潮蟹更是說話
彈塗魚說話，濕地說話
而我，是靜默的島

從夜晚翩翩而來
佇在燈塔最高的視界
你所給我的
粼粼波光照影，曾是驚鴻[27]

On Wanggong Fishing Port　　Lin Ming-Li

The windmill is singing in the fishing harbor
And the fishing harbor is aloud in the tide
One after another bamboo raft on the sea
Are swaying like the neat black knight.

---

[27] 王功漁港是臺灣彰化縣八景之一。據記載，早在三百八十多年前，先民從福建渡海來臺灣，即在此定居。漁港裡有座黑白條紋的芳苑燈塔，是台灣本島最高的燈塔；還有十座風力發電機組、造型獨特的圓拱橋、望海寮、濕地生態、夕照等景色。

Water birds talk — mangroves talk
And fiddler crabs talk
Mudskippers talk, wetlands talk
And I am an island of silence

Coming elegantly from the night
To the highest view of the lighthouse
What you give me
Is the reflection of rippling waves, which has been graceful[28]

❀ ❀ ❀

40 ·

別老母 　　　　　　　　　　　　黃景仁

搴帷別母河梁去，白髮愁看淚眼枯。
慘慘柴門風雪夜，此時有子不如無。

Parting With My Old Mother　Huang Jingren

Lifting the curtain, parting with
my old mother, I cross a bridge

after another bridge; white-crowned,
sorrow-laden, she cries her eyes dry.

---

[28] Wanggong Fishing Port is one of the eight scenic spots in Changhua County, Taiwan. According to records, as early as 380 years ago, the ancestors crossed the sea from Fujian to Taiwan to settle here. There is a black and white striped Fangyuan lighthouse in the fishing harbor, which is the highest lighthouse on the island of Taiwan; and there are also ten wind turbines, unique round arch Bridges, Wanghailiao, wetland ecology, sunset and other scenic spots.

The darkish wooden gate seems
to be swallowed by the night stormy

with wind and snow — with a
son is no better than without a son.

蘿蔔糕[29] 　　　　　　　　　林明理

在鯉魚山市集
我瞥見了——
　　腦海中的畫面
那是蘿蔔糕
在爐灶上
四溢。

每逢佳節
我常吮吸著
那怦然的氣味
貼進大地風是甜的
勤奮的母親輕煽著
　　　　柴火……

而月彎垂，透過
半開的　木門
還有夢中雞啼——
啊，童年

---

[29] 「蘿蔔糕」的台灣話稱為「菜頭粿」。印象中，母親會將米洗淨泡水，隔夜再用石磨製成米漿，又把白蘿蔔去皮刨絲，加水再入鍋悶煮至蘿蔔軟爛。最後填入圓型蒸籠中。待涼脫模，可感覺到，一種原樸的味道。母親會切塊煎香，食用時，沾點醬油膏或甜辣醬。天冷時，還可將之切成條狀，用高湯煮，加些香菇、芹菜及茼蒿，十分可口。

記憶已成斑駁
我不得不重新刷新

Turnip Pudding[30]   Lin Ming-Li

At the Lei Yue Shan Market
I caught a glimpse —
A mental image
Of turnip cake
Spilling over
The stove.

Each festival
I often suck
The palpitating scent
Stuck to the earth the wind is sweet
Diligent Mother gently fanning
The firewood....

And the moon bent, through
The half-open wooden door
And the chicken crowing in my dream —
Ah, my childhood
Memories have become vague and mottled
And I have to refresh them

---

[30] "Radish cake" is called "caitou kueh" in Taiwanese. In my impression, Mother washes the rice and soaks it in water, and then uses stone grinding to make rice pulp overnight, and peels the white radish, before adding water to boil it into the pot until the radish is soft, finally to fill the circular steamer. Wait for the cool mold, and you can feel a kind of primitive taste. Mother would cut them into pieces to fry them. When she eats them, she dips them in soy sauce or sweet spicy sauce. When the weather is cold, you can also cut it into strips, cook it with stock, add some shiitake mushrooms, celery and chrysanthemums, which is very yummy.

清詩明理思千載
古今抒情詩三百首
漢英對照

41 ·

新雷 張維屏

造物無言卻有情，每於寒盡覺春生。
千紅萬紫安排著，只待新雷第一聲。

The First Thunder of Spring Zhang Wei-ping

The Creator is speech-
less, yet perceptive:

cold ending, spring
on the growing. One

thousand flowers, red
or purple, are ready

to bloom — until the
first thunder of spring.

春之歌 林明理

春天，你唱著穿過了花城
那是什麼樣的仙樂
讓鳥獸都在歡欣中來到你面前
讓遍地花木草葉都有了語言
那是什麼樣的仙樂
讓我一遍又一遍四處尋覓
一心要用韻律譜寫你的神秘
以及你眼裡的溫存

那是時間鳴奏著你搖映發光的臉
還是你細細端詳塵世裡的悲

噢，春天，你毋須告別
你是夢裡的雲朵
輕微的　輕微的
拂拭每個人的傷口和淚水
你是不涸的泉源
滋潤著世界萬物
任誰也譜不出你悠遠的清音
任誰也描不出你綻開的笑意

The Song of Spring　　　　　　　Lin Ming-Li

Spring, you sing through the flower city
What kind of heavenly music
For birds and animals to come to you joyfully
For flowers and grassy leaves all over ground to be wordy
What kind of heavenly music
For me to search here and there time and again
To single-mindedly write about your mystery
As well as the tenderness in your eyes
That is the time to play on your face
Or you carefully look at the sadness of the world

Oh, spring, you do not have to say goodbye
You are a cloudy blossom in the dream
Gently　so gently
To wipe the wounds and tears of everybody
You are an inexhaustible fountain
To moisten myriads of things in the world
Nobody can trace your distant and melodious sound
Nobody can describe your blossoming smile

※ ※ ※

清詩明理思千載
古今抒情詩三百首
漢英對照

42.

己亥雜詩（之五） 龔自珍

浩蕩離愁白日斜，吟鞭東指即天涯。
落紅不是無情物，化作春泥更護花。

Miscellanies Composed in 1839 (No. 5)
Gong Zizhen

The sun declining, my boundless grief refuses to decline;

urging with a horse whip —
an eastbound journey —

to the horizon. Falling &
fallen red is not a heartless

thing: turned to earth, it
nurtures & nourishes flowers.

湖畔冥想 林明理

沒有什麼更讓我雀躍，當我像一隻黑鳥
　　飛過青青大草原
　　　　或那片嫣紅的毛地黃
歇在湖水映著濛濛的山嵐
　　在冬日微涼的霞光之中
　　在初升太陽於太平洋之中⋯⋯我夢見
自己騎著單車，緩緩在湖畔的草垛旁
　　欣喜和你相遇

遠眺週遭樸實寧靜的原野
我會掠過山林深處連續不斷的蟲鳴
　在觀海聽潮之後又開始歌著
只要風　再引我走一趟舊路
我就會看見盡收眼底的花叢
　有鳳蝶與我一同飛起
白鷺翩翩，在白雲的光影中
啊，我可以什麼都不要，如果──
能抓得到夢，我期待已久的旅程就會來到

Lakeside Meditation　　　　　　Lin Ming-Li

Nothing makes me happier than flying like a black bird
　　Across the boundless green prairie
　　Or the pink patch of foxglove
Resting in the mountain misty in lake water
　　In the cool rosy light of winter
Watching the sun rising above the Pacific Ocean... I dream
Myself slowly riding a bicycle on the grassy shore of the lake
　　Joyfully meeting with you
　　Looking down at the plain and the quiet field
I pass through the insects' chirping in the depths of the mountain
　　After watching the tide, I begin to sing again
As long as the wind leads me to the old road
I will see an eyeful of clusters of flowers
　　There is a swallowtail butterfly flying with me
The egret flying elegantly, in the light and shadow of white clouds
Ah, I don't want anything, if —
I can hold fast to the dream, my long-awaited journey will begin

🌷 🌷 🌷

清詩明理思千載
古今抒情詩三百首
漢英對照

43.

己亥雜詩（之一二五） 龔自珍

九州生氣恃風雷，萬馬齊喑究可哀。
我勸天公重抖擻，不拘一格降人才。

Miscellanies Composed in 1839 (No. 125)
Gong Zizhen

A great thunder is in great
need for the rejuvenation

of our country; lamentable:
thousands of horses are

standing mute. I urge the
Lord of Heaven to cheer

and brace up again: talented
people are to be greatly valued.

寫給屈原之歌 林明理

今夜，我在汨羅歌唱
用我粗獷的語言和深情
　　你的眼神加注了
　　真實節奏
　　在風中，彷彿江水
投射出高貴的氣質

而我的歌不說你的傷心
只順著江畔奔跑
星海曉得

你的才華豐盈深厚
流浪心靈中
完成了中國不朽的辭賦

我看見歲月流逝
也聆聽出你歌裡的
沉默與堅韌
你擎起一盞燈
照亮了
人類絕世的光芒

今夜，我在汨羅歌唱
　　屈原
　　這名字迴盪著我
　　你的詩園是我四季的庇護所
　　而留給我們的詩句
如迎向曙光的百合

A Song for Qu Yuan　　　　　　Lin Ming-Li

Tonight, I sing by the Miluo River
With my rough language and deep feeling
　　Your eyes add to
　　The real rhythm
　　In the wind, as if the river water
Has projected a noble temperament

And my song does not speak your sadness
Only running along the river
The star-sea knows
Your talent is boundlessly profound
In the wandering soul
To complete the immortal Chinese poem

I see the years slipping by

And have heard the silence and the tenacity
In your songs
You have held up a light
To enkindle
The light of humanity

Tonight, I sing by the Miluo River
   Qu Yuan
     The name is echoing with me
       Your garden of poetry is my shelter through four seasons
     And the poems left to us
Are like lilies bathed in the flush of dawn

⚘ ⚘ ⚘

44 •

日本雜事詩   黃遵憲

拔地摩天獨立高，蓮峰湧出海東濤。
二千五百年前雪，一白茫茫積未消。

Mount Fuji of Japan   Huang Zunxian

By itself, Mount Fuji rises
from the ground as a sky-

scraper, and the Lotus Peak
towers over the East Sea.

The snow, through two
thousand and five hundred

years, still remains pure
white, refusing to thaw, to die.

嵩山[31]之夢　　　　　　　　　　　林明理

高高地
在如此多的山之間
我迷失了
如一隻歌雀奔向叢林
銜著綠色的夢
當七彩的靈光　耀滿山頭

啊，我飛翔
當沉睡的地殼呼喚我
真的嗎
這是夯土築城的亳都
真的嗎
這是站成永恆的佛寺

這奇異的峻峰
是夢，又不是夢
我迷失了
連秋月與星空
嵩陽書院
也溶進了我遐想的心

啊，我飛翔
北瞰黃河和洛水
南覽潁水和箕山
面對林立宮觀
我合十
是的，我還要跟山水對話

---

[31] 嵩山位於河南省，是五嶽的中嶽。古詩曰：「嵩高維嶽，峻極於天」，無論從自然地質還是文化遺存上，嵩山都堪稱五嶽之尊、萬山之祖，也是儒釋道共處的聖地之一。

飛過博物院和觀星台
飛過古城、關隘和戰場
穿過白雲和山風
心　卻一直醒著
聽戲曲聲聲
一顆心　也被鎖住了

啊，我飛翔
在茶樓
在巷弄
我翹首向來路張望
那些早已過去
如煙的往事已化為微笑

深深地
聽見了海峽的呼吸
感到了月亮的孤獨
我匆匆地來
卻迷失了
迷失在讚美嵩山的那一瞬

The Dream of Songshan Mountain[32]

Lin Ming-Li

Tall and towering
Among so many peaks
I am lost
Like a song sparrow running to the jungle

---

[32] Mount Song, located in Henan Province, is the middle one of the five mountains, as in the ancient poetic lines: "lofty is Mount Song, high-rising is the sky". Whether from natural geology or cultural relics, Mount Song can be called the ancestor of the five mountains, and it is one of the sacred places where Confucianism, Buddhism and Taoism coexist.

With a green dream
When the seven-colored ethereal light is brilliant all over the mountain

Ah, I fly
When the slumbering earth calls me
Is it real
This is the capital constructed with rammed earth
Is it real
This is a Buddhist temple standing into eternity

The eerie lofty peak
A dream, and not a dream
I am lost
Even the autumn moon and the starry sky
The Songyang Academy
Has also dissolved into my heart of reverie

Ah, I fly
Northward view of the Yellow River and Luoshui River
Southward view of Yingshui River and Jishan Mountain
Before a forest of palaces
I cross my hands
Yes, I also want to talk with the landscape

Flying over the museum and the observatory
Over the ancient city, the pass and the battlefield
Through the white clouds and the mountain wind
The heart is always awake
Listening to the opera
A heart is also locked

Ah, I fly
In the teahouse
In the alley
I lift my gaze at the way where I come from
Those dim and distant
Past events have turned into a beaming smile

Deeply
I have heard the breath of the strait
I have felt the loneliness of the moon
I come in great haste
And I am lost
In the moment of praising Mount Song

❀ ❀ ❀

45 ·

山村夜雨   祁寯藻

山村寂歷夜深清，夢醒涼雲枕簟生。
三百人家燈火裡，一時齊聽灑窗聲。

Night Rain in a Mountain Village   Qi Junzao

The mountain village is
isolated when night is pure

and deep; awakening from a
dream, cool clouds are born of

the bamboo mat. Three hundred
households, lit with lamps,

are giving ear to the raindrops
dropping against the window.

當愛情靠近時   林明理

我動作猛迅
　毫不遲疑

也絕不懊惱或怕嘲笑
只記得曾一塊兒談心
一塊兒追逐夢想

我會像小鹿斑比
　　在湖邊跳躍
嬌羞而美麗
彷若遊蕩雲間
心扉也因傷感而澄淨

當愛情靠近時
我會像一支小提琴
　　嘰哩嘩啦地自鳴起來
我選擇相信它的傳說
　　雖然愛得還不算深

When Love Approaches   Lin Ming-Li

I move fast and speedily
　　Without hesitation
Without any annoyance or fear to be ridiculed
I remember our talking to each other
Chasing the dream together

Like little deer Bambi
　　Leaping by the lake
Shy and beautiful
As if wandering through the clouds
My heart is limpid with sorrow

When love approaches
Like a violin I will
　　Sing to myself noisily
I choose to believe its legend
　　Though the love is not adequately deep

清詩明理思千載
古今抒情詩三百首
漢英對照

🌷🌷🌷

46 ·

邯鄲旅店　　　　　　　　　　　王星誠

滿衣塵土晚停車，洗腳升堂一碗茶。
自撿松枝蒸粟飯，不知清夢落天涯。

The Inn of Handan　　　　Wang Xingxian

Covered and soiled with dust,
the evening sees a carriage

coming to a stop; washing feet
before going to the hall for a

bowl of tea. Picking pine twigs
as firewood to cook food, the

lodger does not know a pure
dream has fallen in the horizon.

冬日神山部落[33]　　　　　　　林明理

冬日大武山的寧靜裡
有神秘清昂的魔力：
柔和的光澤與雀榕樹的斑斕，

---

[33] 神山部落（Kabalelradhane）位於臺灣屏東縣霧臺鄉。大武山，最高峰也稱北大武山（Kavulungan），是屏東縣境內唯一超過三千公尺的高山。五色鳥（Taiwan Barbet）是臺灣的特有亞種鳥類。魯凱族（魯凱語：Drekay），為臺灣原住民族。

院牆小貓慵懶的哈欠聲。
霧裊裊的岩板巷,
環繞部落孤遺的地……

有時一隻五色鳥飛起,
宛若預告幸福的閃現,
又像是萬物靜止的終點。
我在魯凱族孩童身上
找回生命中不悔的歡愉。

Sacred Mountain Tribe in Winter[34]

Lin Ming-Li

In the winter tranquility of Dawu Mountain
There is a mysterious great magic:
The soft luster and the gorgeous banyan trees,
The lazy yawn of kittens beneath the courtyard wall.
The foggy slate alley
Encircles the tribe's abandoned land...

Occasionally a five-colored bird flies,
As if heralding a flash of happiness,
Again like the end of all quiet things.
In the children of Lukai ethnic group
I trace the unregretted joy of life.

☙ ☙ ☙

---

[34] The Kabalelradhane tribe is in Wutai Township, Pingtung County, Taiwan. Dawu Mountain, whose highest peak is also called Kavulungan, is the only mountain in Pingtung County with a height of more than 3,000 meters. The five-colored bird, or Taiwan Barbet, is a subspecies of bird endemic to Taiwan. Drekay is an indigenous people of Taiwan.

清詩明理思千載
● 古今抒情詩三百首
漢英對照

47 ·

新霽　　　　　　　　　　　　　　郭慶藩

纖雲四卷碧天遙，霧散江清凍未消。
萬樹梅花香似海，因風吹送過溪橋。

Letup of a Snowfall　　　　　　Guo Qingfan

Flimsy clouds are massing
and scattering in the bound-

lessly blue sky; fog dispersed,
river clear, yet still frozen.

Myriads of plum trees are
fragrant like a sea and, blown

in the wind, the flowery scent
is carried across the creek bridge.

憶阿里山　　　　　　　　　　　　林明理

站在天堂也似的山上
清溪潺潺，天色泛紅
萬物都讓我想起你
還有那櫻花，晚霞，鐵道
奔馳的小火車
諦聽繽紛四季的風
讓我用羽翼貼近你
在山之巔，棲息在古木旁
悠然觀賞雲海變幻
四周的一切已然淡忘
看這水清山秀

看這怡人之鄉
漫步在山的雲端
我沉浸於你周圍的景色
你已撥動了我靈魂
像是在對我高歌

Memory of Ali Mountain Lin Ming-Li

Standing atop the mountain which is like heaven
The brook gurgling, the sky reddish
Everything is suggestive of you
And the cherry blossoms, sunset, railway
The little train which is running
Listening to the wind through the four seasons
Let me approach you with wings
Atop the mountain, perching beside the ancient tree
While leisurely watching the changing clouds over the sea
Everything around me has faded to be dim and distant
Look at the limpid water and fair mountain
Look at the pleasant land
Ambling through the clouds over the mountain
I am immersed in the scenery around you
You have stirred my soul
As if to be singing to me

❀ ❀ ❀

暮春 席佩蘭

十樹花開九樹空,一番疏雨一番風。
蜘蛛也解留春住,宛轉抽絲網落紅。

Late Spring

Xi Peilan

Out of ten flowering
trees nine are standing

bare, barely-clothed —
a gust of wind, a spell

of rain. Even the spider
knows well how to retain

spring: it spins a cob-
web to net the falling red.

龍田[35]桐花祭之歌

林明理

今年四月間
我又走上桐花紛飛的舊路
妳舞在芳香的風中
把霧谷染白
在步道旁
似仙女輕撫青草
喚醒綠芽,讓繆斯甦醒

林明理攝
A photo taken by Lin Ming-Li

我在林間漫步
觀看穿著大衿衫的婦女跳舞
頓時被周圍的一切迷住
這是客家桐花祭
有音樂注入這片愛情之樹
還有孩童的歡呼
而妳的靜默是令人陶醉的頌歌

---

[35] 龍田社區位於臺灣臺東縣鹿野鄉。

像不可忘卻的福鹿茶
杯沿上還殘留著一份甘醇
這是歌唱的山野
我站在這兒對妳凝神睇看
每一片花瓣都是故事
是詩
也是愛,像母親的叮嚀。

The Song of Tong Flower Festival[36]

Lin Ming-Li

In April of this year
Again I have walked on the old road alive with flying flowers of paulowi
You are dancing in the scented wind
To whiten the foggy valleys
Along the footpath
Like a fairy to gently stroke the grass
To awaken the green buds, to awaken the Muse

I am walking in the woods
Watching women dancing in their loose clothes
And I am mesmerized by everything around me
It is the Hakka Tong Flower Festival
Music infused into this tree of love
And the cheering of children
And your silence is an intoxicating ode

Like the unforgettable deer tea
The cup is still with a lingering sweet
This is a singing field in the mountain
I stand here and look at you
Each petal is a story

---

[36] Longtian Community is located in Luye Township, Taitung County, Taiwan.

清詩明理思千載
● 古今抒情詩三百首
　　漢英對照，

Is a poem
And love, like Mother's exhortation

❀ ❀ ❀

49 ·

夏夜示外　　　　　　　　　　　　　　　席佩蘭

夜深衣薄露華凝，屢欲催眠恐未應。
恰有天風解人意，窗前吹滅讀書燈。

The Summer Night　　　　　　　　Xi Peilan

Deep night, thin clothes,
heavy dew; time and

again, an urge to be
persuasive of going to

bed, yet afraid of no reply.
A spell of heavenly wind,

knowingly, comes to blow
out the reading lamp.

在真實世界裡　　　　　　　　　　　林明理

「Dad, happy birthday！」
珍的手機上有這些字：
　「我要給您一個大擁抱。」
此刻，傑克卻在電腦鍵盤前
　苦於公司正要精簡人事，
並夾在「雇主和員工抗爭」中間。

在真實世界裡，
幾乎每個人的工作
　　永遠像堆疊而上的盒子，
且爬得愈高，責任愈是繁重。
多數的人為了生存，
　　寧可忍受浮世的擁塞，
不與親友欣賞雲朵和山水；

誰能偶遇奇蹟的美的存在，
誰能在大自然中吟詩，
誰能再讓愛情發生，
誰就是那位不可思議
　　卻懂得品味人生的人。

In the Real World　　　　　　Lin Ming-Li

"Dad, happy birthday!"
Jane has these words on her phone:
"I want to give you a big hug."
At the moment, Jack is in front of the computer keyboard
　　The company is downsizing,
And is caught in the "employer and employee entanglement".

In the real world,
Almost everybody's work
　　Is always like a stack of boxes,
The higher you climb, the greater responsibilities.
Most people, in order to survive,
　　Would rather endure the congestion of the floating world,
Rather than enjoy clouds and mountains with their relatives and friends;

Whoever can encounter the miraculous beauty,
Whoever can write poetry in the great nature,

Whoever can make love happen again,
He is the incredible person
Who knows how to taste life.

🌷 🌷 🌷

50 ·

聽鶯　　　　　　　　　　　　　　　　孫蓀意

空庭過雨曉煙新，恰恰鶯啼楊柳春。
好語如簧須自惜，世間識曲已無人。

The Oriole　　　　　　　　　　　　Sun Sunyi

Raindrops drop through the empty
yard, the morning fog fresh; the

oriole is chittering, chirping, twittering,
and tweeting in the willowy spring.

Keep your slick and silken tongue
to yourself — no, there is no bosom

friend, in the mortal world, who is
appreciative of your musical notes.

安義[37]的春天　　　　　　　　　　　林明理

金花開了
老村醒著

---

[37] 安義縣在江西省，是南昌市所轄的一個縣。

遠方的雲呵
你思念的是什麼

千畝櫻花　把鄉路呵暖了
我的腳印像雀鳥般
從遠方而來
落在春雨中
落在回憶裡

你的容貌
像灰瓦上的白鴿
在風中飛翔
溫柔的羽衣
飛在思念的閨樓
飛在嬉戲的石牌坊
飛在黎明的薄霧裡

那漫漫的歲月
留下了多少動人的故事
見證了多少悲歡的歷史
一種簡單的感覺
在此相會的一瞬

這是你坐過的戲台
是你走過的小巷
是你眺望的梅嶺
而你的回眸
總是令人心醉

啊，我懷著滿腔熱情
與你漫步古塘
這是你熟悉的地方
即使在夢中也能把它找到

瞧，這越冬的田又欣欣向榮
你的歌聲是百合的模樣
你的眼裡有月亮的溫存
你的背影
在青石板小徑
就是無數旅人的家

金花開了
老村醒著
遠方的雲呵
是我思念的孤獨

The Spring of Anyi[38]   Lin Ming-Li

The golden flowers are blossoming
The old village is awake
Oh the distant clouds
What are you longing for

Thousands of acres of cherry blossoms have warmed the village road
My footprints are like birds
Coming from afar
To fall in the spring rain
In the memory

Your visage
Like a dove on gray tiles
Flying in the wind
Gentle feather
Flying in the pining boudoir

---

[38] Anyi County, in Jiangxi Province, is a county under the jurisdiction of Nanchang City.

Flying in the frolicking stone archway
Flying in the thin mist of dawn

The long years
Have left behind many moving stories
Have witnessed many joys and sorrows of history
A simple feeling
Of meeting here in a moment

This is the stage you have ever sat on
This is the alley you have ever walked through
This is the plum ridge you have ever looked at
And your backward glance
Is always intoxicating

Ah, I walk with you about
An ancient pond with passion
A place with which you are so familiar
That you can trace it even in your dream

Look, the wintering field is thriving again
Your song takes the posture of the lily
Your eyes have the tenderness of the moon
Your back form
Along the blue stone path
Is the home of countless travelers

The golden flowers are blossoming
The old village is awake
Oh the distant clouds
Are the solitude of my longing

⚘ ⚘ ⚘

清詩明理思千載
古今抒情詩三百首
漢英對照

51·

書懷   周寶生

小草雨露偏,欣欣便得意。
才吐一枝花,臨風學嫵媚。

Inspired in an Instant   Zhou Baosheng

Tender grass lies prostrate
under a shower of rain;

it is freshly dewy and at
great ease. A blossom is

bursting and blossoming,
when the view assumes

to be charming, ravishing,
delightful, and wonderful.

我原鄉的欖仁樹   林明理

喔,我原鄉的欖仁樹,
樹中之樹!
你的清碧枝葉,
為何眷顧著我?
在微雨的四月,
你的生命之歌,
使我深深感動。

每日晨昏,
都看祢獨步街頭,
在滿月的夜裡,

在禪那的護念中移足。

喔,我的欖仁樹啊,
每當與你同在
就忘卻外界的煩囂,
你是臺東站前最美麗的一景,
那兒有百鳥的啼囀,
清風、群山和雲彩
我無比的豐足與幸福。

An Olive Tree of My Hometown

Lin Ming-Li

Oh, my native olive tree,
The tree of trees!
Why are your green twigs and leaves
Solicitous of me?
In April of slight rain,
Your song of life
Has moved me deeply.

Every morning and night,
I see you walking alone in the street,
At the night of a full moon,
To move your feet in the care of Zen.

Oh, my olive tree,
Whenever I am with you,
I forget the noise of the outside world.
You are the most beautiful sight before Taitung Station,
Where there are hundreds of birds twittering,
The breeze, mountains and clouds,
I am extremely rich and happy.

⚘ ⚘ ⚘

清詩明理思千載
古今抒情詩三百首
漢英對照

52 •

對月   徐韋

愁心化為水,蕩漾明月光。
將心寄明月,墮地忽成霜。

Facing the Moon   Xu Wei

Sorrowful mind into
water, and the light

from the bright moon
is rippling & poppling.

My heart leans toward
the bright moon,

whose beams fall
aground into hoar frost.

秋夜   林明理

又是一個秋夜
幽深的長巷
消融了喀什老城的夜聲.
星雲低垂
遮沒了河谷
胡楊和白樺林

啊,朋友
天池飄下
第一場雪了嗎
我在土屋一切平和

有酒
足以重溫你我相知的故事

Autumn Night　　　　　　　　　　Lin Ming-Li

Another autumn night
The deep long lane
Has swallowed the night sound of Kashgar as an old city
The stars and clouds drooping low
To veil the valleys
Poplar trees and birch forests

Ah, my friend
Has the first snow
Fallen over the Heavenly Pool?
I am at peace in the mud house
There is wine
Enough to relive the story known between you and me

❦ ❦ ❦

53 ·

鄉思　　　　　　　　　　　　　　胡友蘭

窗外瀟瀟響，孤燈淡五更。
鄉思如碧草，一夜雨中生。

Homesickness　　　　　　　　　Hu Youlan

Without the window
it is noisy; a solitary

lamp fades into the
fifth watch of the night.

清詩明理思千載
● 古今抒情詩三百首
　　漢英對照,

My homesickness
is like the green grass,

which grows over-
night in the rain.

回憶 　　　　　　　　　　　　　　　　　　　　　林明理

回憶
就像一池秋水中
最後激起的一絲漣漪

你的笑聲讓我停止做夢
你的憂傷如一場雨
讓我垂下了頭

啊，朋友，
相知一輩子肯定不夠
請用陽光、雨露和詩句
注滿我生命之河

Memory 　　　　　　　　　　　　　　　　Lin Ming-Li

Memory
Is like the last ripples
In a pool of autumn water

Your laughter stops me from dreaming
Your sorrow is like a rainfall
Which bows down my head

Oh, my friend,
A lifetime of acquaintance is not enough
Please fill the river of my life
With sunshine, rain and poetry

❀ ❀ ❀

54 ·

桐江夜泊 彭孫貽

一路春山江影空，雨添新翠落孤蓬。
微茫小徑入雲去，寺在半天疏樹中。

Tongjiang River at Night Peng Sunyi

Spring mountains all the way, the
shadows of the river are empty; the

rain, falling on the solitary pond-
weed, adds to the new green. A

narrow path, dim and distant, leads
upward into the clouds; a temple

is in mid-air, where sparse trees, like
shepherd's purse, set off its quietude.

七股潟湖[39]夕照 林明理

在夕陽下閃爍的潟湖
宛如一簇簇紫丁香
灰藍的影子沒入了
白鷺的喁喁情話中

---

[39] 七股潟湖位於臺灣臺南市七股區境內，為臺灣第一大潟湖，昔日鹽場最忙碌的季節是陽光普照、雨水較少的三月至五月，鹽民稱為「大汛季」，收之可達年產量的一半。

清詩明理思千載
● 古今抒情詩三百首
漢英對照,

而我回憶起大汎季年代
一窪窪鹽峰,晶耀如玉
依稀可以看見
包花布巾的勞工在鹽場奔忙

那紅樹林的每次顫動
都是美麗的靜默
也是我永遠的凝思

林明理　畫
A Painting by Lin Ming-Li

Evening Glow Over the Seven Lagoon Lake[40]

Lin Ming-Li

The lagoon lake glinting in the sunset
Is like clusters of lilacs
The grayish blue shadows dissolve
In the sweet murmuring of white egrets

And I recall the Great Season
A low stretch after another stretch of salt peak, crystal like jade
Faintly visible
The workers wrapped in cloth towels are busy in the salt field

Each tremor of the mangroves
Is beautiful silence
And my eternal contemplation

❦ ❦ ❦

---

[40] The Seven Lagoon Lake, as the largest lagoon lake in Taiwan, is located in Qigu District of Tainan City. In the past, the busiest season of the salt farm was from March to May when the sun shines adequately with comparatively less rain.

山行詠紅葉（其一） 蔣超

誰把丹青抹樹陰，冷香紅玉碧雲深。
天公醉後橫拖筆，顛倒春秋花木心。

Red Leaves in the Mountain (No. 1)
Jiang Chao

Who applies pigment to the
mass of trees — cold scent and

red jade against white clouds
in the depths of green woods.

Drunken, the Lord of Heaven
wields his brush capriciously,

to confuse and mix up spring
blossoms and autumn flowers.

關山[41]遊 林明理

我想畫一條溪
山巒夾著山坳
輕輕的
有白鷺掠過
或者
畫油菜花的靜默
一波波雲霧裊裊

---

[41] 關山鎮土地肥沃水源充沛，因此開發很早，清咸豐年間就有西部漢人李天送招佃入墾，今為臺灣臺東縣內較為發達的大鎮。

清詩明理思千載
● 古今抒情詩三百首
　　漢英對照,

但我框不住這片
青山
也框不住紅紅落日

我還想畫一縷炊煙
穿過灰鳥的方位
掬飲
一片幽雅的涼意
在祈求神明將我保佑前
悄悄地
將詩裡的小註
埋藏在閃亮的
褐色的土地裡

林明理　畫
A painting by Lin Ming-Li

Visiting Guanshan Town[42]　　Lin Ming-Li

I want to paint a stream
With hills and valleys
Gently
Egrets are flying by
Or
With the silence of rape flowers
Waves upon waves of lingering fog and clouds
But I fail to frame this stretch of
Green mountain
Or the red sunset

---

[42] Guanshan Town, rich in fertile land and abundant in water resources, has been developed early. During the Xianfeng Period of Qing dynasty, Li Tiansong, a Han from the west, has recruited tenants for cultivation here. Now it is a relatively developed large town in Taitung County, Taiwan.

I also want to draw a wisp of smoke
Across the grey bird's direction
To drink
A stretch of elegant cool
Before I pray to the gods to bless me
Quietly
To bury the notes
Of the poem in the
Shining brown earth

❀ ❀ ❀

56·

舟中戲題 徐悼

雪後微風捲浪遲,緩搖柔櫓怕鷗知。
舟中倦客閒憑幾,不見舟移見岸移。

On the Boat Xu Zhuo

After a snowfall, a gentle wind
slowly rolls up the waves; gently

rowing the oar, lest the seagulls
know it. On the boat, the weary

travelers sit in idleness before
a tea table, without feeling

movement of the boat —
except that of the river banks.

清詩明理思千載
古今抒情詩三百首
漢英對照

富岡海堤[43]小吟　　　　　　　　　林明理

我在海上擁抱渴望
世界已無關緊要
且讓我拾一枚思索之果
望一舟　從遠古攜浪而來

啊，加路蘭港——
多少星轉斗移
全在夢幻裡
留下一聲浩嘆

啊，逝者如斯
多少生生靈靈
全在歲月裡
隨風飄向你的襟懷

是誰穿透一部詩史
讓我悠悠思念
這藍碧的水，稀微的風與
白色的光

Ode to the Tomioka Seawall[44]　　Lin Ming-Li

At the sea I embrace longing
The world is irrelevant
Let me pick up a fruit of thought
Watching a boat　carrying waves from ancient times

---

[43] 富岡漁港是臺東縣內的第二大漁港。
[44] Fugang Fishing Port is the second largest fishing port in Taitung County, Taiwan.

Ah, Port Galuran —
How many turning stars
All in the dream
Leaving behind a long sigh

Ah, so many souls of the dead
Have thus been swept by the wind
To your bosom
Through the years

Who penetrates a history of poetry
For me to long and pine
The blue water, ethereal wind and
White light

❀ ❀ ❀

57 ·

偶成　　　　　　　　　　　　　　　沈守正

望裡平林高復低，征車兀兀走長堤。
楊花似欲留人住，亂向東風裏馬蹄。

An Impromptu　　　　Shen Shouzheng

A vista of woods high and
low; a wagon is dragging

itself forward along the long
bank. The poplar filaments

seem to detain the travelers:
the filaments, in the east wind,

清詩明理思千載
● 古今抒情詩三百首
　　漢英對照。

mass themselves into a ball after
another ball, to bind the hooves.

野地　　　　　　　　　　　　　　　　　　林明理

大清早
從草原上出發
鹿從林裡來
狐狸在湖邊遊蕩
水面擠滿了青蛙
那是白鷺在冰上打滑
秧雞和天鵝每天兩次
帶著青魚回家

此刻
濕地漸漸醒來
石楠和荊豆
是否還在水沼旁
千湖之陸
仍繼續保持著秘密
而有時，一個槍火
劃破靜寂－

獵季已開始
所有的動物都豎耳驚悸
在暈紅的碎石路上
肥沃的平地
映出發白的雲
和吉普車，音樂，搖滾般
向太陽方向駛去
下谷，上坡

只有我

一個孤獨的旅客
正耐心等待巴士啟動
別了,水塘
別了,野地和狗兒
在蒙著微光的蜻蜓翅芽上
一群鶴正準備遷徙遠去
牠們的身影也有絲絲落寞

The Wild Field   Lin Ming-Li

In early the morning
Starting off from the prairie
Deer come from the woods
Foxes stray by the lake
The surface of the water is alive with frogs
Aigrettes are gliding on the icy lake
Corncrakes and swans twice a day
Go home with herrings

At present
The wetland gradually wakes up
Heather and vitex beans
Whether or not still standing by the marsh
The land with a thousand lakes
Still keeps their secrets
Occasionally, a sound of gunfire
Breaks the silence —

The hunting season begins
All the animals are vigilant of their ears
On the road of red rubble
The fertile plain
Reflecting the pale clouds
And jeeps, music, rockingly

清詩明理思千載
● 古今抒情詩三百首
　　漢英對照

Running towards the sun
Down the valley, up the slope

Only I
A lonely traveler
Waiting patiently for the bus to start
Goodbye, the pond
Goodbye, the wild field and dogs
On the glimmering wings of the dragonfly
A bevy of cranes are ready for distant migration
The silhouette of their form appears to be solitary

✿ ✿ ✿

58 ·

鉛山河口即目（其一）　　　　　王奐曾

一重芳草一重沙，幾縷新煙幾片霞。
雨後篷窗關不得，村村屋角有梨花。

A Glimpse of Hekou Town in Yanshan County (No. 1)
Wang Huanzeng

A stretch of fragrant grass
after a stretch of sand; a few

wisps of fresh fog upon a few
blossoms of clouds. After a

rainfall, the window refuses to
be closed — pear flowers are

flowering and spreading against
the wall, from village to village.

致雙溪[45]　　　　　　　　　　林明理

夜霧瀰漫小山城，
雙溪河在我眼底喧響。
風依舊蕭索，
送來一地的寒。
那叢綠中的野薑花，
彷彿來自星群，
從平林橋下的親水公園
飛出無數白蝶，
飛向水田
飛向和悅清澈的鏡面。
忽地，一隻孤鷺飛進我的愁緒。
而明天
陽光將仍在花間跳舞，
這鄉景的光華，
寂靜，如秋。

To Shuangxi[46]　　　　　　Lin Ming-Li

The night mist fills the small mountain city,
When the Twin Creek River is noisy under my eyes.
The wind is still bleak,
Sending a groundful of cold.
The wild ginger flowers in the green cluster,
As if from the stars,
From the hydrophilic park under the Pinglin Bridge
Countless white butterflies fly out,

---

[45] 雙溪區，位於臺灣新北市東部，境內多山。
[46] Shuangxi Dist is in the east of New Taipei City, Taiwan, and it is a mountainous area.

清詩明理思千載
古今抒情詩三百首
漢英對照

Toward the water field,
Toward the pleasant and limpid mirror.
Suddenly, a lone heron flies into my melancholy.
And tomorrow
The sun will still be dancing among the flowers;
The light of the country scene,
So silent, like autumn.

❀ ❀ ❀

59·

鉛山河口即目（其二）　　　　　王奐曾

嫩綠初生枝漸新，灘頭春漲正粼粼。
一群白鷺誰驚起？有個殘陽喚渡人。

A Glimpse of Hekou Town in Yanshan County (No. 2)
Wang Huanzeng

Tender green newly born, twigs gradually fresh;the head of

the beach is alive with spring water which is rippling and

poppling. A bevy of white egrets are startled into flight — who

is the startler?Bathed in the declining sun — a ferryman.

淡水黃昏[47]　　　　　　　　　　林明理

我偏愛淡水
偏愛碼頭
偏愛踏上的暮色
遠遠，帆影搖紅
有飛鳥逗著圈子掠過
風的輕漪，讓愛燃燒起來
霞光晃漾在長波裡
有人感到很幸福
有人陷入自憐或沉思
而我搖擺的記憶
隨風揚起，像蜿蜒的河

Tamsui Dusk[48]　　　　　　　　Lin Ming-Li

I prefer fresh water
I prefer the dock
I prefer the twilight on way ahead
In the distance, the shadows of the sails are shivering with red
Some birds are flitting by in circles
Ripples of the wind, for love to burn
The rosy light is rippling in the long waves
Some people feel happy
Some people fall into self-pity or contemplation
And my swaying memories
Are blown up in the wind, like a meandering river

♈ ♈ ♈

---

[47] 臺北的淡水河風景秀麗，為臺灣美景之一。
[48] Tamsui River in Taipei is one of the most beautiful scenic spots in Taiwan.

清詩明理思千載
古今抒情詩三百首
漢英對照

60．

西池　　　　　　　　　　　　　　　　曹寅

曉風吹動木蘭橈，兩岸無人過板橋。
幾日不來春水闊，滿河葦葉雨瀟瀟。

The West Pool　　　　　　　　　Cao Yin

The morning wind blows the
orchid oar; boating through

the slab bridge, the banks are
peopleless. A few days' absence,

spring water is overbrimming
and overflowing, and a riverful

of reedy leaves are shivering
and rustling in showers of rain.

竹子湖[49]之戀　　　　　　　　　　林明理

霧裊裊在斜坡上，在竹子湖附近嬉戲不歇……當我把耳朵貼進七星山，我就聽見那百鳥在夢中振翼飛舞的旋律，那些老農在訴說著半生的酸甜，那蓬萊米原鄉的故事和不斷起伏稻浪的和絃。

臺北樹蛙鳴叫，珍貴而奇美，在水池邊跳躍。樹蟬用盡力氣嘶鳴了整個夏天。當月光灑落小油坑前，一種富於

---

[49] 竹子湖，是臺灣北部大屯山與七星山之間的一個山谷，位於臺北的陽明山公園轄區內。

音樂性的思想忽地而起,在天籟中交織——啊,飛去吧,
——那兒有沉睡中的夢土,風、海芋和清泉。

在這樣的夜,一樣的露水,啊,我甦醒,而空茫之景如水。也許那兒的光和可遇不可求的秀麗又鐫刻心動,——只為人間,而我徜徉在這島嶼東緣,在眼睛明暗交接處迎出了樹影靜怡後的思念。

Love of Zhuzihu[50]   Lin Ming-Li

The mist is curling along the slope, on the playing and frolicking by the Bamboo Lake... When I put my ears in the direction of the Seven Star Mountain, I hear the melody of hundreds of birds flying in the dream; the old farmers are telling the joys and sorrows of half a life, the story of the Penglai rice village and the chord of the undulating waves of rice.

Taipei tree frogs are chirping, precious and beautiful, leaping and jumping about the edge of the pool. The tree cicadas have shrieked with all their might through the whole summer. When the moonlight falls into the pit, a musical thought is suddenly arising, to be mingled with the sounds of nature — ah, fly away — there is the sleeping dreamland, as well as wind, arum, and clear spring.

On such a dewy night, O, I awaken, and the empty landscape is like water. Perhaps the light there and the rare beauty is engraved in the heart — only for the world, and I am wandering in the east edge of the island and, in the eyes of the intersection of light and dark, to greet the pining after the shadows of the trees quiet down.

---

[50] Zhuzihu is a valley between Datun Mountain and Qixing Mountain in northern Taiwan, within the jurisdiction of Yangmingshan Park in Taipei.

61 ·

題畫三首（其一） 　　　　　　　　　　曹寅

群山滴翠雨初收，渡口無人灌木稠。
茅屋數間門自掩，桃花深處有行舟。

Three Poems on Paintings (No. 1) Cao Yin

A crowd of hills are dripping
with green, initial letup of rain;

the ferry is deserted of travelers,
and the shrubs are thick. A few

thatched cottages whose doors
are closed from day to day; in

the depths of pear blossoms,
a small boat is slowly sailing.

水沙連[51]之戀 　　　　　　　　　　　　林明理

總想駕一葉輕舟，來到群巒浸拂著水霧的河岸，
去尋找你軀體裡彌漫的柔情與豁達。
那波紋暮光底下，遊艇徐徐緩緩。片片落葉，誕生了朵
朵漣漪，

---

[51] 日月潭風景區位於南投縣中部魚池鄉水社村，因潭景霧薄如紗，水波漣漣而得名為「水沙連」，四周群巒疊翠，全潭以拉魯島（光華島）為界，南形如月弧，北形如日輪，遂改名為「日月潭」。

154

都在你多情的懷抱裡。
總想聆聽各方風的呢喃,弄清各方魚的噤聲,
總想請時間的雨佇留,請歲月不再迅馳……
是的,在此休憩片刻吧。
就像這月光包裹著我,日月潭又名水沙連,彷彿那片野薑花,
是一首抒情的詩。在老鷹之舞,在祭神與戰舞之間,慢慢開展……
恍惚間,我已是伊達邵的一隻白鹿。
一隻白鹿,在水裡尋找生命的源頭,或者邵族的根,根在這兒延伸,
枝繁葉茂,禽鳥們在拉魯島上得以快樂地飛躍。
一隻貓頭鷹,在枝頭看著我,也在蒼穹看著我,像是要訴說什麼?
啊,沒有一種痛能夠將牠怠忽,沒有任何騷動能夠改變牠的言辭。
牠的寬容,如聖者,助族人習於堅毅,從黑夜到黎明,
在某個密葉裡安全地守護,在湖泊前,寂靜而耀眼。
不只在我心田種下了一湖新詩,還留下呼-呼的高音。

Love of Shuishalian Pool[52]   Lin Ming-Li

I always want to take a leaf of boat, to the river bank towered with mountains veiled in mist,
To find your body filled with tenderness and open-mindedness.

---

[52] The Riyuetan Pool scenic spot is located in Shuishe Village, Yuchi Township in the middle of Nantou County, which is aliased as Shuishalian Pool, or the Pool of Sandy Water for its rippling water through a filmy mist. All about it is enclosed with green hills. The whole pool is divided by Lalu Island (or Guanghua Island) as the boundary; to the south it is shaped as the arc of moon, and to the north it is shaped as the wheel of sun, hence the name of the Riyuetan Pool, or the Sun-and-Moon Pool.

清詩明理思千載
古今抒情詩三百首
漢英對照

Under the rippling twilight, the yacht is moving slowly. A falling leaf after another leaf, giving birth to a blossom after another blossom of ripple,
All into your affectionate arms.
I always want to listen to the murmurs of wind from all directions, to make clear the silence of fishes from all directions,
I always want to stay and remain the rain of time, for the years not to be so speedy......
Yes, let's have a rest here.
Like the moonlight wrapping me, the Riyuetan Pool is also known as the Pool of Sandy Water, like that piece of wild ginger flowers,
Which is a lyrical poem. Between the dance of the eagle, the dance of offering sacrifices to gods and the dance of war, slowly spreading......
In a trance, I am a white deer of Idashao.
A white deer, looking for the source of life in water, or the roots of Idashao, which are extending here,
With luxuriant foliage, the birds can fly joyfully over Lalu Island.
An owl, looking at me in the branches, also in the sky, as if to say something?
Ah, no pain can neglect him, and no disturbance can change his words.
His tolerance, like a sage, helps his people to learn to be firm, from night to dawn,
Safe guard in some Miyari; in front of the lake, silent and dazzling.
Not only to plant a lake of new poetry in my heart, but also to leave a shrieking high pitch.

✿ ✿ ✿

62．

漫興   魏基

東風昨夜到山家，岸柳依依欲放芽。
只是春寒猶未解，一簾細雨夢梅花。

An Impromptu   Wei Ji

Last night witnesses the
east wind arriving at a

mountain village, where
the bankside willows, lank

and long, are bursting with
buds. Yet spring cold lingers,

when a curtainful of fine rain is
dreaming about plum blossoms.

驀然回首   林明理

我努力捕捉
那守在雲堆裡的陽光如流星的眼波

白鳥齊飛，空餘的笑聲低迴
在我感動的一刻
山盡的茅屋又多了份凝重，那是
這一地金黃自雨後沖刷的青石階上
只聞微風向甜美的小草殷勤問候

前路一直延伸著
而我已別無所求

清詩明理思千載
● 古今抒情詩三百首
　　漢英對照

只要拐個彎
就會看見栩栩如生的楓紅

Looking Back Suddenly   Lin Ming-Li

I try to catch
The eye of the sun which is like a meteor in the clouds

White birds flying, vacant laughter echoing low
At the moment when I am touched
The mountain hut is solemn, which is
A groundful of golden yellow along the bluestone steps washed by rain
Only to smell the breeze greeting the sweet grass

The road stretches on
And I have nothing to desire
With a turning of the corner
I'll see the vivid maple red

☙ ☙ ☙

63 ·

下堯峰   閔華

上堯峰接下堯峰，石路無塵滿谷松。
行盡清溪人不見，萬修篁里一聲鐘。

The Lower Yao Peak   Min Hua

The Upper Yao Peak connects the
Lower Yao Peak; the stony road

is free of dust, all the valleys filled
with pine trees. The limpid creek

is traced to its very source, still
nobody in sight; from among the

bamboo groves, chiming or ringing
of the bell is melodiously traveling.

修路工人 　　　　　　　　　　　林明理

幾個工人,揮汗如雨,
　　小心修補長長的路——
開車的,揮旗的,發號施令的,
　　還有一隻小黃狗,
各盡其責,緊密相依。
　　只有天空注視著這一切。
一場驟雨,來得太急,
被無端撞飛的小夥子
　　血流不止,斷了氣。
是的,天空的雲彩依舊,
施工繼續進行,
　　含著淚,修補著最後一段路。
啊命運之神,你不可能不關注
　　這些底層勞動者,
也不可能不回答他們的狂喜和悲痛。
是的,哪怕人生短暫如滄海一粟,
黑暗終究無法隱蔽黎明的曙光。
當朝陽的浪濤,又輕輕地拍擊……
　　海鷗振翅騰起
　　沒時間哭泣。

　　　　　　　　　　　　　　　－2018.11.3

Road Workers   Lin Ming-Li

A few workers, sweating,
    Carefully repairing the long road —
Driving, waving, giving signals,
    As well as a little yellow dog,
All work as a team,
    Under the watchful eye of the sky.
In the middle of a sudden shower
A young man has been accidentally hit by a truck
    Bleeding until death.
Yes, the clouds in the sky are the same,
The construction goes on.
With tears, they are repairing the last section.
Ah, god of destiny, how can you watch without attention
    These underclass workers,
It is also impossible not to answer their ecstasy and grief.
Yes, even if life is as tiny-brief as a grain in the sea,
After all, darkness cannot hide the morning light.
When the waves of the sunlight are gently beating…
    Seagulls spread their wings
    There is no time to cry.

    —Written on November 3, 2018

✿ ✿ ✿

64 ·

黃昏   黃任

亂鴉繞樹雀爭喧，寂寂牆陰小院門。
人自離思花自發，一庭秋色近黃昏。

Dusk

Huang Ren

Bevies of crows & sparrows
are riotous about the trees;

in the lonely gloomy wall
there is a gate to the small

yard. Departing sorrow lingers
in the mind when flowers

are blooming; a gardenful of
autumn tints are nearing dusk.

回眸恆春夕照

林明理

這片海域一望無際——
　　寧謐如秋
只有雨，在騷動著
我一如從前
信步走近欄杆
　　看水鳥輕吻波面

我曾攀登過許多山林
也曾痴迷過滿天星斗
　　但我知道
你的微笑帶著暖意
　　光潔而可愛：
　　總是那麼熟悉
就像這夕照
　　流溢著迷人的光輝
讓我把詩鏤入夢中

清詩明理思千載
● 古今抒情詩三百首
　　漢英對照

Backward Glancing at the Sunset of Hengchun
Lin Ming-Li

The sea is boundless —
　　Peaceful and serene like autumn
Only the rain is noisy
As usual I
Approach the railing
　　To watch waterfowls kissing the waves

I have climbed many mountains
And have been infatuated with brilliant stars
　　But I know
Your smile is warm
　　Pure and lovely:
　　　Always so familiar
Just like the setting sun
Which is suffusing with charming light
For me to embed poetry into the dream

✿ ✿ ✿

65 ·

獨遊上帶溪二絕句（其一）　　　　黃任

翠壁千層澗道低，樵人歸塢日初西。
山花數片吹落石，野鳥一聲飛過溪。

Two Quatrains Composed During Solitary Touring Shangdai Creek (No. 1)
Huang Ren

Thousands of emerald cliff
walls, the creek road is low；

back to the dock, the woodcutter
sees a westering sun. A few

petals of mountain flowers are
falling from the stones, when

a wild bird, uttering a single
note, is flying across the creek.

牡丹水庫[53]即景 　　　　　　　　林明理

挾著天光的雲朵在壩頂
停留
九重葛和美麗的橋梁
讓週遭景物都恬然自足
走過哭泣湖來吧
隨我步上這老村
望著裊裊白煙升起
凝聽排灣族的生命故事

連鳥兒都緘默了
而原古的歌聲像流水
徐徐緩緩
不經意地在我身後迴響

每當夏風吹拂時
我聽到
那水聲日夜拍打著山巒
不管站在島嶼何方
都在旅人心中長存

林明理 攝
A photo by Lin Ming-Li

---

[53] 牡丹水庫是屏東最大的水庫，於 1995 年興建完成，供應著恆春、核三廠、屏南、墾丁國家公園等用水。周邊為原住民部落，而哭泣湖的排灣族語，是指水流匯集之地。

從黃昏的四重溪落到東源村
從煙雨中的野薑花谷到水庫
啊！這湛綠的寶石
水波蕩漾
夢一般的觸動，引我相思

View of Mudan Reservoir[54]   Lin Ming-Li

The cloudy blossoms tinctured with heavenly light linger over the damn
Bougainvillea and the beautiful bridge
For the surrounding scenery to be restful and serene
Walk over the crying lake
Follow me to the old village
Gazing at the white mist curling up
Listening to the life story of Paiwan people

Even the birds are silent
And the primitive song is like running water
Slowly and sluggishly
Carelessly echoing behind me

Whenever the summer wind blows
I hear
The water sound beating the mountain day and night
No matter where the island is standing
It is in the heart of the traveler

---

[54] Mudan Reservoir, the largest reservoir in Pingtung, was completed in 1995 and it supplies water to Hengchun, Nuclear No. 3 Plant, Pingnan and Kenting National Park. It is surrounded by indigenous tribes, and the Paiwan language for Crying Lake means the place where water overbrims.

From the twilight through four-layered waterfalls to the Tungyuan Village
From the wild ginger valley in misty rain to the reservoir
Ah! The emerald gem
Rippling with waves
Touching like a dream, hence homesickness

🌷 🌷 🌷

66 •

夜過夢溪   張如炯

南來夜夜還家夢，行到夢溪不見溪。
漏盡更殘眠未定，林間時有子規啼。

Night Passing by Mengxi, or Dreamy Creek   Zhang Ruxia

Heading south, from night
to night a dream of returning

home; coming to the Dreamy
Creek, but no creek is seeable.

The night waning, still rest-
less and sleepless, when the

woods is noisy, occasionally,
with the singing of cuckoos.

清詩明理思千載
● 古今抒情詩三百首
　漢英對照

相見居延海[55]　　　　　　　　　林明理

我喜歡西海的暮雲
秋日的胡楊
它們的美麗與憂傷
讓千里戈壁為之動容
雪水的注入
牧者的祈禱
阿拉善的官兵在營房周圍
尋找自然的豐饒

我想橫渡黑河
看白鳥棲息，鴨浮碧波
那藍色的蒼穹
心靈所受的感動
源自一個深邃的古老的夢
哪怕路途迢迢
哪怕烈日風暴
西海，是我苦苦追尋的去處

Meeting in Juyan Lake Basin[56] Lin Ming-Li

I like the dusk clouds of the West Sea
And the poplars in autumn
Their beauty and sorrow
Touch thousands of miles of Gobi
The pouring in of snow water
The prayers of the shepherd

---

[55] 居延海，位於內蒙古自治區阿拉善盟額濟納旗北部，漢代稱「居延澤」，後也稱「西海」。

[56] Juyan Lake Basin is located in the north of Ejin Banner, Alxa League, Inner Mongolia Autonomous Region, and it was called Juyanze in the Han dynasty and later called the West Sea.

The officers and soldiers of Alxa are looking
For the richness of nature around the barracks

I want to cross the Black River
To see white birds roosting, ducks floating in blue waves
The blue vault of heaven
The heart which is touched and moved
From a deep and age-old dream
In spite of the long road
In spite of the scorching sun and storm
The West Sea is the place I am searching for

❀ ❀ ❀

67 ·

舟望　　　　　　　　　　　　　　　黃家鳳

半山雨氣半山晴，江上人家樹作城。
插遍早秧收盡麥，枝頭猶自喚催耕。

Gazing From the Boat　　　Huang Jiafeng

Half a mountain is bathed
in rain and, the other half,

in sunshine; riverside homesteads, trees as the town.

Early seedlings planted and
wheat harvested, from the

treetops birds are still calling
for sowing and ploughing.

清詩明理思千載
● 古今抒情詩三百首
　　漢英對照，

你繫著落日的漁光　　　　　　　林明理

你繫著落日的漁光
在我白色的星砂邊緣
一彎下腰，
我就忘了時間是何物
而不必裝作若有所思

我曾是追夢的捕手
也曾蹉跎過歲月
如今，一切都將重來
村裡的老船長已不再掌舵
我只有，把你的形象
披滿在木琴的憂鬱之中

You Are Tied to the Fishing Light of the Setting Sun
　　　　　　　　　　　　　　Lin Ming-Li

You are tied to the fishing light of the setting sun
At the edge of my white starsand
When I bow down
I forget what time is
Without pretending to be thinking

I have been the catcher of dreams
And have ever wasted my life
Now, it is all over again
The old captain of the village is no longer at the helm
And all I have to do, is to spread your image
In the melancholy of the xylophone

68 ·

題方邵鶴琴鶴送秋圖   馬曰琯

一聲鶴唳沁寥天,坐對高空思渺然。
試向孤亭彈別調,白雲黃葉滿山前。

Inscription on a Painting of Autumn
Ma Yueguan

At the crane's crying in the crisp
and clear sky, I, sitting at a height,

feel remote, far-flung, and wide-
ranging of mind. Against a solitary

pavilion, tentatively I play a farewell song, when the mountain

is filled and filling with white
clouds & yellow leaves.

劍門蜀道遺址   林明理

我想登上那劍門關
憶起所有三國的故事
像隻貓頭鷹
傾聽百花凋零
還有萬株古柏和
明月峽,是恆久的夢想

峰巒裡,有我的呼吸
瀑流裡,有我的情感
遠從千佛崖

清詩明理思千載
● 古今抒情詩三百首
　　漢英對照，

望斷皇澤寺
步容在
老城，留戀這環境

我相信，每一個傳說
也相信每一次邂逅
在偉大的時間裡
呵，請聽我說
這是雄奇的創造
——而我卻有一絲感傷

Ruins of Jianmen Shu Road　　Lin Ming-Li

I want to climb up the Sword Gate
To recall all the stories of the Three Kingdoms
Like an owl
Listening to hundreds of flowers withering
And the ten thousand cypress trees
And the Bright Moon Gorge, which is an eternal dream

In the mountain, there is my breath
In the waterfall, there is my emotion
Far from the one-thousand-Buddha cliffs
To look at Huangze Temple
Steps remain
In the old city, love for the environment

I believe, every legend
As well as every encounter
In the great time
Oh, please listen to me
This is a magnificent creation
—And I am with a touch of sadness

⚘ ⚘ ⚘

69.

杭州半山看桃花   馬曰琯

山光焰焰映明霞,燕子低飛掠酒家。
紅影倒溪流不去,始知春水戀桃花。

Admiring Peach Flowers in Banshan Mountain of Hangzhou   Ma Yueguan

Peach flowers are flaming
and flaring against the

twilight glow, when swallows
are flying low over wine-

shops. The red shadows
are working against the

current — spring water is
in love with peach flowers.

大好河山張家口[57]   林明理

啊,多美麗的河流
橋下亮閃閃
站在八角台上
一邊是側柏、丁香和油松
一邊是山桃、海棠和沙果
有的在盛開
有的在凋落
那斜陽如此美

---

[57] 張家口市,位於中國河北省西北部。

清詩明理思千載
古今抒情詩三百首
漢英對照

彷彿是南飛雁的夢
總是那麼輕輕地
把我的思念
輕輕牽引
安靜,舒暢,柔和

光正耀眼,松柏更繁茂
站在牌坊前
我默默傾聽
有音樂緩緩流入
有的美
從不需要歌
莊嚴的山
讓這片自然
處處充滿了神色
大水泉
清澈甘美,終年不涸
能浸潤於這森林的魅力中
就是幸福

巨大的草海啊
你為誰如此歡騰
多少逝去的帝王將相
曾在此佇立觀望
而我的相思
也從草原的那頭傳到這頭
閃電河上
舟影朦朦朧朧
遠處花草蔓延
駿馬奔馳
啊,這初秋
載不動我歡欣的蹄音
在永恆的凝望中

The Great Rivers & Mountains in Zhangjiakou[58]

Lin Ming-Li

Ah, what a beautiful river
Under the bridge it is brilliant
Standing on the octagon
One side is cedar, cloves and pines
The other side is mountain peaches, crabapple and sand fruits
Some are in bloom
Some are withering
The setting sun is so beautiful
As if it is the dream of the southbound geese
Always so gently
To pull my thoughts
So gently
Quiet, soft, comfortable

The light is glaring, pines are thriving
Standing in front of the archway
I silently listen
To the music flowing slowly
Some beauty
Never needs a song
The solemn mountain
Fills the nature everywhere
With a touch of deity
The large water springs
Are clear and sweet, never dry year round
It is happiness
To be steeped in the charm of the forest

Oh great sea of grass
For whom do you rejoice

---

[58] Zhangjiakou is located in the northwest of Hebei Province of China.

清詩明理思千載
● 古今抒情詩三百首
　　漢英對照,

How many kings and generals of the past
Have ever stood here to watch
And my love
Has passed from the end of the prairie to another end
Over the river of lightning
The boats are misty and shadowy
In the distance grass and flowers are spreading and sprawling
Horses are galloping
Ah, the early autumn
Cannot carry the sound of my happy hoof
In the eternal gaze

♅ ♅ ♅

70 ·

蟋蟀　　　　　　　　　　　　　　　　李四維

山郭江村雨後涼，西風吹冷豆花香。
疏籬草徑行人少，蟋蟀吟時正夕陽。

Crickets　　　　　　　　　　　　Li Siwei

Mountain villas and riverside villages are cool from

a rain; the west wind blows
cold the fragrant bean flowers.

Sparse hedges and grassy
paths, few travelers, when

the crickets are chirping
against the westering sun.

遠方傳來的樂音 　　　　　　　　林明理

像歌詠謬斯的
古希臘詩人一樣
牠，顯得那麼溫柔又帶點憂鬱
那藍紅的翅羽
還有橄欖綠的眼睛
竟唱出一生最美的一曲——愛情
裊裊不絕，如同泉響

The Sound of Music From Afar Lin Ming-Li

Like the ancient Greek poet
Singing praises of Muse
He looks so tender, with a touch of melancholy
The blue-red wings
And the olive green eyes
Should sing the best song in his life — love
Lingering and enduring, like a fountain

山中雪後 　　　　　　　　鄭燮

晨起開門雪滿山，雪晴雲淡日光寒。
簷流未滴梅花凍，一種清孤不等閒。

In the Mountain After Snowing Zheng Xie

Arising in the morning to open
the door, I find the mountain

清詩明理思千載
古今抒情詩三百首
漢英對照

white with snow, which is sunlit
against the cold sun through pale

clouds. The eaves drops fail to
drop or drip when plum flowers

are frozen; a current of pure
solitude — no common thing.

二月春雪 林明理

這場雪景，
　來自遙遠的芝加哥——
卻讓我感到無比的親切。
　一排小樹，像一群
要去遠足的小孩，
屋內的詩人也不甘寂寞，
目不轉睛地打量著外面的世界。

夜晚
　當大地睡着了。
雪啊，就繼續飛翔吧……
　在後院裡飛翔，
飛入你深邃的眼睛，——
　讓燈火點亮
　　　你的詩意，
　讓鳥獸們安息，
讓我整夜為你歌唱。

　　　　—此詩獻給非馬，寫於臺灣，2020.02.14

詩人非馬寄來家中後院的雪景
William Marr, a famous Chinese-American poet, sends a photo of the snow scene in his backyard.

Spring Snow Lin Ming-Li

This scene of spring snow,
　Is from the remote Chicago —

Yet it makes me feel so familiar.
　　　　A row of young trees, like a group
Of children ready for a hike,
The poet in the room does not want to be kept out of the company,
And he is closely looking at the world outside.

At night,
　　　When the earth falls asleep
Snow continues to fly ....
　　　Flying in the backyard,
Flying into your profound eyes, —
　　　Let the lamp light up
　　　　　Your poetry
　　　Let the birds and beasts sleep soundly,
Let me sing for you through the night.
　　　　　　　—The poem is dedicated to William Marr, written in
　　　　　　　　　　　　　Taiwan on February 14, 2020

♃ ♃ ♃

72 ·

芭蕉　　　　　　　　　　　　　　　　　　　鄭燮

芭蕉葉葉為多情，一葉才舒一葉生。
自是相思抽不盡，卻教風雨怨秋聲。

Plantain Trees　　　　　　　　　　Zheng Xie

Plantain trees are affectionate,
lovey-dovey: when a leaf is

spreading, another new leaf
is on the budding. Pining and

177

清詩明理思千載
古今抒情詩三百首
漢英對照

longing are lasting and lingering
— when the sign of autumn

reigns, winds & rains are
plaintive on plantain trees.

曇花[59]的故事

林明理

昨夜,霧散漫如煙
秋又向我伸出雙手
千百年來
風雨中等候
冰雪中吟詠
而我
總是在黎明前
消失於霎時
難道
你未曾察覺
我在書頁裡用心寫著
在你途經的每次回眸
你可以再靠近一點
就會看個清楚

---

[59] 近日,詩友非馬 Dr. William Marr 傳來親種的曇花,恬淡絕塵的風采令我傾倒。相傳,曇花和佛祖座下的韋馱尊者有一段哀怨纏綿的故事,所以曇花又叫韋馱花。她原是天上的小花仙,卻愛上了每天為她鋤草的小夥子,玉帝知道後震怒,並把花神貶為一生只能開一瞬間的花,不讓他們相見,還把那個小夥子送去靈柩山出家,賜名韋馱,讓他忘記前塵,忘記花神。可是花神卻忘不了那個年輕的小夥子,她知道每年暮春時分,韋駝尊者都會上山採春露,為佛祖煎茶,就選在那個時候開花,希望能再見韋馱尊者一面。遺憾的是,春去秋來,花開花謝,韋馱終究不認得她了。因此,就有了「曇花一現,只為韋陀」的愛情傳說。有感為詩。
—2016.8.31

也許你　一無驚奇
也許我　仍在夢中

The Story of Night-blooming Cereus[60]

Lin Ming-Li

Last night, the mist disperses like smoke
Autumn holds out its hands to me
Through thousands of years
Waiting in winds & rains
Singing in ice & snow
And I
Always disappear
In a blink before dawn
Have you
Not noticed that
I have written with my heart on the page
Each time you pass by and glance back
You can get a little closer

---

[60] Recently, my poet-friend Dr. William Marr sent me the night-blooming cereus planted by him, whose beauty enchants me. As legend has it that the night-blooming cereus and the Waxbill Seat of the venerable great Buddha have a sad story, hence the name of waxbill flowers. Originally she was a small flower fairy in the sky, but fell in love with the young man who weeded for her every day. The Jade Emperor was furious when he knew it, and reduced the flower deity to a flower that could only open for a moment in his life, and did not let them meet; in addition, he also sent the young man to the Coffin Mountain to be a monk, naming him Waxbill, so that he could forget the past and forget the flower deity. But the flower deity failed to forget the young man — knowing in late spring every year Waxbill would go up to the mountain to collect spring dew and boil tea for the Buddha, she chose to bloom at that time in hope to encounter Waxbill. Unfortunately, spring out and autumn in, flowers blossoming and withering, Waxbill did not recognize her, hence the love story of "transitory flowering only for Waxbill". The poem is thus inspired.　—August 31, 2016

And you can see clearly
Perhaps   you are not surprised
Perhaps   I am still dreaming

❀ ❀ ❀

73 ·

小廊   鄭燮

小廊茶熟已無煙，折取寒花瘦可憐。
寂寂柴門秋水闊，亂鴉揉碎夕陽天。

The Small Corridor   Zheng Xie

The tea is well-prepared, without
any wisp of smoke from the teapot;

standing in the small corridor, I carry
a lovely twig of chrysanthemums

freshly plucked. The lone wooden gate
leads to a great expanse of autumn

water, over which riotous crows
seem to break the sky of a setting sun.

秋暮   林明理

冬山河[61]　鹹草鳴蛩
濱鷸　兩兩

---

[61] 冬山河為臺灣宜蘭縣的第五大河。

惟有小水鴨
擾亂了整個水面
喚起白霧飛脫
留下溪口外
一片明霞

An Autumn Dusk Lin Ming-Li

Dongshan River[62]　angelica grass noisy with crickets
Riverside dunlins　in pairs
Only little ducks
Have disturbed the whole water surface
To arouse the white mist flying in all directions
Leaving a stretch of bright glow
Beyond the mouth of the stream

❀ ❀ ❀

74 ·

登長溪嶺 葉元坊

獨行殘日下空山，樹色炊煙曲水彎。
兀立孤峰一回首，萬家明滅亂雲間。

Climbing the Changxi Ridge Ye Yuanfang

Against the setting sun, solitary
walking down the vacant mountain;

the trees are veiled in mist suffusing
over the bend of running water.

---

[62] Dongshan River is the 5th longest river in Yilan County, Taiwan.

清詩明理思千載
● 古今抒情詩三百首
　　漢英對照,

A lonely peak is towering heavenward; backward glance — thousands

of homes appear and disappear
from among masses of clouds.

踏青詠春　　　　　　　　　　　　　　林明理

金色楓林下，白雪木
團團簇簇
如聖誕初雪
路的盡頭
紅櫻藏身樹林
魚兒嬉遊野溪石縫

但我不能久留
春天的眼睛
閃爍著童稚的快樂
萬花又紅遍枝頭
而我聽見白冷圳
輕輕哼唱故鄉的小調

從賞花到玩踩水
從酒莊到虹橋
我聆聽薰衣草說話
也夢見那些原野和搖閃的
螢火蟲，幾隻白鷺掠過——
安然自得

Ode to Spring and Spring Outing
　　　　　　　　　　　　　　Lin Ming-Li

Under the golden maple forest, snow flake pascuita
Masses of them

Like the first snow at Christmas
The end of the road
The red cherry hidden in the woods
Fish frolicking in the stony cracks of wild brooks

But I cannot stay for long
The eyes of spring
Flashing with childish joys
Myriads of flowers are red all over the branches
And I hear the White Cooling Canal
Gently humming melodies of the hometown

From admiring flowers to treading water
From wineries to Hongqiao Bridge
I listen to lavender speaking
And dreaming of fireflies in the fields which
Are flickering, a few egrets passing by —
At great ease

❀ ❀ ❀

鸛鵲樓   喬光烈

何處西風鸛鵲樓，煙沙蕭瑟滿汀洲。
人間俯仰成千古，到海黃河日夜流。

The Stork Tower   Qiao Guanglie

The Stork Tower is blown in
the west wind from somewhere;

the isles, veiled in sandy mist,
are dismal and desolate. Up and

清詩明理思千載
● 古今抒情詩三百首
　漢英對照

down in the mortal world — it
has been through the sages; the

Yellow River keeps flowing day
and night, seaward, night and day.

緬懷億載金城[63]　　　　　　　　　林明理

城門上，獨留風
　　輕微地呢喃——
勿忘我……勿忘我
還有時光編織的
小故事
交織成我胸中一股暖流

喔，老城矗立——
如此從容
既無畏風雨，也不再有痛
周圍只有細葉落簌簌
和這廣大中庭、群樹環繞…
　…小河嘩嘩地流向遠方

我認出了那傾圮的紅磚
　　是從熱蘭遮城取來的
它　是我小小的等候
我輕輕撫摸著

---

[63] 位於臺南安平區的二鯤鯓砲臺，舊稱安平大砲臺，俗稱為「億載金城」，建於清朝（1874年），完工於1876年，由法國工程師參考巴黎的外圍防禦工事而設計，是臺灣第一座西式砲台；它在中法戰爭和抗日時，都曾對敵砲擊，發揮其防禦外敵的功能。而安平古堡又稱「熱蘭遮城」（荷蘭語：Zeelandia），是一座曾經存在於臺南市的堡壘，最初建於1624年，是臺灣最早的要塞建築。

如一部史書——
翻閱的　是說不完的歷史

Cherishing Memory of the Erkunshen Turret[64]

Lin Ming-Li

On the gate, the wind alone
　Is murmuring gently —
Forget-me-not... forget-me-not
And the little stories
Woven by time
To weave into a warm stream in my bosom

Oh, the old town stands —
So calm, not afraid
Of wind and rain, and no more pain
Only the fine leaves falling about
In the vast yard, enclosed with trees...
　...The little river rushing to the distance

I have recognized the dilapidated red bricks
　Taken from the city of Jelanzia
It is my little waiting
Which I gently touch

---

[64] Located in Anping District, Tainan, the Erkunshen Turret, formerly known as the Anping Grand Turret, is commonly known as the "Hundred Million Carrying Gold City", and it was built in the Qing dynasty (1874) and completed in 1876. It was designed by French engineers with reference to the outer fortifications of Paris. It was the first Western-style turret in Taiwan. During the Sino-French War and the Anti-Japanese War, it had bombarded the enemy and played its function of defense against invading enemies. Anping Castle, also known as "Zeelandia City" (Dutch: Zeelandia), is a fort that once existed in Tainan City, originally built in 1624, is the earliest building of fortification in Taiwan.

清詩明理思千載
古今抒情詩三百首
漢英對照

Like a history book —
What is leafing through   is an endless history

❀ ❀ ❀

76.

盤豆驛　　　　　　　　　　　　　　　　　　楊鸞

盤豆驛前日欲沉，高高新月映疏林。
一溪澗水數聲雁，何處能消關外心？

Pandou Post　　　　　　　　　　　　　　Yang Luan

Before Pandou Post, the sun is
on the slow sinking; a crescent

moon, high in the sky, is shining
on sparse woods. A creekful

of water is punctuated with
a few cries of wild geese;

an uneasy mind beyond the
pass, how to make it restful?

等著你，岱根塔拉[65]　　　　　　　　　　林明理

等著你，岱根塔拉
盛夏的草原沒有塵世煩瑣

---

[65] 岱海位於內蒙古烏蘭察布盟南部境內；宋元時代稱「鴛鴦泊」，清代蒙古人稱之為「岱根塔拉」，後稱岱海沿用至今。

186

鷗鳥領我飛入寬廣的懷抱
這樣我可以哭泣了
　　　噢我的愛
馳騁天際的王子
　思念　著迷　清澄　我的愛
　　　　我等著你
那湖的四周、灘川遼闊的
林木光影中
　　天鵝扮成詩人
　　蘆葦恍惚飄搖
浪沫與風濤　　交會成
　　　　絕勝
我瞇著眼睛
準備佇立涼城的山峰
啊雪融之時　　請與我一起
那時，天地將會遺忘是何物事
而我也會仰天而視至臥佛眼瞳

Waiting for You, Dagentara[66]　Lin Ming-Li

Waiting for you, Dagentara
The height of summer witnesses no earthly worries
The hagdon leads me into the wide arms
For me to cry
　　Oh, my love
The prince of the horizon
Longing　infatuated　limpid　my love
　　I am waiting for you
Around the lake, in the vast forest

---

[66] Lake Dai is located in the southern part of Ulanqabu League, Inner Mongolia. In the Song and Yuan dynasties, it was called "Yuanyang Bo", or the lake of lovebirds, and in the Qing dynasty, the Mongols called it "Dagentara", which is later called as Lake Dai until today.

Light and shadow of the beach and river
　　The swan dressed as a poet
　　The reed in a trance floating
Foam and wind　converging into
　　　　Absolute victory
I narrow my eyes
Ready to stand atop the mountain of Liangcheng
Oh when the snow thaws　please be together with me
By then, heaven and earth will forget what it is
And I will look up into the eyes of the reclining Buddha

❀ ❀ ❀

77 ·

偶成　　　　　　　　　　　　　朱一蜚

碧雲乍合夕陽沉，石徑人稀酒獨斟。
萬疊樓臺千樹雪，一繩寒雁沒遙岑。

An Impromptu Poem　　　　Zhu Yifui

Upon green clouds closing, the
sun is on the sinking; few travelers

along the stony path, solitary drinking
of wine. Layers upon layers of

towers & pavilions, thousands
of treefuls of snow; a rope of

cold wild geese are disappearing
behind the remote mountain.

睡吧,青灣情人海[67]

　　　　　　　　　　　　　　林明理

睡吧,青灣情人海
你的音樂緩緩流過
我的血脈
那七彩的玻璃石
是光的寶藏

你歌中的每一句
都甜蜜自在
你眼底的清純
澄澈深邃
無論懷著關愛或憂傷
閃光的你
是春之憧憬
引我徘徊

Fall Asleep, Green Bay Lovers' Sea[68]

　　　　　　　　　　　　Lin Ming-Li

Fall asleep, Green Bay Lovers' Sea
Your music slowly flows by
My blood vessel

---

[67] 在臺灣澎湖縣「仙人掌公園」附近的風櫃與青灣之間,有片約長五十公尺的白色小沙灘,這沙灘由珊瑚遺體、貝殼、石英砂、七彩的玻璃石等堆積而成。陽光下的玻璃石,常呈現耀眼的光線,煞是迷人,因而吸引許多情侶在此駐足,稱此地景為「青灣情人海」。

[68] Between the windbox and Green Bay near the Cactus Park in Penghu County, Taiwan, there is a small white beach about 50 meters long, which is composed of coral remains, shells, quartz sand, and colorful glass stones. The glass stone in the sun often shows dazzling, charming light, thus to attract a host of lovers to linger here, hence the name of Green Bay Lovers' Sea as a scenic spot.

清詩明理思千載
古今抒情詩三百首
漢英對照

The colorful glass stones
Are the treasures of light

Each word of your song
Is sweet and leisurely
The pure clarity of your eyes
Is limpid and profound
Whether with love or sorrow
You are brilliant
As the hope of spring
Which makes me loiter and linger

❀ ❀ ❀

78 ·

山行 姚範

百道飛泉噴雨珠，春風窈窕綠蘼蕪。
山田水滿秧針出，一路斜陽聽鷓鴣。

A Mountain Trip

Yao Fan

Hundreds of cliff-side springs are
splashing with pearls of rain; tender

is the spring wind, which blows
green the scented grass. The mountain

field, brimming with water, is studded
with rice seedlings like needles, when

the slanting sun, along all the way, is
giving an ear to the songs of partridges.

南庄[69]油桐花開時　　　　　　　林明理

每年春夏
清早
在親水步道上
露珠在草尖上滾動
順著山稜線慢行
桐花簇簇綻放
五色鳥在林梢
溪魚躍出水面的波紋

在這兒
寧靜的山中小村──
世間一片芬芳
我感到
太陽從山丘的深處躍起
風在林間奔馳
在老街上掠過
在桂花巷尾穿梭著

就這樣
來回尋找歷史過往之中
我感到
客家庄的光華
和樸實的美德
如果
部落不曾存於我心頭
我又怎能在風中歇息片刻

---

[69] 苗栗縣南庄鄉（Nanzhuang Township, Miaoli County）是臺灣四大慢城之一。

清詩明理思千載
● 古今抒情詩三百首
　漢英對照,

如果
不去瞅瞅這美麗的山城
又怎能
重現兒時記憶中桐花飄落……
最動聽的聲音
又怎能
讓老街的建築和美食
俘獲了無數旅人的心

When Tung Tree Flowers Are Flowering in Nanzhuang[70]　　Lin Ming-Li

Each spring and summer
Early in the morning
On the hydrophilic trail
Dewdrops are rolling on the tips of the grass
Walking slowly along the edge of the mountain
The Tung tree flowers are blooming in clusters
The five-colored birds are atop the trees
The creek fishes leap out of the rippling water

Here
In the quiet mountain village —
A fragrance is overflowing in the world
I feel
The sun is rising from the depths of the hills
The wind is racing through the trees
And is passing through the old streets
Shuttling through the lane of osmanthus flowers

Thus
Looking back and forth in the past
I feel

---

[70] Nanzhuang Township of Miaoli County is one of the four slowest cities in Taiwan.

The glory of Hakka village
And the simple virtue
If
The tribe fails to live in my heart
How can I rest a moment in the wind

If
We do not have a look at the beautiful mountain city
How can we
Represent the falling of Tung tree flowers in our childhood memories?
How the most touching
Sound
For the architecture and food of the old street
To capture the hearts of countless travelers

☙ ☙ ☙

79 •

即景（其一）　　　　　　　　　　　慶蘭

碧天雲淨雨初收，水滿平橋卻礙舟。
忽聽屐聲叢竹裡，是誰先我上層樓？

Inspired by the Sight (No. 1)　　Qing Lan

The blue sky is fresh from
clouds and a recent letup of

rain; the bridge, filled to its
top with rising water, is hard

of boating. A sudden string
of sounds of clogs from the

bamboo grove — who ascends
the tower earlier than me?

東勢林場[71]

林明理

漫天櫻舞
讓整個森林安靜下來
陽光在枝上舞動
隙縫中
我最為愜意
溪水環繞，鳥聲啁啾

當四季的芬芳由遠而近
在綠蔭間
全都框進我的眼眸
花蕾的影像也投射於
林場的光芒
和流螢飛舞於草叢之中
你便揚起愉悅的歌謠

當時有快樂的境遇
未來也將被提起
而我似四角林中的老樹
用心靈飛
因為我在浪漫的旅途
遇見一個美麗的邂逅

---

[71] 東勢林場，古名「四角林」，人稱中部的「陽明山」，位於臺灣台中縣東勢鎮東南隅之大安溪畔。

Dongshi Forest Farm[72]
Lin Ming-Li

A skyful of sakura dance
Has quieted down the whole forest
The sun is dancing in the branches
In the crevices
I feel most comfortable
Surrounded by streams, chirping of birds

When fragrance of the seasons from far and near
In the shade of green
All framed in my eyes
The image of the buds is cast
In the light of the forest
And the fireflies are dancing in the grass
When you are singing joyful songs

There were happy circumstances
The future will be remembered
Like an old tree in the four-cornered forest
I fly with my heart
Because I am on a romantic road
To have a beautiful encounter

❦ ❦ ❦

---

[72] Dongshi Forest Farm, with the ancient name of "Forest of Four Corners", known as the central "Yangming Mountain", is located by the Da'an River to the southeast corner of Dongshi Town, Taichung County, Taiwan.

清詩明理思千載
古今抒情詩三百首
漢英對照

80・

即景（其二）   慶蘭

新柳才青鳥未遮，釣竿好趁夕陽斜。
園中細草憑他長，多恐鋤時誤去花。

Inspired by the Sight (No. 2)   Qing Lan

The fresh willows are on the greening, hard to screen off

the birds; a fishing rod is at leisure in the slanting setting

sun. The fair grass in the yard is let alone to grow by itself,

lest a flower seedling, instead of a blade of grass, is weeded.

米故鄉——池上[73]   林明理

花田正值冬之美，
溪谷雨量充沛，
正月的霞光下，白鷺
　　輕掠
　　　　再躍起
於天堂路的起點；

---

[73] 臺灣台東池上位於花東縱谷中部偏南，在清澈甘甜的新武呂溪所沖積而成的肥沃平原中，造就了聞名全台的「池上米」；每年的一月中旬，沿途的油菜花田與隱身其間筆直的伯朗大道，搭配藍天白雲，是不可錯過的旅遊勝地。

唯一渙渙的
　　水畔，
涵映殘絮般的雲天。

哦，只在夢中，
　　我的影子帶我，
游動如呼吸的
　　星子。
直到綠稻展揚前，
　　再把時間折疊
讓我回到最初吧，
那一個米國──
　　池上的晨輝。

林明理　畫
A Painting by Lin Ming-Li

The Land of Rice: Chishang[74]　Lin Ming-Li

The flower field is in the height of winter beauty,
And there is an adequate rain in the valley.
Under the light of the first month, the egret
Is gently flying
Down to be up again
At the beginning of Paradise Road;
The only rippling
Water edge,
Reflecting the massive cottons of the cloudy sky.

Oh, only in dreams,
My shadow carries me,

---

[74] Taitung Chishang of Taiwan is located in the south middle of Huadong Longitudinal Valley, in the fertile plain formed by the alluvial of the clear and sweet Xinwulu River, creating the famous "Chishang rice" in the whole Taiwan. In the middle of January each year, the rapeseed flower fields along the way and the hidden straight Burang Avenue, with blue sky and white clouds, are ideal scenic spots for sightseeing.

Swimming like the breathing
Star.
Until the green rice is spreading,
Then to fold the time
Let me return to the beginning,
That land of rice —
The morning glow on the pool.

🌷 🌷 🌷

81 ·

嘉禾寓中聞秋蟲   謝垣

何處瓜畦絡緯聲，虛堂欹枕正三更。
旅人本少思鄉夢，都被秋蟲暗織成。

Katydids in Autumn   Xie Yuan

In rectangular pieces of field,
from where travels the chirping

of katydids? In an empty
room, against the pillow, it

is the depth of night. It is rare
for a wanderer to have a dream

of home, when it is stealthily
woven by katydids in autumn.

寄霍童古鎮[75]　　　　　　　　　　林明理

霍童抱線獅，甦醒映雪月；
為我伸展手，如聽冰崖水。
客心織夢景，有幸話當年。
再聚支提山，冬風念故人。

To Ancient Huotong Town[76]　　Lin Ming-Li

Huotong holds a string lion in his arms;
awake, the snowy moon is reflected.
Stretching hands for me, as if listening
to water dropping and dripping against
the icy cliff. A wanderer's heart is fond
with a dream, luckily with the events in
those years. Gathering in the Chiti Mountain,
through winter winds, to pine for old friends.

🌱 🌱 🌱

82 ·

漁父　　　　　　　　　　　　　蔣浩

雪後初歸塞北鴻，荻芽抽碧軟東風。
收罷釣絲渡湖去，一枝柔櫓月明中。

---

[75] 霍童鎮位於福建省寧德市。傳說周朝時有霍童真人，居霍林洞，由此得名。境內不僅植被良好，以國家森林公園、峽谷瀑布和眾多植物園著稱。

[76] Huotong Town is located in Ningde City, Fujian Province. Legend has it that during the Zhou dynasty, Huotong lived in Huolin Cave, hence the name. The territory is not only well vegetated, it is famous for the national forest park, canyon waterfalls and a host of botanical gardens.

清詩明理思千載
古今抒情詩三百首
漢英對照

An Old Fisherman Jiang Hao

After snow the wild geese
return from the north; the

silvergrass is budding green
in the gentle east wind.

The fishing rod with-
drawn, to cross the lake;

an oar is softly swaying
under the bright moon.

噶瑪蘭之歌 林明理

美麗的噶瑪蘭
誕生在福爾摩沙小島中
為了生存
所漂之處
都帶著大葉山欖
無畏風雨和激流
他們划過海洋的邊緣
來到太平洋東岸
歷經多次遷徙
成千個日夜的煎熬
卻個個樂觀明朗
尊重長輩，懂得分享的美好

為了證明自己的存在
多少年已經過去
仍固持各項祭典和傳統
耕地打魚或上山狩獵
堅持守護自然生態

不讓化學物質隨河川入海
讓族人對山海的尊敬
成為延續傳承的一部分
讓山泉溪流保有純淨
讓手作的竹籐
魚筌或香蕉絲工藝
代代留傳，光耀千古

啊，美麗的噶瑪蘭[77]
友善土地的大海子民
我祈禱：
所有 Kebalan
都能被山海之神保佑
聆聽生命的壯闊
我願此刻聽到
傳唱耆老的勇士
唱出部落族人的虔誠
願年年豐年祭
在悠揚的樂聲中
帶我走進這些夢境

Song of Kebalan   Lin Ming-Li

Beautiful Kebalan
Born in the small island of Sanasai
For existence
Wherever it drifts about
It is with big-leaf olives

---

[77] 噶瑪蘭的意思是「住在平原的人」，是臺灣的平埔族原住民，祖先居住已超過千年。噶瑪蘭族（Kebalan、Kbalan）是海洋民族，原居於宜蘭蘭陽平原，後因漢人爭地壓力而逐漸南遷，族群多分佈於宜蘭、花蓮、臺東縣，目前人口約一千多人。

清詩明理思千載
● 古今抒情詩三百首
　　漢英對照,

Fearless of wind, rain and currents
They cross the edge of the ocean
To the east coast of the Pacific Ocean
After many migrations
And suffering through thousands of days and nights
Yet they are bright and optimistic
Respecting their elders, knowing how to share the beauty

In order to prove their existence
Many years have elapsed
Still adhering to the rituals and traditions
Of farming or fishing or mountain hunting
To protect the ecology of nature
And to prevent chemicals from flowing into the sea
Let the people's respect for the sea and mountains
Become a part of the continuity and inheritance
Let the mountain springs and streams remain pure and clear
And let the handmade bamboo rattan
Fishing net or banana silk art
Be passed down from generation to generation, shining through the ages

Oh, beautiful Kebalan[78]
The sea people of the friendly land
I pray
That all Kebalan
May be blessed by the gods of the sea and mountains
And hear the magnificence of life
I would love to hear
The old warriors

---

[78] Kebalan means "people living in the plain", and they are the Pingpu indigenous people of Taiwan, whose ancestors have lived there for over 1,000 years. Kbalan is a maritime ethnic group, originally living in the Lanyang Plain of Yilan, and then gradually moved southward owing to the pressure of the Han people fighting for land. The ethnic group is mostly distributed in Yilan, Hualien, and Taitung counties, with the current population of about 1,000 people.

Singing about the piety of the tribesmen
May the Festival of Harvest
In the melodious music
Take me to the land of dreams

☸ ☸ ☸

83 ·

中秋無月   德普

誰道秋雲薄，中宵掩桂輪。
姮娥開鏡懶，愁殺倚樓人。

Mid-autumn Moon Festival Without Moon
De Pu

Who says autumn clouds are
thin? The height of the night

sees a wheel of moon completely
veiled. The Moon Goddess

is lazy to open her bright
mirror — the solitary person

leaning against the balustrade
in the high tower is saddened.

坐在秋陽下   林明理

坐在秋陽下
就這樣不慌不忙地

聽著木琴聲
我忽然明白了一些事

原來生命像只風箏
雖然微不足道
仍想放飛到高空
看看自己想要什麼

然而,金光依然柔媚
剛灑在油桐樹上
這部落的心跳還在這裡
就像以前那樣,是我溫暖的歸屬

Sitting in the Autumn Sun　　Lin Ming-Li

Sitting in the autumn sun
Thus in no hurry
I listen to the sound of the xylophone
Suddenly I understand something

Life is like a kite
Although insignificant
Still want to fly to the sky
To see what I want

Yet, the golden light is still soft
On the Tung trees
The heartbeat of the tribe is still here
Just as before, is my warm belonging

觀水　　　　　　　　　　　　旺都特納木濟勒

傍岸攜筇獨步行，秋來一色碧澄清。
無情水與人情似，隨處翻波隨處平。

Watching the Water　　　Wangdu Tena Muzil

Along the bank, solitary
walking with a walking stick,

in autumn it is the same
color of green limpidity.

The unfeeling water, like
an affectionate person, is

rippling or surging here —
and is level or calm there.

布拉格之秋　　　　　　　　　　林明理

千塔輝映著晚霞，
繆斯的眼眸
　　繼續延伸。

被世界歌誦過無數的單詞，
從天文鐘塔塔頂
　　飄到另一個國度。

一個詩人
聆聽穿廊下莫札特的樂音，
讀到片片秋葉的心事。

清詩明理思千載
古今抒情詩三百首
漢英對照

Autumn in Prague
Lin Ming-Li

A thousand towers are glowing in the sunset,
Muse's eyes
Continue to extend.

Countless words have been sung by the world,
From the top of the astronomical clock tower
Floating to another country.

A poet
Listens to the music of Mozart in the hallway,
And reads the thoughts of autumn leaves.

⚘ ⚘ ⚘

85·

桐廬道中雜詩（其一） 程同義

春風吹客又天涯，帆轉青山一葉斜。
日暮愁生江水急，荒亭細雨濕梅花。

Miscellaneous Poems Along the Tonglu Road (No. 1)
Cheng Tongyi

Blown in the spring wind, the
wanderer is again at the edge of

the sky; turning around the blue
mountain, a leaf of sail is sailing

aslant. At dusk, sorrow is born
at the sight of speedy river water,

when a fine rain above the deserted
pavilion is moistening plum flowers.

聽泉 　　　　　　　　　　　　　　　林明理

步移松林徑，陶然景色鮮。
山中無仙音，聽泉思故人。

Listening to the Spring　　　　Lin Ming-Li

Steps moving along
the path of pines;
leisurely, the scene
— looks so fresh.
The mountain boasts
no immortal music,
Listening to the spring,
pining for the deceased.

⚘ ⚘ ⚘

86 ·

桐廬道中雜詩（其二）　　　　　程同義

江邊艇子小於棱，雪灑烏蓬白漸多。
水淺更無魚可網，老漁晝臥抱寒蓑。

Miscellaneous Poems Along the Tonglu Road (No. 2)　　　Cheng Tongyi

The riverside boat is smaller
than a shuttle; snowing on

清詩明理思千載
● 古今抒情詩三百首
　　漢英對照,

the awning, it is white and
whiter. The water is shallow,

without any fish to catch, when
an old fisherman, in daytime,

is lying in his boat, covered
with a palm-bark rain cape.

聽海　　　　　　　　　　　　　　　　林明理

憂鬱的藍
像是起伏的心海
當它消隱之時
暮色旋踵即至
塔的幽影，玫瑰色的紅
還有浪濤砰砰擊響

啊西子灣[79]
像母親的殷盼
哼一曲鄉居小唱吧
每當冬季來臨
你高歌如鷹
騰飛到我身旁

Listening to the Sea　　　　　Lin Ming-Li

The melancholy blue
Is like the undulating sea of heart
When it fades and retreats
Dusk is soon approaching

---

[79] 西子灣位於臺灣高雄市柴山西南端山麓下，是個以夕陽及天然礁石聞名的海灣。

The shadows of the tower, the rose-red
And the pounding of the waves

Ah, Xizi Bay[80]
Like Mother's earnest expectation
Hum a little countryside song
Whenever winter nears
You sing like an eagle
Soaring to me

✿ ✿ ✿

87 ·

聞雁 徐志源

已是蕭蕭落葉聲，更聞孤雁客心驚。
關山到處多矰繳，冷月淒風況獨征。

The Honking of Wild Geese   Xu Zhiyuan

Falling leaves are eddying, rustling,
soughing and swirling; hearing the

honking of wild geese, the wanderer
is startled in the heart. From hills

to hills, from rills to rills, there are
tools to shoot birds, coupled with

the chilly wind & the cold moon —
take care, in your solitary flight.

---

[80] Located in the southwestern foothills of Chai Mountain in Kaohsiung City, Taiwan, Xizi Bay is a bay famous for its beautiful sunset and natural reefs.

清詩明理思千載
古今抒情詩三百首
漢英對照,

大冠鷲的天空　　　　　　　　　　　林明理

這麼多的雲
追逐
分秒
一如斑蝶
一如我
旋轉
在熟悉的山岬中

遠遠的
紅波瀾　舞動
那山邊微茫的紅瓦石屋
雨豆樹下
揮了又揮的
春藤，都由遠而近
想穿越　無數暗藍的
霧晨

遠遠的
東北角前方
一隻
大冠鷲
在漁村前頭
似飛似飄地
朝塔林投去

想不到
那空漠的天空
都聽到了

都捕捉到了
牠的一勻
笑容

The Sky of the Crested Serpent Eagle
             Lin Ming-Li

Great masses of clouds
Chasing
Seconds
Like butterflies
Like me
Spinning
In the familiar promontory

In the distance
Red waves   dancing
The dim and distant red-tile stone house beyond the mountain
Under the rain-bean tree
The spring vine
On the waving, nearing from afar
Intending to pass through countless dark blue
Fog morning

Far away
In the northeast corner ahead
A great
Crested serpent eagle
Before the fishing village
As if flying or floating
Toward the forest of towers

Beyond imagination
The boundlessly vacant sky
Has heard

清詩明理思千載
古今抒情詩三百首
漢英對照

And caught
A ladle of
His smile

88 ·

嘲燕　　　　　　　　　　　　　　　　　金和

海燕將雛分外忙，呢喃終日向華堂。
生兒盡學江南語，秋後如何返故鄉？

Jeering at the Sea Swallows　　Jin He

Sea swallows are busy caring
about their babies; murmuring

and whispering, daylong and
nightlong, in the gorgeous room.

When their babies are raised
through learning southern accent,

how can they return to their native
north after the northern winter?

重生的棕熊　　　　　　　　　　　　林明理

空曠山脈的邊緣，——
春天，歌聲輕輕掠過
雪、土壤與樹，
萬物也融洽於一切靜寂。

噢，美麗的珍博莉娜[81]，
在岩間微笑，像陽光般
閃耀，還輕吻了星辰，
同小花沐浴於廣野。

她探出身子，——看見
雲躲在微曦裡。接著對風
說說話，驚喜的神情…
…彷若大地的史詩。

林明理 畫
A painting by Lin Ming-Li

A Reborn Brown Bear Lin Ming-Li

On the edge of an empty mountain —
In spring, the songs sweep gently
Over the snow, soil, and trees,
All things are in harmony with ubiquitous silence.

Oh, beautiful Jean Bolina[82],
Smiling among the rocks, shining
Like the sun, and kissing the stars,
And bathing the fields with little flowers.

She leans out — to see
Clouds hiding in the light. Then talking

---

[81] 報載，今年十二歲的母棕熊珍博莉娜（Jambolina）生於烏克蘭，之前都生活在馬戲團的籠子和表演場來回；因疫情造成馬戲團經營不善，幾經波折及國際動保團體出面救援，如今，牠已在瑞士阿爾卑斯山脈的大片土地上，擁有了自由的天空，因而有感為詩。
　－2021.6.27.

[82] It is reported that a 12-year-old female brown bear named Jambolina was born in Ukraine and has spent her life in circus cages and performances. Due to the poor operation of the circus caused by the epidemic, after twists and turns, and owing to the rescue of international animal protection groups, now it enjoys a free sky in a large area of the Swiss Alps, hence this poem. －June 27, 2021.

清詩明理思千載
古今抒情詩三百首
漢英對照

To the wind, surprised look…
…Like the epic of the earth.

❦ ❦ ❦

89 ·

十一日夜坐 　　　　　　　　　　　易順鼎

人間不過隔關山，天上樓臺遠莫攀。
今夜舉頭唯見月，才知最遠是人間。

Night Sitting 　　　　　　　　　Yi Shunding

The human world is simply
beyond the pass; no —

not to climb the distant
towers in heaven. Tonight,

upward looking, only a
solitary moon is seen —

the furthest distance in the
world is the mortal world.

歲暮 　　　　　　　　　　　　　　林明理

1.
數千隻帝王斑蝶
　總在加利福尼亞州過冬。
此刻尤加利樹林
是個庇護之地，
在求偶舞中

214

忙著繁衍下一代,
不受海風吹落。

2.
美麗的小海象
　　誕生在沙灘上,
偉大的公海象跋涉了五千公里,
偉大的母象抵達沙灘準備分娩,
　　再一次開始,
　　　繁衍胖寶寶。

3.
雪地、地下隧道和迷宮中的
田鼠,
　　避開
掠食者略施的詭計,
　　並向鏡頭中的我們哈哈大笑。

4.
啊,這地球村
　　所有生物,和逝去的生靈
都正在循著
　　一定的軌跡更迭、輪替,
如去年的融雪
　　不知去了何方?
但都喜歡同大地母親說說話。

The Close of the Year　　　　　　Lin Ming-Li

1.
Thousands of monarch butterflies
　　Are wintering in California.

清詩明理思千載
古今抒情詩三百首
漢英對照,

Now the Eucalyptus Forest
Is a place of refuge,
And in courtship dances
   They are busy procreating the next generation,
And they protected from the sea wind.

2.
The beautiful baby walruses
   Are born on the beach,
The great male walruses travel 5,000 kilometers,
The great female elephants arrive on the beach, ready to give birth,
   And once again,
      To breed chubby babies.

3.
The voles in snow, underground tunnels
And mazes,
   Dodging
The tricks of predators
   And laughing at us on camera.

4.
Ah, in this global village
   All the living creatures, and the deceased
All are following
   A certain track to change and replace,
Such as last year's snow
   Where is it now?
But they all like to talk to Mother Earth.

90・

天童山中月夜獨坐（其一） 易順鼎

青山無一塵，青天無一雲。
天上惟一月，山中惟一人。

Moonlit Night, Solitary Sitting in Tiantong Mountain (No. 1) Yi Shunding

The blue mountain
is spotlessly clean;

the blue sky is free
from any single shred

of cloud. The sky nurses
a solitary moon, and in

the mountain: nothing,
nobody — except me.

四草[83]湖中 林明理

我聽過天空
嘎嘎這嘎嘎那的雷響，還有
消失三十餘年的鳥蚶重回四草湖懷抱
我歡喜，因為我知道寧靜
如這群白鷺
正緊跟著夕陽而且習以為常了

---

[83] 四草位於臺灣臺南市安南區，以擁有豐富的紅樹林、溼地景觀、水鳥及觀光竹筏等著名。據報導，因水質變好，鳥蚶（cockle）在消失卅餘年後，又重新回到四草湖，遂有而作。—2014.6.10

那紅樹林就在前方
映照出深淺不一的藍

不過，我喜愛的
不只是招潮蟹招展在泥灘
或是氣定神凝的彈塗魚
我關注的
其實只有復育的榮耀
我尋覓，再尋覓
嘎嘎這嘎嘎那的雷響，我用心觀察——
並沉湎於最遠那閃光的河道

In Sicao Lake[84]

Lin Ming-Li

I have heard the rumbling
Thunder of the sky, as well as
The birds which have disappeared for over 30 years, returning to Sicao Lake.
I am glad, because I know the silence
Like the bevy of egrets
Which are closely following the sunset as a custom

---

[84] Located in Annan District of Tainan City, Taiwan, Sicao Lake is famous for its rich mangrove forest, wetland landscape, water birds and sightseeing bamboo rafts. It is reported that owing to the improved water quality, the cockle, which has disappeared for more than 30 years, has now returned to Sicao Lake. – June 10, 2014

The mangrove forest is ahead
Shining in different shades of blue

But what I like most
Is not only fiddler crabs spreading in the mud
Or the mudskipper calm of mind
What I care about
Is actually the glory of regeneration
I seek, and I search
The rumbling thunder, and I observe with my heart —
While indulging in the farthest, brilliant channel

91 ·

天童山中月夜獨坐（其二） 易順鼎

此時聞松聲，此時聞鐘聲。
此時聞澗聲，此時聞蟲聲。

Moonlit Night, Solitary Sitting in Tiantong Mountain (No. 2)   Yi Shunding

Now audible is —
the soughing pines;

now audible is —
the tolling bells;

now audible is —
the babbling creek;

now audible is —
the chirping crickets.

清詩明理思千載
古今抒情詩三百首
漢英對照

新埔柿農[85]   林明理

黑夜裡，當九降風吹起，
在旱坑里山丘上，
……輕輕地喚醒柿農。
整個客家村開始忙碌。

這是黃金的隊伍。
這是薪傳的驕傲。
而風在低音區接續
一個又一個古老的故事。

月光下，他們徐疾有序，
屋簷內充滿
微笑、期待與知足。
那雙手的智慧，散溢著成熟的
甜甜果實，正是我心頭的歌。

Farmers of Persimmons in Xinpu Town[86]
                                             Lin Ming-Li

In the dark night, when the strong gale blows,
On the hill in the dry pit,

---

[85] 臺灣新竹縣新埔鎮客家村，是臺灣的柿餅之鄉，每年的九月旱坑里九降風吹起，直到十二月，是曬柿餅的季節。傳統的柿餅製作經由削皮、日曬、脫水等程序後，排成黃金的隊伍在架上等熟成。

[86] Hakka Village in Xinpu Town of Hsinchu County, Taiwan, is the land of persimmons. Each year, the wind blows in the dry pit from September to December, and it is the season for drying persimmons. Traditional processing of persimmons goes through peeling, sunning, dehydration and other procedures, lining up as a golden team on the rack and waiting to ripen.

…Gently to awaken the farmers of persimmons.
And the whole Hakka village begins to be busy.

This is the golden team.
This is the pride of passing on.
And the wind continues in the low register
One after another old story.

In the moonlight, their movement is orderly slow,
The eaves are filled with
Smiles, expectations and contentment.
The wisdom of a pair of hands, overflowing with ripe
Sweet fruit, which is the song of my heart.

⚘ ⚘ ⚘

丙戌十二月二十四日雪中游鄧尉三十二絕句（其二十三） 易順鼎

湖天光景入空濛，海立雲垂瞑望中。
記取僧樓聽雪夜，萬山如墨一燈紅。

A Trip to the Snowy Dengwei Mountain (No. 23)
Yi Shunding

The scene of a lakeful of sky
is ethereally foggy;a misty sight:

the sea standing and the clouds
drooping. Remembered is the night

to listen to snowing in the Buddhist
monastery — myriads of mountains

清詩明理思千載
古今抒情詩三百首
漢英對照

like ink, alive with a single dot
of red — from a glowing lamp.

海煙 　　　　　　　　　　　　　　　林明理

我行在
北回歸線界標上
哪怕
只有黑色的翅膀
仍緊密
把我的靈魂包纏

我踱著步
這只不過
是白雲的故鄉
而舞鶴台地[87]
卻還給寧靜世界
它原有的安詳

漸漸地
透明的光在增強
停留在海面
月亮昇起的地方
只有時間延續
只有煙霧孃娜

這時我終於知道
知道我那沉深的悲愴
也曾輕觸
也曾迷惘

---

[87] 舞鶴台地是花蓮縣的旅遊景點，全臺灣有三座北回歸線標，花蓮縣就有兩座。

一切不再虛矯
虛矯正是真實的浮相

The Sea Mist   Lin Ming-Li

I am walking
Along the Tropic of Cancer
Even if
Only black wings
Are still tightly
Wrapped around my soul

I am pacing
This is simply
The land of white clouds
And Wuhe Platform[88]
Restores the quiet world
To its original tranquility

Gradually
The transparent light is increasing
To stay on the sea
Where the moon rises
Only for time to last
Only for mist to curl up

Now I come to know
That my profound sorrow
Has ever been lightly touched
Has ever been confused
Nothing is false or pretentious
Pretention is the floating image of truth

---

[88] Wuhe Platform is a tourist attraction in Hualien County. There are three Tropic of Cancer markers in Taiwan, and two of them are in Hualien County.

清詩明理思千載
古今抒情詩三百首
漢英對照

93.

邠州七絕　　　　　　　　　　　　譚嗣同

棠梨樹下鳥呼風，桃李蹊邊白復紅。
一百里間春似海，孤城掩映萬花中。

A Quatrain Composed in Binzhou

Tan Sitong

In the birch-leaf pear trees birds
are twittering against the wind;

the path-side peach trees & plum
trees are now red and then white.

Through hundreds of miles,
spring is like a boundless sea,

where a solitary town is veiled in
great masses of myriads of flowers.

時光裡的和平島　　　　　　　　　林明理

為了愛，我又回來
你，純淨無邪的野百合
在回憶的波上
在我嚮往已久的岸邊踱步唱歌
高山阻擋不了你的魅力
峽谷隱藏不了你的柔情
河流帶不走你的憂鬱

大海為你永遠守誓
我在尋找你走過的路
岩縫間都長滿了苔衣

聽,金風蕭瑟,塵海起伏
那飛逝的季節裡
你仍是你
無懼驚世駭俗
多少冬夏與春秋
多少痛苦或歡笑
我愛你,天然的模樣
愛你不用讀唇的細語
愛你無需翻譯的沉靜

林明理 攝
A photo by Lin Ming-Li

今夜,我是詩人
我看到了傳說中的傳說
看到了鷗鳥從岸畔飛起
瞬時,浪花有了節奏
隨你起伏跌宕
我看到了漁舟唱晚
心是如此幸福

當月兒停坐在尖石上
聆聽浪濤時
你的光芒湧動
而時間過去了,你的愛留了下來
讓記憶抵達過往吧
讓島嶼凝聚成祥和
重複講述你我相遇的故事

啊,tuman
光的細鱗在你四周

清詩明理思千載
古今抒情詩三百首
漢英對照

你的美麗
已戰勝了腐朽
秋波渺渺,暮靄重重
多少豪情在世間激蕩
多少淚水在世間漂流
你度盡風雨
又從火紅中孵出新綠
一如往年
島嶼的命運仍在轉動

當夜越顯漆黑時
你像玉山剛下的雪
白而光明
而我在懸崖的寧靜中
呼喚你
從這裡到光的盡頭[89]

Heping Island in Time

Lin Ming-Li

For love, I am back,
You, pure and innocent wild lily
On the waves of memory
To pace the shore of my long longing while singing songs
The mountain fails to stop your charm
The valley fails to conceal your tenderness
The river fails to carry away your melancholy
The sea always keeps the oath for you

---

[89] 和平島是離臺灣最近的離島,位於基隆港北端、港口東側,距基隆市約四公里,佔地六十六公頃餘。在清朝前期時稱「雞籠嶼」或「大雞籠嶼」,為北臺灣最早有西方人足跡之地,也是基隆最早有漢人入墾所在之一。附近海域是基隆外海有名的磯釣場,每到入夜時分,一艘艘海釣船停泊在基隆嶼附近,是基隆嶼夜晚最美麗的一面。—2016.10.30 寫於台東

I am in search of the path trodden by you
The rocks are covered with moss

Listen, the golden wind is bleak, the dust sea up and down
In the fleeting season
You remain changeless
Unafraid to shock the society
How many winters, summers, springs and autumns
How many joys or pains
I love you, the natural appearance
I love your whisper without reading lips
I love your quiet which entails no interpretation

Tonight, I am a poet
I have seen the legend of legends
I have seen seagulls flying from the shore
Instantly, the waves are with a rhythm
With your ups and downs
I have seen fishing boats returning in the evening
And I feel so happy in my mind

When the moon sits on the sharp rock
To listen to the waves
Your light is surging
Time has elapsed, and your love remains
Let the memories travel to the past
Let the island gather into peace
To repeat the story of the meeting of you and me

Oh tuman,
The scales of light are all around you
Your beauty
Has triumphed over the decay
The autumn waves are boundless; the dusk is dimly veiled
How many passions are stirring in the world
How many tears are drifting in the world
You have weathered the storms
And have hatched green from the fiery red

Like the past years
The fate of the island is still turning

When the night is getting darker
You are like the snow freshly falling over the Jade Mountain
White and bright
And in the quiet of the cliff I
Call you
From here to the end of the light[90]

🌷🌷🌷

94 ·

獄中題壁　　　　　　　　　　　　　　譚嗣同

望門投止思張儉，忍死須臾待杜根。
我自橫刀向天笑，去留肝膽兩崑崙。

Inscription on the Wall of the Prison
Tan Sitong

Stopping over for shelter wherever
there is a house, in hope of being

---

[90] Heping Island is the closest outlying island from Taiwan, which is located in the north of Keelung Port and the east of the port, about four kilometers away from Keelung City, covering an area of over 66 hectares. In the early Qing dynasty, it was called "Jilongyu" or "Big Jilongyu", which was the first place where Westerners had footprints in northern Taiwan and one of the earliest Han settlers in Keelung. The nearby sea is a famous rock fishing ground off Keelung Island. Each nightfall, one after another sea fishing boat is moored near Keelung Island, forming the most beautiful scene of Keelung Island at night. —October 30, 2016, written in Taitung

welcomed like Zhang Jian — and
like Du Gen, to patiently wait for an

opportunity to fulfil the Constitutional
Reform and Modernization. Facing a

sword, ready to die a martyr, I laugh
heartily heavenward; those who leave

and those who stay — they are honest
and aboveboard, like Kunlun Mountains.

鵝鑾鼻燈塔 　　　　　　　　　　林明理

你凝視天空
恍若永恆的祈禱者
世界沉默著
你却何等剛毅——
讓巴士海峽之夜都亮了
不再畏懼七星岩暗流

飛吧，我願是鷹
嗖嗖地飛向你鼻尖前
耳畔只有潮汐起落聲
天空如明鏡無影
安閒地俯視著
所有生靈

我願在波光中
宿命地飛著
唱吧
唱出我戰鬥的幸福
請引領我
跨越黑夜，迎向光明

清詩明理思千載
古今抒情詩三百首
漢英對照

The Eluanbi Lighthouse   Lin Ming-Li

You stare at the sky
Like an eternal prayer
The world is silent
Yet you are so stouthearted —
And the night in the Bashi Channel is brilliantly lit
Unafraid of the undercurrents of the Seven Star Cave no more

Fly, I wish I were an eagle
To whirl about your nose
In the ears is the rising and falling tide
The sky is as clear as a mirror
Leisurely overlooking
All creatures

I would like to fly fatefully
Through the waves
And sing
To sing the joy of my struggle
Please lead me
Across the night, toward brightness

❁ ❁ ❁

95 ·

偶題　　　　　　　　　　　　　　姚永概

西風吹雨似輕埃，零落殘芳尚亂開。
秋蝶向花無意興，繞叢三匝卻飛回。

An Impromptu Poem Yao Yonggai

The west wind blows
powder-like rain; remnant

flowers, scattered, are
still flowering riotously.

Autumn butterflies fly
among flowers without

any zest — hither & thither
— before it flies back.

美在大安森林公園[91] 林明理

雨，細細密密，在高枝上傾訴
這條長長的步道
穿越了我數千個日夜
今晨，那熟悉的茶園儷影
竟瞬間擊中我的心
啊，新生的梔子花多麼嬌柔
憂傷的天空，無盡的奔馳。

而我溫柔的目光，凝注著紅土
記憶的空隙，漫無目的地飄浮
延著我的傘尖看去，幾度寒暑
大安森林公園——記錄我的憶念
在草木鳥獸，美麗的景象之中。

---

[91] 大安森林公園位於臺北市大安區，是座草木濃密的生態公園，被譽為臺北市的「都市之肺」，為市民最喜愛休閒場所之一。友人余玉照教授近日電郵告之：「我走在大安森林公園的紅土上散步，有如走在家鄉農地上親切打拼的過往年代裡那般踏實、自在、自得。」，有感而作。—2016.8.16

Ode to Da'an Forest Park[92]   Lin Ming-Li

Raindrops, here and there, are dropping & dripping in high branches
The long footpath
Through my thousands of days and nights
This morning, the familiar fair form of the tea garden
Instantly strikes my heart
Oh, how fair and tender is the new gardenia
The melancholy sky, endless running.

And my gentle eyes, focusing on the red earth
The gap of memory, floating aimlessly
To see along the tip of my umbrella, several cold and summer days
Da'an Forest Park has one by one recorded my memory
In the beautiful scene of vegetation, birds and animals.

🌷 🌷 🌷

96 ·

西樓   黃節

晨炊殘月掛西樓,樹頂朝陽綠尚稠。
短短秋風才領略,困人煩暑又淹留。

---

[92] Da'an Forest Park, located in Da'an District of Taipei City, is a lush ecological park, known as the "city lung" of Taipei City, and it is one of the most popular leisure places for local citizens. Professor Yu Yuzhao, a friend of mine, recently emailed me: "Walking on the red earth of Da'an Forest Park, I feel as down-to-earth, comfortable and contented as walking on the farmland of my hometown in the past years of efforts and struggle." This poem is thus inspired. —August 16, 2016.

The West Tower

Huang Jie

Morning cooking, a remnant
moon hanging above the

west tower; the morning
sun atop the trees shines

on green masses. After
a brief spell of autumnal

cool wind, the tiring and
vexing heat is still lingering.

小野柳漫步

林明理

此時陽光穿透雲層　俯覽
　　各種奇岩怪石──
海那邊，三十二公里之外
　──綠島如雄獅俯臥

林蔭覆蓋的沿途風景
太平洋、白水木或草海桐
　　岩層呈波浪狀褶曲⋯⋯
讓心之所向，便是宇宙

偶有一隻攀木蜥蜴
　　藏在石縫處
蟬比鳥還要激昂地嘶叫著
蜂迎蝶聚，翩翩而來──

啊，大海開始低吟──
　　　抒情而雋永
啊，園中的清香盤旋不去
　　我雀躍　如鳥出籠

臺東小野柳風景區／林明理 攝
A photo of Xiaoyeliu Scenic Area,
Taitung by Lin Ming-Li

清詩明理思千載
古今抒情詩三百首
漢英對照

Promenade in Xiaoyeliu Scenic Area

Lin Ming-Li

Now the sun shines through the clouds to overlook
　　Various strange rocks —
Across the sea, thirty-two kilometers away
　　— The green island lies prostrate like a lion

The scenery along the way covered by trees
The Pacific Ocean, White Water Wood or Grass Sea Tong Trees
　　The rock formation is wavy of folds...
Let the heart go wherever it wants, and it is the universe

Occasionally there is a wood-climbing lizard
　　Hiding in a crevice in the rock
Cicadas are chirping more passionately than birds
Bees greeting and butterflies gathering, flitting and flying —

Oh, the sea begins to croon —
　　Lyrical and meaningful
Oh, the fragrance in the garden is lingering
　　I leap and dance　like a bird out of its cage

☙ ☙ ☙

97 ·

詠梅十首（其九）　　　　　秋瑾

一度相逢一度思，最多情處最情癡。
孤山林下三千樹，耐得寒霜是此枝。

Ode to Plum Blossoms (No. 9) Qiu Jin

Annual meeting, annual
pining; where it is the most

affectionate, it is the most
lovey-dovey. Among three

thousand trees in the Solitary
Mountain Woods, only the

tree of plum blossoms is
cold-proof and frost-proof.

一顆瑩潔的燦星——悼葉嘉瑩教授[93] 林明理

此時，我只想到，
天使在大殿上吟唱，
妳，帶給人間的歡樂。

瞧，妳的一生，
讓這世上懂得古典詩詞的人
要比熟悉其他旋律的人來得
多。

但我願傾聽妳的所有詩句，
在北方平靜的冬夜裡，
向宇宙中迴響……

---

[93] 葉嘉瑩（1924-2024），號迦陵，蒙古族旗人，大學教授，中國古典文學研究學者，獲授加拿大皇家學會院士等殊榮，享年百歲；其詩句「池水一泓碧，天光萬古涵」，已成絕響。—2024 年 11 月 26 日近午，寫於天津市南開大學張智中教授電郵告知葉教授的逝世消息後，有感而作。

A Bright, Brilliant Star: Mourning Professor Chiaying Yeh[94]

Lin Ming-Li

Now, I only think
Of the angels singing in the hall,
And the joys brought by you to the world.

Look, with your lifetime efforts,
You familiarize more mortal people with classical Chinese poetry
Than any other tune or melody.

But I would like to give an ear to all your poems,
On the quiet winter night in the north,
Echoing through the universe.

❀ ❀ ❀

98 ·

詠梅十首（其十）

秋瑾

冰姿不怕雪霜侵，羞傍瓊樓傍古岑。
標格原因獨立好，肯教富貴負初心？

---

[94] Chiaying Yeh (1924-2024), styled as Jialing, Mongolian nationality, is a distinguished professor of Nankai University, a scholar of classical Chinese literature, and academician of the Royal Society of Canada. She died at the age of 100, yet her poetic lines "the water in the pool mirrors a skyful of blue, / the heavenly light is eternal in its brilliance" linger forever in the world. —Inspired at the noon of November 26, 2024, upon reading professor Zhang Zhizhong's email about professor Yeh's passing away.

Ode to Plum Blossoms (No. 10)   Qiu Jin

The icy posture dreads no snow
& frost; shy away from sumptuous

mansions, the plum blossoms
blossom against age-old hills. A

lofty model of independence which
is detached from the other flowers

—how can the original aspiration
be abandoned for the sake of wealth?

朱鷺   林明理

遠遠的朱鷺飛來了,
好像詩人丁尼生的門生。
牠鼓翼緩緩——
羽冠在微風中
好像浪聲如影隨行……
而漢水總是那麼浩瀚。

我到過許多城市,
數這裡的感覺最傾心。
古木低昂若一個戰士。
山勢高危,水石激盪,
把牠雪亮的羽也釉上了一層光。
瞧,牠目光凝定——
彷彿整個世界已然無關。

至少,我自己這樣地想。
這領地是多麼

寬廣。還有萬壑之中
或近或遠的清響──
啊,牠是連山岳都要動容的
──熱愛鄉土的姑娘。

The Crested Ibis   Lin Ming-li

From far away flies the crested ibis,
Like the pupil of Tennyson the famous poet.
It flutters its wings slowly —
In the breeze the crest
Is like the sound of waves...
And the Han River is always so vast.

I have been to many cities,
And this is the most charming one.
The ancient tree hangs low, like a warrior.
The mountains are high, the rocks are stirring in water,
To lend a sheen to its bright feathers
Lo, its eyes are fixed —
As if the whole world is irrelevant.

At least, that is what is on my mind.
How vast is
The territory. In myriads of valleys
There is a clear sound, near and far —
Oh, she is the girl who loves the country
— And for whom even the mountains are moved.

99・

登山六首（其一）   周實

長江浩浩日夜東，豪傑落落古今同。
四顧寂寥萬籟絕，眾山皆小天地空。

Mountaineering (No. 1)   Zhou Shi

The Long River is running
day and night, racing eastward;

heroes, since time of yore, are
roughly the same. Looking

around: it is solitary when
silence reigns supreme, and

all the mountains seem small —
both heaven and earth are empty.

在下龍灣島上[95]   林明理

古老的懸崖，
島上的葉猴，躲過了戰火，
從灰燼中鑽出。

地洞裡的一窩小鼠。
喀滋喀滋地咀嚼著竹根，
黑夜的繁星。

---

[95] 下龍灣（Ha Long Bay）位於越南東北部，其水域被列為聯合國教科文組織世界遺產。

清詩明理思千載
● 古今抒情詩三百首
　　漢英對照，

一隻鋸緣龜
兜著尾走在森林
鳥鳴溪畔之地。

蝙蝠媽媽飛回說：
那條蛇放棄埋伏了。
窩裡的蝙蝠寶寶歡欣鼓舞。

啊，地球生態危機的年代。
我仍聽得見
海灘上獨木舟的水聲穿過來。

On Ha Long Bay Island[96]　　　Lin Ming-Li

The ancient cliff,
Leaf monkeys on the island have escaped from the war flames,
Out of the ashes.

A nest of mice in the burrow.
Chewing and crunching the bamboo roots,
The stars of the night.

A turtle named cuora mouhotii
Is walking with its tugged tail in the forest
Where birds are singing by the stream.

The mother bat flies back, saying :
The snake has given up its ambush.
The baby bats in the nest are rejoicing.

Oh, the age of the earth's ecological crisis.
Still I can hear
The sound of canoes traveling on the beach.

---

[96] Ha Long Bay is located in northeast Vietnam and its waters are listed as a UNESCO World Heritage Site.

100·

詠紙鳶 　　　　　　　　　　　　　方芳佩

剪紙為形骨相寒，常依稚子博悲歡。
偶然得藉微風力，卻要旁人仰面看。

Ode to the Paper Kite　　　Fang Fangpei

Paper is carefully cut into
a formlessly formed kite

to bring joys and sorrows
to children. Occasionally,

the paper kite, under the force
of wind, flies high into the

sky, which entails upward
looking to see and admire it.

二林舊社田龜夢　　　　　　　　　林明理

黃昏，我看到白鷺
成群舞躍
伴著收割機的聲響
自由輕啄
全村的農作物
都在田裡

清詩明理思千載
古今抒情詩三百首
漢英對照

我看到了
土地靜默的力量
落日降臨
在大池，在小鴨戲水的
悠遊時刻
如此美好。農舍也欣幸地睡覺
而月亮漫步著
傾聽耆老的訴說[97]

The Field Turtle Dream of Erlin Old Society
Lin Ming-Li

At dusk, I see egrets
Dancing in bevies
In the sound of harvesters
Pecking freely
All the crops of the village
Are in the field

I have seen
The silent power of the earth
As the sun sets over
The big pond, in the leisure hour
When ducklings are swimming
So beautiful. Farmhouses are sleeping happily

---

[97] 臺灣彰化縣二林舊社是「田龜計畫」的故鄉，據史書的記載，二林地區原為荒蕪之處，是平埔族的居住地，荷蘭人進據臺灣之前，即有二林社。這項計畫源於一位中山大學資管系退休的黃慶祥教授，為協助當地農村再生轉型，並協助老農拓展農產品網路銷售。「田龜」意指老農像烏龜般彎腰駝背在田間工作，他想打造家鄉成為「全穀之鄉」。最近這項計畫繼二林舊社故事館成立、電視台亦拍攝紀錄片《農夫與他的田》，值得繼續關注，因而為詩。—2016.7.29

While the moon is ambling
And listening to the tale of elders[98]

✿ ✿ ✿

101·

樂府體　　　　　　　　　　　　　　　　馮班

別日花盈盈，今來蟲嘖嘖。
蒼苔滿階前，封君去時跡。

A Folk Song　　　　　　　　　Feng Ban

Bidding adieu, flowers are fair
to flare;coming back, insects

are cheeping and chirping.
The steps are overgrown with

---

[98] Erlin Old Society in Changhua County, Taiwan is the hometown of "Field Turtle Plan". According to historical records, Erlin Aea, originally a barren place, is the residence of Pingpu nationality, before the Dutch entered Taiwan, there was Erlin Society. The project was initiated by Huang Qingxiang, a retired professor in the Department of Information Management at Sun Yat-sen University, to assist the local rural regeneration and transformation, and to help elderly farmers expand online sales of agricultural products. "Field turtle" refers to the old farmer hunching over the fields like a turtle, and he wants to make his hometown "the land of the whole valley". Recently, following the establishment of the Erlin Kuosha Story Museum and the filming of the documentary "The Farmer and His Field" by the TV station, this project deserves continued attention. Hence this poem. ─ July 29, 2016.

清詩明理思千載
● 古今抒情詩三百首
　　漢英對照，

moss, which covers up and
erases your departing traces.

給岩上的信　　　　　　　　　　林明理

我的朋友，
今天，頭一次
抬頭看著天空，看著您。
驚奇於您離得這麼遠，
卻依然能挺起腰板兒，──
高貴地
走路，恰如壯年。

啊，我的朋友，
人間最幸福的，
是相知的美麗
和常懷悲憫心；
而您生命之光
將存在於所有思念的人的記憶裡，
您不朽的豐功，
亦將與神的榮耀同在。

－2020.9.10

A Letter to Yan Shang　　　Lin Ming-Li

Dear friend,
Today, for the first time
I look up into the sky and look at you.
I am surprised you are so far away,
But still able to stand up straight, ─
Nobly
Walking as of in the prime of your life.

Oh dear friend,

The happiest thing in the world,
Is to know each other
With compassion;
The light of your life
Remains in the memory of all those who pine for you,
Your long-lasting achievements,
Are to be with the glory of God.

❁ ❁ ❁

102．

春感　　　　　　　　　　　　　　王崇簡

雲暗春猶冷，一簾煙雨斜。
舊懷千萬緒，牆角見桃花。

Spring Inspiration　　　　　Wang Chongjian

Dim clouds see a spring
with lingering cold; a curtain

of misty rain aslant. Old
memories recall and throng,

when the corner of the wall
is flaring with peach flowers.

北極熊　　　　　　　　　　　　林明理

一隻飢餓的北極熊
躲在岸邊的雪地上
沿著海灣
徘徊在工作站旁

清詩明理思千載
古今抒情詩三百首
漢英對照

當牠被麻醉劑射中
救難員用直升機將牠載走
昏睡了九十分鐘後的牠
哪裡才能找到回家之路
哪裡才能找到覓食的天空[99]

The Polar Bear   Lin Ming-Li

A hungry polar bear
Hiding itself in the snow on the shore
Along the bay
Wandering by a work station
When it is shot by an anesthetic gun
And carried away by a rescue helicopter
After a ninety-minutes profound sleep
It wakes up to face a question
Where to find the spot for food[100]

🌷 🌷 🌷

103．

絕句   林古度

客來自何處？為言南山頭。
昨夜片時雨，新添春澗流。

---

[99] 最近看 BBC 影片中，科學家們憂慮，因地球冰山融化加劇，讓北極熊面臨找不到食物而想接近人類掠取食物的悲歌。因而為詩。—2017.6.9

[100] In a recent BBC film, scientists worry about the melting iceberg which is on the exacerbating, so much so that polar bears cannot find foodstuff, and they go to humans for food. Hence the poem. —June 9, 2017.

A Quatrain
Lin Gudu

Where is the visitor from?
—from the Southern Mountain.

Last night a shower of rain
lasts for a short while,

and the spring stream is
swollen with spring freshet.

給 Bulgarian poet Radko Radkov[101] （1940-2009）

林明理

在如風般逝去的日子懷抱裡
任何天使之翼
也不能捎去我的訊息
枝上那只夜鶯
已不再唱牠的妙曲
可是，就在這片刻之間
你從金馬車上翩然回首
在星辰中，堅韌如昔
身影從容優閒
彷彿回到玫瑰谷的重逢

To Bulgarian Poet Radko Radkov[102] (1940-2009)

Lin Ming-Li

Gone are the days like the arms in the wind
No angel's wings

---

[101] Radko Radkov 是任教於保加利亞大學教授，著名詩人。
[102] Radko Radkov is a professor and a famous poet at the University of Bulgaria.

清詩明理思千載
● 古今抒情詩三百首
　漢英對照．

Can carry my message
The nightingale on the branches
No longer sings her wonderful song
Yet at this moment
You glance back from the golden coach
Among the stars, you are as tough as ever
Your form is so leisurely, at great ease
As if a returning to the reunion in Rose Valley

⚘ ⚘ ⚘

104·

池上　　　　　　　　　　　　　　　　張光啟

倚杖池邊立，西風荷柄斜。
眼明秋水外，又放一枝花。

Over the Pool　　　　　　　　Zhang Guangqi

Leaning against my walking
stick, I stand and stare by

the pool; lotus stems, withered
with dead leaves, are aslant

in the west wind. A bright
and brilliant sight: beyond

the autumn water, another
stem of flower is blossoming.

秋收的黃昏   林明理

紅霞一抹,歸雁
嫻雅地劃破天際
岸柳,蘆花的豐白仍甦醒中
在槐葉轉黃裹 隨風飄動
並邀請秋葵與栗樹
——互訴靈趣
於是那幹活的佃農
早已忘卻露水冰凍
啊,挺身
眼前是金黃的稻穗,笑望田壠

Dusk of the Autumn Harvest   Lin Ming-Li

With a touch of red glow, returning geese
Gracefully cut through the sky
Bank willows, the rich white of reeds is still awake
In the yellowing of pagoda leaves fluttering in the wind
And the okra and chestnut trees are invited
—To confide in each other
And the working tenant farmer
Has forgotten the frozen dew
Oh, to stand up
Before the eyes are the golden ears of rice, beaming at the ridges

⚘ ⚘ ⚘

清詩明理思千載
● 古今抒情詩三百首
　　漢英對照

105・

早起　　　　　　　　　　　　　　宗渭

宿雨散涼色，竹林煙未醒。
流鶯三四語，啼破半窗青。

Early Rising　　　　　　　　　Zong Wei

An overnight rain incurs
coolness, when the mist

atop the bamboo woods
still sleeps and persists.

Flowing orioles produce
three or four melodious

notes, which pierce half
a windowful of green.

愛的禮讚　　　　　　　　　　　林明理

偶然回首，
歲月悠悠以還
一種空靈的秘密，
在記憶中時時晃動；
登上直覺的台階，
和妳撞個滿懷……

該如何努力構思？
想像天涯海角飄零，
妳鬢髮已泛白；
我只能木立，

對望——
那張稚氣未失的臉,
沉在心底。

妳孜孜追求的,
不正是期待普照的光明;
而我也報予妳
生命中最熱烈的掌聲。
然後,
憑著愛的無邊力量,
在光亮中繼續前行。

In Praise of Love　　　　　　　Lin Ming-Li

I wish I were a small sailboat
　　　Mooring beyond the sunset
Each encounter with the sea
　　　There are lingering memories
If the rain falls down
　　　When loneliness visits from time to time
I sing like that…
　　　…To myself
Am I just living my life
　　　Without seeing clearly what life is
All the waves are humming
All the stars are shining
But I keep yearning —
　　　The tung flowers are blooming
And there are stories
Coming from afar
Yes, no matter how long I sail
How far　is home
In my heart, there is a kind of love
Which often brings me back to my hometown
　　　The gentle and massive embrace

清詩明理思千載
古今抒情詩三百首
漢英對照

106.

曉雨 　　　　　　　　　　　　　　　　　　王庭

獨鳥鳴南園，曉來雨初息。
空庭生秋陰，莓苔長寒色。

Morning Rain 　　　　　　　　　　　　Wang Ting

A solitary bird chirping
in the south garden;

a letup of rain in the
early morning. Autumn

gloom is born in the
empty yard, when

the moss is over-
grown with chilliness.

細密的雨聲 　　　　　　　　　　　　　　林明理

你在哪裡逗留？
——在雨中，穿過
時間的荊棘；

是什麼樣的愛情，
把你凝成
樹痂般的岩顏，

要你如此伏臥
不停震顫到另一個明天？

The Thick Sound of the Rain   Lin Ming-Li

Where are you staying?
— In the rain, through
The thorns of time;

What kind of love,
To turn you into
A scabby rock,
For you to lie and keep trembling
Till another tomorrow?

☘ ☘ ☘

107 ·

宿山中   張履祥

明月不改色，青山留舊顏。
故人零落盡，臥聽水潺潺。

Lodging in the Mountain   Zhang Lüxiang

The bright moon refuses
to changes its complexion;

the blue mountain retains
its old visage. Old friends

and relatives are departing
to the nether world, one by

one; sitting or lying in idleness,
I lend an ear to the babbling water.

致摯友非馬 　　　　　　　　　　　　林明理

我佇立於福爾摩沙
望穿中央山脈到大西洋
穿過海流和茂林
穿過巨石和礫灘
去追逐你奔馳的方向
我寄給你的信
是我小小的憂鬱
而你的容顏，璨爛明亮
彷彿黑暗中冉冉升起的太陽

－2017.06.15

To My Best Friend Dr. William Marr

Lin Ming-Li

I stand in Formosa
Gazing over the central mountains toward the Atlantic Ocean
Through waves and lush forests
Through boulders and sand beaches
To follow your running direction
My letter to you
Carries my melancholy
And your visage, bright and brilliant
Like the sun rising slowly from darkness

－June 15, 2017

108·

五夜 陳一策

五夜入孤村,冒寒人語少。
雞鳴兩三聲,殘月掛林表。

The Fifth Watch of Night Chen Yice

The fifth watch of
night, or the early

dawn, entering the
solitary village; cold

overflowing, few words
from people. Two or three

cockcrows, a remnant
moon atop the woods.

今夜,我走入一星燈火 林明理

那顆星子已逝,渺無人跡
我凝視遠方——
遠方似前又後,懸宕成一拱門
而藍灰的廣場似浸在水中
我在小鐘塔裡
同螞蟻般緩緩步移
那金色劍河正引發懷古思愁

當點點輕舟亮起燈火
城光延伸著,院落連著院落

清詩明理思千載
古今抒情詩三百首
漢英對照

飄浮自濃密林裡閃閃躍動
我忽然記起
若不是那北風嗚咽著
我幾乎遺忘一個流逝的跫音
自千哩外拓了回來，又消失很遠很遠了

Tonight, I Walk Into a Star of Light

Lin Ming-Li

The star is gone, to be traceless
I gaze into the distance —
The distance seems to be backward and forward, hanging into an arch
And the blue-gray square seems to be submerged in water
In the little bell tower
I walk slowly like an ant
The golden Sword River is incurring nostalgia

When dots of little boats flare up
The city light extends, a courtyard connecting another courtyard
Floating from the dense forest shining and twinkling
I suddenly remember
If not for the sobbing north wind
I almost forget a passing sound of steps
From thousands of miles away, to be dying away, far away

❀ ❀ ❀

109·

山行 施閏章

野寺分晴樹，山亭過晚霞。
春深無客到，一路落松花。

A Mountain Trip

Shi Runzhang

A temple in the wilderness
parts the sunlit woods; the

mountain pavilion seems
to be flying through the evening

clouds. Spring advances to
its depth without any visitor

and, along all the way, piny
flowers are falling and fallen.

當陽光照耀達娜伊谷[103]

林明理

當陽光照耀達娜伊谷
群魚不慌不忙
　　從曾文溪上游
　　游經山泉和吊橋
在微風裡
　　　蝶鳥飛舞

山美村的天空純藍
種種和諧的聲響
　　　是我心靈的歡呼
啊，所有鄒族人

林明理 畫
A Painting by Lin Ming-Li

---

[103] 「達娜伊谷」Tanayiku 是鄒族語，意指「忘記憂愁的地方」，也是聖地。在阿里山鄉山美村族人的同心協力下，全村對達娜伊谷進行封溪保育；最後高山鯝魚（俗稱苦花魚）復育有成，因而成為鄒族人的驕傲。

都曾那樣祈禱
每一條溪徑都純淨
鯝魚悠游
在可愛的黎明之中

When the Sun Shines Into Tanayiku[104]

Lin Ming-Li

When the sun shines into Tanayiku
The schools of fish swim unhurriedly
From the upstream of Zengwen Creek
Past mountain springs and suspension bridges
In the breeze
Birds and butterflies flying

The sky of Shanmei Village is pure blue
Various harmonious sounds
Are the cheer of my soul
Ah, all the Zou people
Have prayed in that way
Each stream path is pure
Fish swimming leisurely
In the lovely dawn

⚘ ⚘ ⚘

---

[104] Tanayiku is Zou language, meaning "a place of forgetting sorrow", and it is also a holy place. With the concerted efforts of the people of Shanmei Village in Alishan Township, the whole village carries out the conservation of Tanayiku. Eventually, Xenocypris catfish (commonly known as bitter flower fish) recovers and becomes the pride of the Zou people.

110．

夜坐天遊峰得月 　　　　　　　施閏章

微雨仍留月，千峰洗更明。
仙雲真可數，片片掌中生。

Night Sitting in Heavenly Mountain to Admire the Moon　　　Shi Runzhang

A slight rain still keeps the moon,
when thousands of peaks are

brighter from the shower. The
flimsy clouds are countably ethereal:

a piece after another piece are
gentle and light in the palm.

光之湖 　　　　　　　林明理

春日帶著白松味
罩在橡樹叢
石岸旁
雨露殘留未散
我在虛空裡逡巡——
那失足的花葉
還有從歌雀銜來的漿果
闖入了自己眼眸
常春藤恆長著
蟲聲起了騷動
一隻赤松鼠忽地躍起
轆轆的馬車呼嘯而過

清詩明理思千載
古今抒情詩三百首
漢英對照

The Lake of Light   Lin Ming-Li

The spring day are tinctured with white pine
Cloaked in the oaks
By the stony banks
The remnant dew & rain still remains
I prowl in the void —
The stray leaves of flowers
And the berries from the songbirds
Come into my eyes
The ivy is growing
There is commotion of insects
A red pine leaps up all of a sudden
When a rumbling wagon is whizzing past

⚘ ⚘ ⚘

111 ·

題畫   吳綺

怪石頹雲勢不平，西風卷出大江聲。
漁郎醉臥蘆花裡，笑指何人觸浪行。

Inscription on a Painting   Wu Qi

Rocks grotesque in shapes
and masses of decaying clouds

— the river sound is born
in the west wind. A fisher-

man, drunk, is lying in a boat
caught in reedy flowers while

giving a laugh: who? who
is surfing against the waves?

在沙巴[105]東岸的谷地 　　　　　林明理

原始森林的生物　幾世代來，
從草原、莽原、濕地
　　向沙巴繁衍茁出。
而一群大象
因森林的風雲變色，不得不遷徙。
牠們穿梭在古老的路上，
心中所盼的，不是未來的夢，
而是回家之路迢迢，
只有嘆息……嘆息……
　　在迂迴不堪的山徑中。

In the Valley of the East Coast of Sabah[106]
　　　　　　　　　　　　Lin Ming-Li

For generations, the creatures of primeval forest
Have flourished in Sabah

---

[105] 沙巴（馬來語：Sabah），是馬來西亞聯邦在婆羅洲領土上的兩個行政區域之一。據報導，沙巴森林中有一群不到 1500 隻的大象，因其森林家園被伐木等因素而變小；如何避免牠們面臨絕種的危機，值得關注。－2024.11.13.

[106] Sabah is Malay, and it is one of the two administrative regions of the Federation of Malaysia in the territory of Borneo. It is reported that Sabah forest boasts a herd of less than 1,500 elephants, and the number is dwindling owing to such factors as logging. It is notable how to prevent them from the danger of extinction. －November 13, 2024.

From grasslands, wilderness and wetlands.
And a herd of elephants
Have to move because of the changing forest.
Shuttling through the ancient road,
What they cherish in the heart, is not the future dream,
But the long homeward road,
Only sigh.... and sigh....
　　Along the winding mountain path.

112 ·

夜坐　　　　　　　　　　　　　　　　孫枝蔚

園中鳥不鳴，鄰女靜彈箏。
只道東牆下，無人看月明。

Night Sitting　　　　　　　　　　Sun Zhiwei

Profound quiet reigns
in the courtyard; the

birds are silent, when
the neighbor girl begins

to play her zither by
the east wall, believing

she is the only admirer
of the bright moon.

螢光與飛蟲 　　　　　　　　　　林明理

闖入窗紙
驚喜黑暗螢光
軀體上的靈魂都葬入了
夢想空浮了嗎?

燈罩上的玻璃
靜守著
丁丁地響
小蟲真的撲火了!

Fluorescence and Fireflies 　　Lin Ming-Li

Breaking into the window paper
Pleasant surprise at dark fluorescent
The soul in the body is buried
In the floating dream?

The glass on the lampshade
Silently keeping watch
Tinkling and jingling
The bug is really flying into fire!

❁ ❁ ❁

113・

微雲移時月出 　　　　　　　　　王士禧

乍散還乍聚,疑煙複疑水。
清光出雲中,皎皎如初洗。

The Moon Peeps Through Thin Clouds

Wang Shixi

Now clouds gather,
then clouds scatter;

seemingly water,
seemingly mist.

A beam of light
through clouds:

clear and pure as
if freshly washed.

追悼——出版家劉振強前輩

林明理

你的名字
是臺灣出版界的豐碑
是萬種圖書的奠基人
在所有親友的追憶中
你,是永不枯竭的泉源
是文學史上永遠的財富
也將得到神的恩惠[107]

In Memoriam of Liu Zhenqiang as a Famous Publisher

Lin Ming-Li

Your name
Is the monument of the publishing industry in Taiwan

---

[107] 二〇一七年三月,三民書局創辦人劉振強先生逝世了,享年八十六歲,留給愛戴他的員工及親友無限懷思。劉老先生在臺灣出版界有不可抹滅的貢獻,而三民書局成立迄今出版了一萬多種圖書,也為文學史立下一個重要的里程碑。因而為詩紀念這位卓越的出版家。

As the founder of ten thousand books
In the memory of all relatives and friends
You are an inexhaustible source
The eternal wealth in the history of literature
And you will be graced by deity[108]

❀ ❀ ❀

114‧

題畫 　　　　　　　　　　　　湯貽汾

此景不知何處，臨溪萬樹梅花。
不是扁舟能到，更誰知有人家。

Inscription on a Painting 　　Tang Yifen

The scenic spot is hard
to be orientated: myriads

of trees are burdened
with plum blossoms by

the creek. If not for the
thoroughgoing boat, who

knows there is a homestead
in such a remote place.

---

[108] In March, 2017, Mr. Liu Zhenqiang, the founder of Sanmin Book Company, passed away at the age of 86, and his beloved staff and friends cherish an everlasting fond memory of him. Mr. Liu has made an indelible contribution to the publishing industry in Taiwan, and Sanmin Book Company has published over 10,000 books since its establishment, which has also set an important milestone in the history of literature. Hence this poem to commemorate him as a remarkable publisher.

清詩明理思千載
● 古今抒情詩三百首
　漢英對照

致巴爾札克（Honoré de Balzac, 1799-1850）

林明理

無人能替代你
引我如此想像
我所記得的
除了一些手稿和繪畫
並聯想到　遠方的
你
有星群守衛著
在花園周圍，還有
幾件雕塑

誰都比不上你
把多種藝術統一
成為神奇體式的小說
而筆下撰寫的
人物
多樣而不可預測
你是一部宏偉的史詩
挺立的身姿
盡顯率性不羈與驕傲

－2019.7.15

To Balzac (Honoré de Balzac, 1799-1850)

Lin Ming-Li

Nobody can replace you
Who can lead me to imaginations
What I remember
Except for some manuscripts and paintings
In association with the remote distance
You

The maze of guarding stars
Around the garden, and
A few sculptures

Nobody can match you
In unifying various arts
To become a magical novel
And under your pen
The characters
Various and unpredictable
You are a magnificent epic
Standing straight
To bespeak your pride and unrestrained character

—July 15, 2019

115 ·

題畫 湯斌

秋林不厭靜，高士自能閒。
盡日茅亭下，開窗到遠山。

Inscription on a Painting   Tang Bin

The autumn woods
are not tired of quiet;

a recluse enjoys
his leisure. Daylong

sitting in the pavilion;
open the window —

a remote mountain
is approaching.

寂靜無聲的深夜 　　　　　　　　　　林明理

1.
閉氣四十分鐘
海底的海鬣蜥
有神乎其技的天賦

2.
自然界中
一隻達爾文雀的歌聲
竟啟發了演化論

3.
此刻
我的思潮在深夜奔騰
像籠中逸出的歌雀[109]

The Silent Night 　　　　　　　Lin Ming-Li

1.
Hold the breath for 40 minutes
The underwater sideburns
Have a miraculous innate skill

2.
In the natural world
The song of a Dalvin finch
Has inspired the theory of evolution

---

[109] 海鬣蜥（marine iguanas），是僅出沒在科隆群島的鬣蜥科物種。達爾文雀（Darwin's finches）大多生在厄瓜多爾西方大西洋中的一座孤懸於海上的火山群島，是第一個被評為世界自然遺產之地。

3.
At the moment
My thoughts are surging in the night
Like the songbirds who have escaped from the cage[110]

❦ ❦ ❦

116 ·

閨情　　　　　　　　　　　　　夏宗沂

庭樹暮棲鴉，秋風入樓角。
誰遣落葉聲，空閨先獨覺。

Boudoir Repinings　　　　Xia Zongyi

The courtyard trees
are noisy with dusk

crows, when autumn
wind invades the

mansions. The falling
of leaves — who,

in the lonely boudoir,
is the first hearer?

---

[110] Marine iguanas are a species of iguana found only in the Colon Islands. Darwin's finches are mostly found on a cluster of isolated volcanic islands in the Atlantic Ocean west of Ecuador, and it is the first to be rated as a World Natural Heritage Site.

清詩明理思千載
● 古今抒情詩三百首
漢英對照

月桃記憶[111]   林明理

每年秋末
月桃花綴滿山野
當果實迸裂
種子又散落山谷時
我總會想起
那一天
在東部濱海的
都蘭部落
我看到
一個個專注編織的老人
在這靜寂的園子
歡迎我

她們高興就唱得甜蜜
偶爾也會皺著眉頭
檳榔和酒香
就成共同的慰藉

她們將曬乾的月桃葉
一片片剝開
捲成圓圈圈
再曬一次
開始編織成籃子或手提包

這是後山的傳奇嗎
我好奇又興奮地問
美麗的鳥兒啊，告訴我

---

[111] 自古以來月桃就深具有民俗味，可用月桃葉包粽子；加以魯凱族、卑南族和阿美族人多會用月桃葉為編織材料。

這周圍的一切
不是夢
那月桃記憶
恰如夜半更深的輕喚親吻
沒有歌詞,卻永不消逝

Shell-flower Memory[112]   Lin Ming-Li

At the end of each autumn
When peach blossoms bloom in the mountains
And the fruits burst
And the seeds scatter all over the valley
I always remember
The day
On the eastern coast
Of the Duran tribe
I see
One after another old man absorbed in weaving
In the quiet garden
To welcome me

They sing sweetly when they are happy
Occasionally they frown
The aroma of betel nut and wine
Is the common comfort

They peel the dried moon peach leaves
One by one
And roll them into circles
To dry them again
And start to weave them into baskets or handbags

---

[112] Since ancient times, the *Shell-flower* is rich in folk flavor; its leaves can be used to wrap dumplings, and the Jarukai, Pinan and Amis people tend to use the *Shell-flower* leaves as weaving materials.

清詩明理思千載
古今抒情詩三百首
漢英對照

Is this the legend of the Back Mountain?
I ask, curious and excited
Oh beautiful bird, please tell me
Everything around here
Is not a dream
The peach moon memory
Is like a gentle kiss deeper in the night
Without words, yet it never dies

🌷 🌷 🌷

117 ·

讀曲歌 　　　　　　　　　　　朱彝尊

素藕生池中，紅荷浮水面。
與汝同一身，本自不相見。

A Song　　　　　　　　　　Zhu Yizun

White lotus grows
beneath the water

in the pool; red lotus
flowers are floating

on water. Both
spring from the

same root, yet they
never meet each other.

丁香花開　　　　　　　　　　林明理

砲聲震過
從驚夢中醒
敵人越來越近

我打傘下山
春天的沿石露凝
破曉的胭脂魚白
草原的生氣不再

鐘響起
慟，我在墓園裏觀禮
送你，悄然地
是一地淡紫丁香的回憶

Flowering Lilacs　　　　　　Lin Ming-Li

The sound of the cannon
Awakes me from my dream
As the enemy are approaching

Holding an umbrella I come down the mountain
Spring is dewy along the rocks
At dawn the mullet white
The grassland animation is no more

The bell rings
Sorrowful, I attend ceremony in the cemetery
To see you off, in silence
A groundful of memory like light lilac

清詩明理思千載
古今抒情詩三百首
漢英對照

118．

惜花（其二）   李經垓

落花飛滿衣，似有留人意。
何處無情風，依然吹落地。

Cherishing Flowers (No. 2)   Li Jinggai

Falling flowers
fill the fold of my

clothes, seemingly
to be fond of me.

A gust of unfeeling
wind, from nowhere,

blows them, one
and all, aground.

我的歌[113]   林明理

在發生災難的
失眠時刻
你的傷痛隱藏於
天使的羽衣之下
如哀傷的銀鷗
長夜漫漫
世界有時變化無常
而我的歌

---

[113] 2016.07.14 法國國慶日遭逢恐怖攻擊，死傷慘重。我致電郵給 Prof. Ernesto Kahan，所幸他安好並回應說：「Dearest Ming-Li, Receive a big huge perfumed with friendship。」因而為詩。

是熱血沸騰的回聲
穿過尼斯的月亮

My Song[114]   Lin Ming-Li

In the event of a disaster
Insomnia time
To hide your pain
Under the feathers of an angel
Like the sorrowful silver gull
All night long
The changeable world
And my song
Is a passionate echo
Through the moon of Nice

❀ ❀ ❀

119 ·

曉起   葛元福

起看庭前花，漸欲舒紅蕚。
不嫌緩緩開，但願遲遲落。

Getting Up in the Morning   Ge Yuanfu

Getting up in the morning
to admire flowers in

---

[114] On July 14, 2016, the National Day of France, there is a terrorist attack with heavy casualties. I send an email to professor Ernesto Kahan, to luckily get the message that he is safe and sound: "Dearest Ming-Li, Receive a big huge perfumed with friendship." Thus this poem.

the yard, which are
on the budding of red

calyx, I do not abhor
their gradual spreading,

with a fond wish of their
slow dropping and falling.

青煙

林明理

天開了──
露珠像明珠似的
掛在瓜棚
笑看著天空

公雞在跳躍
跳在泥牆邊
跳在綠竹旁
跳在水田間
跳在污泥上

青煙升了──
一縷縷同爐香似的
在老農夫的心

風中，彷彿聽見……
聲聲呼喚
老伴兒，回來呀──
吃飯囉──

Blue Smoke

Lin Ming-Li

The sky slowly opens —
Dewdrops like a bright pearl

Hanging in the melon shed
Smiling skyward

Roosters are leaping about
By the mud wall
By the green bamboos
In the paddy field
And over the mud

Blue smoke arising —
Wisps of incense
In the old farmer's heart

In the wind, seemingly to hear…
A call after another call
My dear wife, come home —
For dinner —

❀ ❀ ❀

120 ·

宿山園   謝芳連

小雨松徑寒，人歸夜深火。
宿鳥棲未安，驚飛落山果。

Lodging in a Mountain Yard   Xie Fanglian

A slight rain lends cold
to the piny path; the roamer

returns and the deep night
lamp remains. Before

清詩明理思千載
● 古今抒情詩三百首
　　漢英對照,

the perching birds settle
themselves, their flight startles

mountain fruits, which are on
the dropping — one, two, three…

剪影 　　　　　　　　　　　　　　　　　　林明理

昨夜夢的矇矓
那等在廣場的靜謐
如今朝的雨色淒迷

走出地鐵,花傘繽紛的街上
妳的影子 捻起我心的律動
在風中,濕潤的空氣混濁
妳的嘴唇似西山的繁霜秋楓

我翩翩的羽翼是無間的力量
愛,讓我展翅,飛向光芒……

Sketch 　　　　　　　　　　　　　　　　Lin Ming-Li

Last night's dream blurs
The quiet waiting in the square
Sad and sentimental like this morning's rain color

Walking out of the subway, on the street of colorful umbrellas
Your shadow twists the rhythm of my heart
In the wind, the moist air is turbid
Your lips are like the frost of autumn maples in the West Mountain

My fluttering wings are the concentrated power
Love, for me to spread my wings, to the light...

121.

密雲望行人　　　　　　　　　　　　　謝芳漣

人行犬更吠，密雲迷村影。
欲扣酒家扉，山橋一蓑冷。

Watching Wanderers in Miyun
　　　　　　　　　　　　　　　　Xie Fanglian

Wanderers walking,
more barking of dogs;

Miyun is lost in the
shadows of the village.

Upon knocking at the door
of a wineshop — a cold

palm-bark rain cape is
passing by a mountain bridge.

銀背大猩猩[115]　　　　　　　　　　　林明理

大地溫柔地看著
　　大猩猩的影子
風與山丘寂靜……
啊，牠躲過各種侵襲

---

[115] 銀背大猩猩（Silverback，Gorilla Tracking）又叫金剛猩猩，是地球上現存的最大、最強壯的靈長類動物，屬於保護類野生動物。

清詩明理思千載
* 古今抒情詩三百首
  漢英對照

可以在森林裡睡得飽
也沒憂慮
　　——我祈禱著

Silverback Gorilla[116]   Lin Ming-li

The great earth looks gently
　At the gorilla's shadow
The wind and the hills remain silent....
Ah, through escaping from various attacks
It can enjoy a sound sleep in the forest
Without any worry
　　— I am praying

✿ ✿ ✿

122 ·

落花   宋犖

昨日花簌簌，今日落如掃。
反怨盛開時，不及未開好。

Falling Flowers   Song Luo

Yesterday the flowers are
flowering in masses; today

the flowers are dropping and
falling in showers. The height

---

[116] Silverback gorillas (also known as Gorilla Tracking) are the largest and strongest primates living on the earth, and they are protected wild animals.

280

of their flowering is no better
than their budding stage.

約克郡[117]的春天 　　　　　　　　　　林明理

一叢叢雪花草開了，
　野兔躍上草原，
紅嘴鷗跟著運作的耕耘機，
　找到了食物。

哦，所有沼澤、海岸
　和谷地中的小動物
開始甦醒、築巢，
　啄木鳥也敲醒了春神。

而我正為一窩小海豹
　在海底瞇眼三十分鐘而著迷。
因為，偉大的生命循環，
　又一次開始。

Spring in Yorkshire[118] 　　　　　　Lin Ming-Li

Clumps of snowflake grass are opening,
Wild hares are leaping in the prairie,
Black-headed gulls follow the tillers,
Until they find their food.

Oh, all the little animals
In the swamps, coasts and valleys
Begin to wake up and build nests;
The woodpeckers have woken up the deity of spring.

---

[117] 約克郡（英語：Yorkshire），又稱約克夏，位於英格蘭東北部。
[118] Yorkshire is located in the North-East of England.

And I'm fascinated by a brood of seal pups
Squinting at the bottom of the ocean for 30 minutes.
For the great cycle of life
Has begun once more.

123 ·

待友 　　　　　　　　　　　　　　　　王敔

小立閒階外，凝眸日已西。
稻苗深一尺，中有水禽啼。

Waiting for a Friend 　　　　　　Wang Yu

Standing in leisure beyond
the steps, the sun is seen

to be slowly westering.
Rice seedlings are knee-

deep, where waterfowls
are cawing and croaking.

寄語哥哥 　　　　　　　　　　　　　林明理

今夜，沉沉的天幕下
窗外一切寂靜，海也酣睡了
雨聲如此純粹。我敬愛的哥哥
我想起童年的我們
微笑單純，在小屋裡讀書寫字
或釣青蛙於田中

往日好似夢幻
又浮現在我眼前……

是啊，生活中無論是甘甜
或辛澀，高低起伏或安逸平順
願主賜給你平安，在未來的
日子裡，有一天
我們又能結伴同遊
而希望是實現的開端
窗外一切寂靜，海也酣睡了
我只能悄悄託付給夜……
用心頭的光　編織成祝禱的言詞

A Message to My Brother   Lin Ming-Li

Tonight, under the heavy canopy of heaven
All is quiet without the window, and the sea is sound asleep
The sound of rain is so pure. My beloved brother
I think of our childhood
When our smile is so simple, reading and writing in the small room
Or fishing frogs in the field
The past is like a dream
Which is emerging before me…

Yes, whether life is sweet or bitter,
Ups and downs, or easy and smooth
May Lord give you peace, in the days
To come, one day
We can travel together
And hope is the beginning of realization
All is quiet without the window, and the sea is sound asleep
I can only quietly entrust it to the night…
With light of the heart to weave words of prayer

清詩明理思千載
● 古今抒情詩三百首
　漢英對照

🌷🌷🌷

124 ·

黃竹子歌　　　　　　　　　　　　　申涵盼

江邊黃竹子，風雨夜悲鳴。
不堪截作笛，亦有斷腸聲。

Song of Yellow Bamboos　　　Shen Hanpan

Riverside yellow bamboos
are soughing and rustling

through the nightlong winds
& rains — when they are cut

into pieces as bamboo flutes,
still they produce plaintive notes.

極端氣候下　　　　　　　　　　　林明理

1.
海水變酸了
像大堡礁殘骸裡逐漸
白化的珊瑚——
無助的泣聲。

2.
從山脈到海岸
濕地越來越少
來來去去的候鳥
都沒有了家。

3.
氣旋和暴雨
讓地球歇斯底里地嘶吼。
一隻赤蠵龜，仍奮力地游回大海，
勇氣的美存在。

4.
啊，下一個世代
誰能繼續頌揚那些
為生命而奮戰的生物？
誰能再次欣賞鯨之舞
美得神聖卻也令人痛苦。

In Extreme Weather Lin Ming-Li

1.
The sea water has turned sour
Like in the remains of the Great Barrier Reef
Gradual bleaching corals —
Helpless cries.

2.
From the mountain to the sea coast
Fewer and fewer wetlands
The migratory birds coming and
Going without homes.

3.
Cyclones and rainstorms
Make the earth roar hysterically.
A loggerhead turtle, still struggling to swim back to the sea,
The beauty of courage still exists.

4.
Ah, in the next generation
Who can continue to celebrate those

清詩明理思千載
古今抒情詩三百首
漢英對照，

Creatures who fight for their lives?
Who can once more admire the dance of whales
So beautiful to be sacred, and so painful.

❀ ❀ ❀

125 ·

溪上 張增慶

輕陰帶斜日，杳靄前山夕。
雙鷺忽飛來，點破一溪碧。

Over the Creek   Zhang Zengqing

Slight shade under a
slanting sun; profound

is the evening glow before
the mountain. A pair of

white egrets suddenly fly here,
to break a creekful of blue.

卑南溪[119] 林明理

靜靜的卑南溪順水而流
線光穿刺天藍的夜色
從小黃山到岩灣河段
浩浩蕩蕩的尖壁望不到盡頭
到了這兒，我聽不見喧聲

---

[119]「卑南溪」是臺灣臺東的第一大溪，卑南之名是為了紀念卑南族的大頭目。

忘了自己身在何處
時間已無關緊要
　愛情之樹常青

讓我緩緩地走向你
　走在很久以前的傳說
多麼堅實的故土上
讓我駛入你深藏眼簾的輕愁
　飛入你寬廣的胸前
靜靜的卑南溪靜靜地流
你的憂鬱是我的戀棧
你的柔波是黎明在舞蹈

The Pinan River[120]   Lin Ming-Li

The quiet Pinan River flows smoothly
And the light pierces the sky-blue night
From Xiaohuangshan to the reach of Yanwan River
The boundless sharp walls stretch endlessly
Here, I cannot hear the noises
　　Forgetting where I am.
Time is insignificant
　　The tree of love is evergreen

Let me walk slowly towards you
　　Walking in the legend of a long time ago
On how solid the native land
For me to enter the light sorrow of your hidden eyes
　　Flying into your broad chest
The quiet Pinan River runs smoothly
Your melancholy is my love
Your soft glances are the dawn which is dancing

---

[120] The Pinan River is the longest river in Taitung, Taiwan, and Pinan is named in honor of the chief of the Pinan ethnic group.

126·

渡江 　　　　　　　　　　　　　　　　　　　文點

青山如故人，江水似美酒。
今日重相逢，把酒對良友。

Crossing the River 　　　　　　　　　　Wen Dian

The green mountain
is like an old friend;

the river water is like
good wine. Today

a meeting again, with
wine to face my friend.

詩與白冷圳的間奏曲[121] 　　　　　　　　林明理

當我讀您
在風中，在您熾熱的靈魂裡
以鷹之姿

---

[121] 二〇一七年三月二十日，我應邀於「飛閱文學地景」採訪錄影於臺北市濟南路的齊東詩舍。歷經集集大地震又被重建的臺中市「白冷圳」（Bailengzhun），迄今已走過九十多年歷史。它堅毅地守護著老家鄉新社等地區的形象，令人動容。那緩緩潺潺的大甲溪，那堅毅凝視的老圳，那群峰環繞的溪谷、水橋，那耀眼明澈的生命之水，在空拍下將聯成一幅動人影像，賦予旅人及遊子更多的生命力。最後，〈白冷圳之戀〉就在導演等團隊的合作下順利完成了這部影片的錄影與採訪。

留給我們無限遐想
您是我生命的溫情
是我千百次
聆聽不厭的豪邁史詩
我讀您的不朽和閃光的眼眸
從翻騰苦難的歲月
到生命中幸福的一瞬

Intermezzo Between Poems and Bailengzhun[122]

Ling Ming-Li

When I read you
In the wind, in your fiery soul
In the position of eagles
To give us boundless reverie
You are the warmth of my life
And the heroic epic which I never tire of reading
Through thousands of times
I read your immortality and shining eyes
From the years of churning suffering
To the happy moment in life

❀ ❀ ❀

---

[122] On March 20, 2017, I was invited to take part in a video interview on "Flying Literature Landscape" at the Qidong Poetry House on Jinan Road, Taipei City. The Bailengzhun in Taichung City, which was rebuilt after the Jiji earthquake, boasts a history of over 90 years. It resolutely guards the image of the old hometown, new society and other areas, which is touching. The slowly gurgling Dajia Stream, the old canal with the firm gaze, the valley surrounded by the peaks, the water bridge, the dazzling and bright water of life, all are taken in the air together into a moving image, giving travelers and wanderers more vitality. Finally, the video and interview of the film *Love of Bailengzhun* was successfully completed under the cooperation of the director and his team.

清詩明理思千載
古今抒情詩三百首
漢英對照

127・

桃花谷 張實居

小徑穿深樹,臨崖四五家。
泉聲天半落,滿澗濺桃花。

The Valley of Peach Flowers Zhang Shiju

A path zigzagging
through deep woods;

by the cliff there are
four or five homesteads.

The spring water falls
from mid-air, when

the ravine is riotous
with peach flowers.

觀霧—雲的故鄉[123] 林明理

輕霧裊裊移動
　在峰谷,以那首古調
掠過天邊又掠過我的眼眸
　山雀在枝椏間倒懸著

哦,美麗的觀霧多寧靜
　夏季已經來臨

---

[123] 位於中高海拔地區的觀霧(Guanwu)森林遊樂區,在臺灣新竹縣五峰鄉與苗栗縣泰安鄉交界,因常有雲霧繚繞,又稱為「雲的故鄉」。

巨木林一片綠意
潺潺瀑布聲轟鳴

多嚮往你四季不同的百景
　純淨的花兒
鳳蝶和山椒魚，還有
　那點綴滿天的星

當月光鋪灑河灘地
　聽鳥獸在岩壁，在溪邊
　在屋宇部落的窗戶
而後，隨著我和那首古調

掠過夜空又掠過我的心頭
你是雲的故鄉
不變的身影，在風中縈繞
像是沉醉在落霞紅日中

Watching Clouds: the Hometown of Clouds[124]
Lin Ming-Li

The gentle mist curling and moving
　Down valley of the mountain, with the old tune
Passing over the horizon and my eyes
　The chickadee hangs upside down in the branches

Oh, so quiet is the beautiful sight of fog
　　Summer has arrived
　Giant woods is a stretch of green
　The running waterfall is roaring

---

[124] Guanwu Forest Recreation Area is located in the middle and high altitude area, at the junction of Wufeng Township of Hsinchu County and Tai'an Township of Miaoli County, Taiwan; owing to the constant clouds, it is known as "the hometown of clouds."

How I long for your different seasons of one hundred sights
    The pure flowers
Butterflies and cryptobranchoidea fish, as well as
    The stars studding the sky

When moonlight paves the beach
    Listen to birds and beasts by the rock, by the stream
    The window of the house tribe
Then, follow me and the old tune

Across the night sky and across my mind
You are the hometown of clouds
Your constant figure, lingering in the wind
As if drunk in the falling rosy colors and red sun

❁ ❁ ❁

128 ·

山居 　　　　　　　　　　洪昇

朝看嶺上雲，夕臥松間月。
醉起復開樽，山花飛不歇。

Mountain Life　　　　　　Hong Sheng

Morning looking at the clouds veiling over the

ridge; evening sitting in the pines to admire the moon.

Getting up, tipsy, to open another bottle of wine, when

mountain flowers are on
the flying and dancing.

詩河   林明理

你來自八荒
激勵我奇思冥想
那叮咚的回聲
時刻盤旋著，搖曳的銀波
輕漾藍調的柔歌

The Poetic River   Lin Ming-Li

You are from wilderness
To motivate me into fancies
That echo of ding-dong
Is on the hovering, the waving silver ripples
Poppling with the soft songs of blue melody

🌷 🌷 🌷

129 ·

採蓮歌   王鴻緒

采采江水濱，荷花照臉新。
莫愁西日晚，明月解留人。

Lotus-Picking Song   Wang Hongxu

Picking and plucking,
plucking and picking

by the river; fair lotus
flowers against fair faces.

The sun is westering
and disappearing —

no worry: the bright
moon is up to shine.

岩川之夜[125]   林明理

野溪
是密林琅琅的樂音

圈圈螢光
披雪守在飛瀑外
一路緊緊相連

黃金雨季不來

而等待
變成阿勃勒花海
來送還它的思念

The Night of Iwakawa[126]   Lin Ming-Li

The wild stream
Is the clear music of the dense forest

Rings of fluorescent light
In blankets of snow to keep watch without the waterfall
Closely connecting all the way

---

[125]「岩川」是臺灣苗栗縣著名的螢火蟲復育勝地。
[126] Iwakawa is a famous firefly breeding resort in Miaoli County, Taiwan.

No coming in the golden rainy season

And waiting
Becomes the Abler flower sea
To return its missing and yearning

🌷 🌷 🌷

130．

別後作　　　　　　　　　　　　劉獻廷

獨立征河岸，蒼茫北去舟。
誰憐此時意，日日到心頭。

Composed Upon Departure　Liu Xianting

Solitary standing by the
river, to see a northbound

boat over boundless water.
Fancy! This scene and

this sight should appear
and reappear in my mind.

致友人李浩　　　　　　　　　　林明理

在遠方，有片起伏的山丘，
發亮的路橋使宇宙陰暗下來。
你說：
上海的天氣，十分舒爽。
公園裡頭的柳堤和池畔，

也懸在我的思維裡發亮了。

在那兒,本想留住溪水,
也留下時間。
我聽到一片海棠跟雨說話,
櫻樹怯怯地
冒出新芽,剎那間:
綠樹,琉璃瓦頂,雲朵,——

直抵深夜,穿過海峽。
上海,一座發亮的大都會,
那兒有許多傳說,
有革命者的足痕和遺跡。
那廣場前來來去去的
身影,何其匆促。

只有你,就像這重複的
雨聲……又像一幅
啜茗沉思者的圖畫。
那瞬息而過的風,
彷若在太平洋上叮囑著:
我的朋友,別來無恙。[127]

To My Friend Li Hao   Lin Ming-Li

In the distance, there is a stretch of rolling hills,
The shining roads and bridges darken the universe.

---

[127] 友人李浩,是《上海魯迅研究》季刊的編委。二〇二二年九月,他寄來一本我在此刊物上發表的文章「尋找恬淡中的感性——以《魯迅圖傳》為視角」,並透過電郵互相問候,也分享幾張他在下班時拍攝的上海魯迅公園、蘇州河的西藏路橋和人民廣場沿線的夜景照。因而有感題詩,以茲留念。

You say:
The weather in Shanghai is very comfortable.
The willowy bank and the pool in the park
Are bright in my mind.

There, initial intention to retain the stream,
As well as time.
I hear a mass of begonias talking to the rain,
The cherry trees are timidly
Budding, in an instant:
Green trees, glazed tile roofs, clouds —
Well into the night, across the channel.
Shanghai, a shining metropolis,
There are a host of legends,
As well as the relics and footprints of revolutionaries.
The forms and figures coming and going
In the square are in such a great hurry.

Only you, like the repeated sound
Of rain... and like a
Picture of a man sipping tea.
The fleeting wind
Seems to be telling and retelling in the Pacific Ocean:
My dear friend, I hope you are well.[128]

🌷 🌷 🌷

---

[128] My friend Li Hao is a member of the editorial board of *Shanghai Luxun Research* Quarterly. In September 2022, he sent me a copy of the magazine where I published an article entitled *In Search of Sensibility in Quietude — from the Perspective of "Lu Xun's Pictorial Biography"*, and through mutual greetings via emails and shared night photos taken during his commuting hours along the Lu Xun Park in Shanghai, the Xizang Road Bridge along the Suzhou River and the People's Square, the poem is inspired for memory.

131 ·

夜宿養素堂東偏　　　　　　　　查慎行

嫋嫋一枝藤，疏疏幾行柳。
籬落吐燈光，鄰家猶賣酒。

Lodging for the Night　　　　Zha Shengxing

A vine which is long
and lean; a few lines of

willows which are sparse
and scattered. Through

fence and hedge the light
penetrates, when the

neighborhood wine-
shop is still in business.

集集站遐想[129]　　　　　　　　林明理

當區間車動身時
偶一回首
我找到軌道旁的一方陽光
是那樣亙古
那樣寧靜
那樣明亮

---

[129] 集集站（1922年1月14日啟用），走過百年的集集站，舊稱集集驛；曾經歷1999年「九二一」大地震襲擊，而今是南投縣旅遊勝地，設有集集鐵路文物博覽館，為台灣歷史建築百景之一，也是從日治時代留下的唯一車站。

月台上的風　習以為常
讓「九二一」都變得淡然
而最能挑起我記憶的
正是庫存的往日——
雖然震垮了
又得以原貌重建

在這裡　一切跟天空十分相像
沒有任何矯情
卻更讓人嘖嘖稱奇
那斷斷續續的
回音
在廣場前飄蕩

是風　在訴說——
歷史的迂廻或淒涼
引我進一步想像
讓我忍不住回轉身軀
望它的背影
是那樣勇敢瀟灑

Reverie of the Jiji Station[130]　　Lin Ming-Li

When the district train starts off
Occasionally I look back
To find a square of sun by the side of the track
So eternal
So quiet
So bright

---

[130] Jiji Station (in use on January 14, 1922), through one hundred years, has experienced "the 921 earthquake in 1999", and is now a tourist resort in Nantou County. With Jiji Railway Cultural Relics Exhibition Hall, it is one of the 100 sights of historical architecture in Taiwan, and the only station left over from the Japanese era.

清詩明理思千載
古今抒情詩三百首
漢英對照,

The wind on the platform is so familiar
For the "921 incident" to be indifferent
The most memorable thing for me
Is the past of the inventory —
Although destroyed
It was rebuilt according to the original appearance

Here everything is very much like the sky
Without any affectation
But more amazing
The intermittent
Echo
Floating in front of the square

It is the wind that is telling —
The detour or desolation of history
Which leads me to further imagination
For me to helplessly turn around
To look at its back
Which is so brave and unrestrained

❦ ❦ ❦

132 ·

舟中書所見　　　　　　　　　　查慎行

月黑見漁燈，孤光一點螢。
微微風簇浪，散作滿河星。

Night Sight from the Boat　　Zha Shengxing

Moonless, fishing light
is seen; a solitary beam

of light as a dot of glow-
worm. Under gentle wind,

waves upon waves are waving
into a riverful of stars.

日出新蘭漁港 　　　　　　　　林明理

那個山海環伺的秋日，
世界像首詩，梭巡蒼穹下。
青春與愛情在沉默中
逝去，又悄悄向前。

但是晨曦依然絢麗，
所有熾熱而純粹的愛——
掠過波光，
忽地變得栩栩如生。
是什麼闖入我眼眸在靠近，
是浪花，是瞭望潮汛的燈塔
還是愛情駝著我在岸邊，
不經意地露出一抹微笑。

Sunrise Over Xinlan Fishing Port
　　　　　　　　　　　　Lin Ming-Li

The autumn day which is surrounded with mountains and seas,
The world is like a poem, patrolling under the sky.
Youth and love remain in silence
Disappear, and quietly moving forward.

Yet the morning light is still brilliant,
All the pure and passionate love —
Flitting by the light of waves,
Suddenly to be so vivid.

清詩明理思千載
古今抒情詩三百首
漢英對照

What is approaching and invading my eyes?
The waving flowers, the lighthouse looking over the tide,
Or me carried ashore by love?
Unconsciously revealing a smile.

☙ ☙ ☙

133 ·

梅花　　　　　　　　　　　　　　　蔣錫震

竹屋圍深雪，林間無路通，
暗香留不住，多事是春風。

Plum Blossoms　　　　　　　Jiang Xizhen

The bamboo house
is enclosed with

knee-deep snow,
and there is no road

through the forest.
The hidden scent is

hard to retain — the spring
breeze as the spoiler.

春雪飛紅　　　　　　　　　　　　林明理

我從月下走過。望一片瑩白的天
松林，雪地，紅櫻矜憐

在宇宙下,無法凝視和把握

是啊,風中之花喁喁飄落……
勘破紅塵。縱然難回首
縱然你眼底有飛揚的虹彩
卻遺忘了我的低眉垂袖

我從石階前坐。望新雁低翔而過
細雨,花飛,冉冉炊煙
在夜夢裏,窗外春雪伴我眠

Spring Snow Flying with Red Lin Ming-Li

I walk under the moon. Looking at the white sky
Pine forest, snow, red cherry pitiable
Under the universe, no way to stare and grasp

Yes, the flowers are fluttering in the wind...
Seeing through the red world. Even though it is hard to look back
Even though with the rainbow flying in your sight
Still I have forgotten my timidity as low brows

I sit in front of the stone steps. To look at the new geese flying low
The drizzle, flying flowers, kitchen smoke slowly arising
In the night dream, without the window I sleep with spring snow

清詩明理思千載
古今抒情詩三百首
漢英對照

134 ·

月橋行秋 　　　　　　　　　　　　　陳仁

秋色涼如水，湖光掩映間。
往來幽意愜，隨月上青山。

The Moon Bridge in Autumn 　　　Chen Ren

The autumn is cool
like water; the lake

light now appears
and then disappears.

Strolling back or forth,
all in leisure; with the

moon, up and upon
the blue mountain.

夢橋 　　　　　　　　　　　　　　　林明理

我從西螺橋[131]下走過，
向最後的殘陽揮手。
橋上只有奔程，只有回歸，
沒有風和雨的旋飛。

我回首望著暗澹天，
想起了那走盡田隴的老爹。
在溪灘沙田的耕作裡，
承受那汗珠滴落的白眉。

---

[131] 「西螺大橋」Hsilo Bridge 位於臺灣雲林縣。

老爹說，
他擔心著暴雨，
又怕颱風來威脅——
他溫柔地種了西瓜，
不怕孤零的疏星和曉月。

今夜，
他把我的童年悄然掀起，
像一只古老的笛琴，
向那紅塵十丈處輕吹⋯⋯

The Dream Bridge Lin Ming-Li

I pass under the Hsilo Bridge[132],
Waving to the lingering setting sun.
There is only running on the bridge, only returning,
No swirling and flying of wind and rain.

I look back at the dark sky
And think of my father who has gone into the field.
In the cultivation of sandy field,
To bear the white eyebrows dripping with sweat.

Dad said,
He is worried about the rainstorm,
And dread the threatening typhoon —
He has gently planted watermelon,
Unafraid of lonely sparse stars and the morning moon.

Tonight,
He quietly lifts up my childhood,
Like an ancient flute,
Gently piping to the depth of red dust...

---

[132] Hsilo Bridge is located in Yunlin County, Taiwan.

清詩明理思千載
古今抒情詩三百首
漢英對照

135·

白髮 翁志琦

朝來攬明鏡,白髮感蹉跎。
畢竟無公道,愁人鬢畔多。

Gray Hairs Weng Zhiqi

Morning looking into
the mirror, hairs graying

through wasted time.
Unfairness reigns —

a sorrowful person tends
to be more gray-templed.

夜思 林明理

與秋空連接的
在一縷行雲間
迴轉往復

縱使無法駕馭長風
卻也甘心化為一棵老松
聽雨在燈下
清音在心境
從流逝不定的靈感
黑暗中尋思光點

任白髮悄然延伸
多少年後
依然瀟灑自如

Night Missing & Pining   Lin Ming-Li

Connected with the autumn sky,
It rotates among
A wisp of clouds

Even if unable to ride the long wind
Yet willing to be an old pine
Listen to the rain in the light
Pure sound in the heart
From the fleeting inspiration
In search of light in the dark

The hair is on the graying
After many years
Still free and unrestrained

✿ ✿ ✿

136.

邦均野寺   慎郡王

僧罷夕陽鐘，客懷正孤絕。
山鳥下空林，自啄茅簷雪。

A Wild Temple in Bangjun   Shen Junwang

After striking the evening
bell, the monk is solitary

清詩明理思千載
古今抒情詩三百首
漢英對照

of mind. Mountain birds
fly away from the empty

forest, to be pecking at
the snow on the eaves.

暮秋裡的春花——讀瓦西里基・德拉古尼詩集《越過夏季》
林明理

妳的話語,多麼明亮無染
　彷若暮秋裡的春花
從雅典靜默的空氣中
　再度綻放在福爾摩沙小島上

妳的眼眸,多麼晶瑩深邃
　彷若一幅碧水錦織的畫
擁有自己靈魂的自由
　在我窗櫺上飛翔

－2024.10.22 寫於臺灣

Spring Flowers in Late Autumn: Reading the poetry collection *Through the Season of Summer* by Vasiliki Dragouni
Lin Ming-Li

Your words are spotlessly bright
　Like the spring flowers in late autumn
In the silent air of Athens
　To bloom again on the island of Formosa

Your eyes are so crystal clear and deep
　Like a painting of embroidered water
With the freedom of your own soul
　Flying on my window sill

- Written in Taiwan on October 22, 2024

137.

長橋 顧於觀

長橋跨通川,明星動川底。
風吹橋上人,雲隨衣帶起。

A Long Bridge Gu Yuguan

A long bridge over a
great river, the surface

of which is surging with
brilliant stars. The watcher

on the bridge is blown
in the wind, when clouds

are born together with
the streaming clothes.

CT273,仲夏寶島號 林明理

夏風吹拂福爾摩沙
吹拂往日聯翩幻想
心卻跟在你前面飛馳
輕輕地牽引我越過山洞
越過無數綠野平疇
越過一甲子時光
像隻自由歡快的黑鳥
盡情飛騰

清詩明理思千載
古今抒情詩三百首
漢英對照

吹著高亢而悠揚的口哨
那麼響亮，最為動聽
是你
威武神奇的身姿
為生命而飛，溫暖而動容
讓我又重溫一次舊夢[133]

CT273, Summer Formosa[134]   Lin Ming-Li

The summer wind blows Formosa
Blowing the past into flights of imagination
Yet the heart flies ahead of you
Gently leading me over the cave
Over boundless green fields

---

[133] 臺灣的台鐵 CT273 仲夏寶島號 Summer Formosa 是蒸汽火車之王，與日本 C57 型車同型，是歷史上不朽的急行火車。台鐵正名為「仲夏寶島號」。當它噴大煙冒白色長龍時，不少鐵道迷跟民眾紛紛拿起照相機、手機，只為捕捉那美麗的復古身影，留下讚嘆不已的珍貴鏡頭與難忘的回憶。2016 年 7 月 2 日黃昏時，CT273 停在鹿野站，令我懷念起國小畢業後離鄉往返於斗六至台北站，父親送別於月台，汽鳴與迴首看到冒白煙的車頭……那熟悉的身姿與搭乘它的美好記憶，因而為詩。

[134] Summer Formosa of CT273 Taiwan Railway, as the king of steam trains, is the same model as the Japanese C57, and it is an immortal express train in history. And Taiwan Railway is officially named Summer Formosa. When it sprays smoke like a white long dragon, many railway fans and the public pick up their cameras and mobile phones to capture the beautiful retro figure, leaving precious shots and unforgettable memories. At the dusk of July 2, 2016, CT273 stops at Luye Station, reminding me of my leaving hometown after graduation from primary school and going back and forth from Douliu to Taipei Station, my father seeing me off on the platform, the noise of the steam and the white smoke in the front of the train... The familiar posture and the fond memory of taking the train. The poem is thus inspired.

Over a little time
Like a free and happy black bird
Flying to your heart's content
Blowing a high and melodious whistle
So loud, and most touching
It is you
Your mighty, wondrous figure
Flying for life, warm and touching
For me to relive the old dream.

❦ ❦ ❦

138 ·

雜詠 　　　　　　　　　　　　　大寧

峰頂屋三間，松邊石一片。
早晚雲飛來，只有樵夫見。

A Random Poem　　　　　　　　Da Ning

Atop the peak there sits
a cottage of three rooms;

by the woods there is a
slate of rock. Between

morning and evening clouds
are flying and fleeting, which

is witnessed exclusively
by the woodcutter.

清詩明理思千載
古今抒情詩三百首
漢英對照

末日地窖　　　　　　　　　　　　　　　　林明理

北極荒野上
那一片巨大冰堤
已消融了……
在繁星下悄然凝立的

幾座石山
和這一片枯林
都側耳傾聽
落葉窸窣的聲響

黑暗裏傳來野鳥
棲落架起的天梯
每朵雲，每顆星
每一個生物
香的花果，樹洞裏的蟲
都哼不出古老的歌謠……

鯨魚
被裂縫中的冰
一塊塊溶解
噴湧出一圈圈
內心的淚

北極熊的天空
變大了許多

望不到岸的
灰藍的淚海裏
只有浪花在沙灘
撿起
一顆與島嶼相連的
蚌殼

The Doomsday Vault
                              Lin Ming-Li

In the Arctic wilderness
The great bank of ice
Has melted...
Standing quietly under the stars

A few rocky mountains
And the dry forest
Are listening attentively
For the rustling of falling leaves

From the darkness comes
The ladder of wild birds
Each cloud, each star
Each creature
Fragrant fruits, insects in the tree holes
Fail to hum the old song...

The whale
Is dissolving
Pieces of ice in the fissure
Spewing out a circle after another circle
Of inner tears

The sky of polar bears
Becomes much bigger

Unseeable is the bank
In the gray-blue sea of tears
Only sprays on the beach
To pick up
A mussel shell
Which connects with the island

❀ ❀ ❀

清詩明理思千載
古今抒情詩三百首
漢英對照

139·

暮春 　　　　　　　　　　　　　　　　　翁格

莫怨春歸早，花餘幾點紅。
留將根蒂在，歲歲有東風。

Late Spring 　　　　　　　　　　　　　Weng Ge

Say not spring dies early:
a few dots of red still

linger. The roots are
retained, waiting to be

budding and bursting
in the coming east wind.

等候黎明 　　　　　　　　　　　　　　林明理

把對岸的屋宇加點光
鐵窗割切成
紙畫

乃至欸乃一聲
方驚醒
今夜月光如利刃
已劃過數不盡的年

風吹散每一聲歎息
都那樣久遠久遠了
是明天，且期待重生
親愛的，妳會來嗎

Waiting for the Dawn Lin Ming-Li

Add some light to the opposite house
And cut its iron window
Into paper drawings

Even a loud sound
Can wake up
Tonight the moonlight is like a sword
Which has cut across countless years

The wind blows away each and every sigh
All so long and so far away
Tomorrow, waiting for rebirth
My dear, will you come

❦ ❦ ❦

140 ·

山中暮歸 張廷玉

林端鴉陣橫，煙外樵歌起。
疲驢緩緩行，斜陽在溪水。

Late Return in the Mountain Zhang Tingyu

Atop the woods lines
of crows are heavy;

beyond the mist wood-
song is arising. A donkey,

travel-worn, is slowly
travelling along a creek

which is brilliant with a
beam of the slanting sun.

阿德湖森林 　　　　　　　　　　　　　　　林明理

三月的雨，悄悄淋落高地。
在新生的風鈴草中，粉腳雁
又要返家了，紅鳶盤旋著，
牧羊人依舊傍著一群小綿羊。
儘管周遭一片荒野苦寒，
一對河鳥仍孵出了牠們的希望。

春天將至，一隻母魚鷹
正凝神孵著待生的鍾愛。
在遙遠的河岸上，水田鼠
得意地躲過了水貂。
此刻，蘇格蘭阿德湖森林
唱歌給我聽了，恰似這場春雨
舞詠在我思念伊的屋簷上。

－2024.11.12

Ade Lake Forest 　　　　　　　　　Lin Ming-Li

The rain of March, quietly drizzle down the highlands.
Among the new-born bluebells, pink-footed geese
Are again returning home, red kites are circling;
A shepherd still sits next to a flock of sheep.
Despite the bitter wilderness around them,
A pair of river birds still hatch their hopes.

When spring is around the corner, a female osprey
Is attentively sitting on her love for life.
On the distant bank of the river, the water vole
Has triumphantly eluded the mink.

Now, the Ade Lake Forest of Scotland
Is singing songs to me, just like the spring rain
Singing and dancing on the eaves of my longing for her.

　　　　　　　　　　　　　－November 12, 2024

141.

偶見　　　　　　　　　　　　　　王文清

雲去山色青，雲住山色白。
去住雲不知，空山自成色。

An Occasional View　　　　Wang Wenqing

Clouds away, the mountains
are blue; clouds stay, the

mountains are white. Away or
stay, the clouds know not where

to linger, when the empty
mountain is the color itself.

燈下讀《田裏爬行的滋味》　　　　林明理

謝謝，你生命的溫情
彷彿曙光下綻開的
百合
在你無瑕的思想裡
慈悲與憐愛贏過一切

清詩明理思千載
古今抒情詩三百首
漢英對照

這是你生命之歌
樸真而堅定
與世長存
我把你的記憶與愛
存於胸中，讓夢想無
限馳騁[135]

余玉照 著
Authored by
Yu Yuzhao

Reading *The Taste of Crawling in the Field* Under the Lamp[136]

Lin Ming-Li

Thank you, the warmth of your life
Is like a lily blossoming
In the light of dawn
In your flawless mind
Mercy and compassion prevail over everything

This is the song of your life
True and firm
And forever
I keep your love and memory
In my bosom, for my dream to be boundlessly flighty

---

[135] 二〇一六年十月二十六日，欣喜於余玉照教授寄贈《田裏爬行的滋味》，深感榮幸；此書除了把作者自幼在農家經歷的事描述得十分感人以外，還能身教言教，讓讀者對農家及食物多分敬意。我深信，他的成功並非偶然，而是一步一耕耘；而在農地裡苦過、打滾過，所衍生的生活智慧，與力爭上游的骨氣，令人敬佩，因而為詩。

[136] On October 26, 2016, professor Yu Yuzhao sent me *The Taste of Crawling in the Field*, which greatly pleases me. Besides describing the author's experience in the farm as a child, the book also teaches readers to respect the farm and food. I am convinced that his success was not by chance, but through his step-by-step efforts. He gains wisdom of life through working hard in the farm, and he strives for better and best, which is admirable. The poem is thus inspired.

🌷🌷🌷

142．

梅花塢坐月　　　　　翁照

靜坐月明中，孤吟破清冷。
隔溪老鶴來，踏碎梅花影。

Admiring the Moon in Plum Blossoms Dock
Weng Zhao

Silent sitting in the bright moon; solitary

crooning to break the pure cold. An old crane

comes from beyond the creek, when the shadow

of plum blossoms is trodden into pieces.

梅花鹿　　　　　林明理

別用深情的雙眸
　注視我
小溪的水聲中
我們分享著細語和
同一夢想
我們分享著牧草和

鹿仔樹苗
邊馳騁，邊聆聽大地的音調[137]

The Sika Deer

Lin Ming-Li

Do not gaze at me
With your affectionate eyes
In the babbling of the stream
We share the whispers
And the same dream
We share the grass
And deer seedlings
While galloping
We listen to the melody of the earth[138]

❁ ❁ ❁

143．

太白樓　　　　　　　　　　　　　　　馬翩飛

黃葉一天秋，青山百尺樓。
樓頭舊明月，夜夜照江流。

---

[137] 臺灣梅花鹿（英文名：Formosan sika deer），為臺灣特有亞種。其野外族群已在 1969 年左右滅絕，目前墾丁公園及綠島的野生族群來自人工復育野放。
[138] Taiwanese deer, English name Formosan sika deer, is a Taiwan-specific subspecies. Its wild ethnic groups have been in extinction around 1969. The current wild population in Kenting Park and the Green Island are from artificial breeding field.

The Tower of Li Bai   Ma Hefei

A skyful of yellow
leaves bespeak the height

of autumn; the blue
mountain faces a tower of

one hundred meters, above
whose eaves an age-old

moon is shining over the river
running from night to night.

緬懷億載金城[139]   林明理

夕陽將至,
老城牆卻益發亮了!

我在夢中把引橋畫在
護河的波上。風咿呀咿呀地
彈唱,
一棵豎著耳朵的苦楝
諦聽稜堡的嘆聲。

我曾到過這裡,──
熟悉的拱門,深濠,
沉默的槍眼、砲臺。

---

[139] 1874 年,日本因琉球漁民遇風漂流至屏東,遭當地原住民殺害,致使日軍出兵侵臺(史稱牡丹社事件,Japanese punitive expedition to Taiwan in 1874);清朝政府指派沈葆楨來臺籌辦加強防務,於是,沈葆楨來臺興建「二鯤鯓砲臺」Erkunshen Fortress,城門四周有護河,並於大門額書「億載金城」Eternal Golden Fort,至此,在臺南鯤鯓 Kunshen 臨海擔負保疆衛土的大任。經臺灣臺南市政府多次整建、保存遺跡,並仿製大砲、小砲,而成今貌。

清詩明理思千載
● 古今抒情詩三百首
　漢英對照，

歷史在盤轉更換……
從臨海綿長海岸到安平港，
以潮汐的力量。

此刻，我不丈量時間，
只願福爾摩沙
永遠向著光明閃耀。

－2024.12.13

In Memory of the Eternal Golden Fort[140]

Lin Ming-Li

The sun is setting;
The old city wall is brightening!

In my dream I draw the bridge
On the waves of the river. The wind is singing and playing,
A neem with upright ears
Listens to the sigh of the bastion.

I have been here before —
Familiar arches, deep walls,
Silent embrasures and batteries.
History is spinning...
From the sea coast to the port of Anping,
With the power of the tides.

---

[140] In 1874, Japanese fishermen from Ryukyu drifted to Pingtung and were killed by local aborigines, resulting in the Japanese punitive expedition to Taiwan in 1874. The Qing Government assigned Shen Baozhen to Taiwan to prepare for strengthening its defense, so Shen came to Taiwan to build Erkunshen Fortress, which was surrounded by a river and inscribed on the front of the gate "Eternal Golden Fort". Tainan Kunshen on the sea to take on the responsibility of protecting the territory and defending the land. After the Tainan City Government of Taiwan has rebuilt and preserved the relics for many times, and imitated cannons and small guns, it finally became what it is today.

Now, I do not measure time,
Only wish Formosa
Always shine through brightness.

　　　　　　　　　—December 13, 2024.

🌷🌷🌷

144・

題畫　　　　　　　　　　　　鄭燮

一節復一節，千枝攢萬葉。
我自不開花，免撩蜂與蝶。

Inscription on a Painting of Bamboos
　　　　　　　　　　　　　Zheng Xie

A section after
another section,

thousands of twigs
heavy with millions

of leaves. They refuse
to blossom, to avoid

the attraction and attention
of bees and butterflies.

鯨之舞　　　　　　　　　　　林明理

一尾座頭鯨
在大海上展放歌喉
二十哩外

清詩明理思千載
● 古今抒情詩三百首
　　漢英對照

一隻母鯨隨著歌聲跳起華爾滋……
寰宇靜寂，
彷彿
只剩這對珍奇的生物，
在一個幸福的國度裡旋舞。

The Dance of Whales　　　　　Lin Ming-Li

A humpback whale
Is singing at the sea
Twenty miles away
A female whale is dancing waltz with the song...
Silence reigns in the world
Seemingly
Only this pair of rare creatures remain,
Waltzing in a country of bliss.

🌷 🌷 🌷

145 ·

田家　　　　　　　　　　　　任瑗

柳陰荷鋤歸，豆莢未出土。
呼兒夜飯牛，昨宵有微雨。

The Farmer　　　　　　　　Ren Yuan

The farmer goes homeward
through the shade of willows

with a hoe on his shoulder,
before the beans sprout

from the earth. He calls
his son to feed the ox in

the night, when the morning
is moist with a slight rainfall.

北門潟湖夕照[141]   林明理

曾經
在井仔腳鹽田,溪口外
有辛勞的曬鹽人

現在出現在潟湖旁
有近二百公頃的蚵田
以平掛式牡蠣養殖
期待今年的豐收

還有操著各種語言
像夢一樣啁啾站著的候鳥
以不斷的努力與勇氣
抵達了這座沙洲

牠們見證了百年來
瓦盤鹽田的興衰
卻也慢慢地習慣
從北方到福爾摩沙
往返遷徙的生活

---

[141] 昔日的臺南北門區係倒風內海急水溪口外的沙洲島,一九二〇年以前此地一直被稱為:「北門嶼」Beimen District。

清詩明理思千載
古今抒情詩三百首
漢英對照,

此時,紅霞映海堤
揮灑出各種自然的面容
讓我不禁笑了,與鳥同飛

－2024.12.13.

Evening Glow Over the Lagoon in the Beimen[142]

Lin Ming-Li

Once
In the Jingzai foot salt field, beyond Xikou
There are hard-working salt makers

Now appearing alongside the lagoon
Nearly 200 hectares of oyster fields
Horizontal oyster farming
In anticipation of this year's harvest

There are also migratory tiptoeing birds
In a variety of languages chirping like a dream
With constant courage and efforts
To reach this sandbank

They have witnessed the rise and fall
Of the salt pans over the centuries
While slowly getting used to
The back-and-forth migration
From the north to Formosa

Now, the red clouds reflecting the sea wall
And a variety of natural faces
For me to laugh in spite of myself, flying with the birds

－December 13, 2024.

---

[142] In the past, the Beimen District of Tainan was Shazhou Island outside the Jishuixi Estuary of the downwind inland sea. Before 1920, it was known as Beimen District.

❁ ❁ ❁

146・

金山寺晚望   郭楷

朝日照河幹,茅屋炊煙起。
時有曬蓑人,依稀紅樹裡。

An Evening View of the Gold Hill Temple
     Guo Kai

The morning sun is shining
over the bed of the river;

the thatched hut is alive
with kitchen smoke.

Now and then there is
a sunner of palm-bark

rain cape, who is dimly
seen through red woods.

東隆宮街景[143]   林明理

在這兒,我感到
寒氣不再滯留

---

[143] 東隆宮主祀溫府千歲,是多數東港人的信仰中心。溫王爺姓溫,名鴻,字德修,東港人慣稱為「王爺公」。東港迎王,俗稱東港燒王船,每三年一科的燒王船,也是臺灣屏東縣極富盛名的宗教盛事與文化祭典。

瞥見的景物為數眾多
陽光如是輕盈
旁人之目不曾冷漠

在喧鬧時刻的伴唱前
我感謝
過去的幸福與自由
我獨自傾聽到
街人滿是歡悅的幽默

The Streetscape of Donglong Temple[144]

Lin Ming-Li

Here, I feel
The cold no longer lingers
A host of scenic spots within a glimpse
The sunlight is so gentle
The eyes of others are not cold

Before the accompaniment of the noisy time
I am thankful
For the past happiness and freedom
Alone I listen to
The street people full of joyful humor

꽃 꽃 꽃

---

[144] The Donglong Temple Lord Wen Fu Chitose is the religious center for most people in Donggang. Prince Wen surnamed Wen, first name Hong, styled Dexiu, and Donggang people used to call him "Prince Gong". Donggang Yingwang, commonly known as Donggang Burning King Ship, every three years a section Burning King Ship, is also a well-known religious event and cultural festival in Pingtung County, Taiwan.

147・

苔 　　　　　　　　　　　　　　　　　袁枚

白日不到處，青春恰自來。
苔花如米小，也學牡丹開。

The Moss 　　　　　　　　　　　　Yuan Mei

When the sun fails
to shine, youth

thrives. The moss,
small like a millet,

opens its blossoms
like the peony.

向科爾沁草原的防護林英雄致敬 　　林明理

曾經，綠茵的草原
　如親臨大海般，——
　都是地沃之地的；
我無法想像：
　那原始的泉河和植被，
無一為茫茫沙地所有。

松林已然消隱，
草場——嚴重退化，
土壤——逐漸鹽化；
屬於科爾沁的，
　除了地域遼闊，
只有營造防護林的英雄
　不願意離開。

清詩明理思千載
● 古今抒情詩三百首
　　漢英對照,

他們無懼地凝視未來，
　　用雙手繼續造夢，
從春夏到秋冬，
　　只盼將來，
當水草豐茂時，
吹拂而過的還是那一清風。

Homage to the Heroes of Horqin Grassland Shelterbelt
Lin Ming-Li

Once, the green grassland
　Was like the sea —
　　The land of the earth;
It is beyond my imagination:
　The original spring river and vegetation
Were not owned by the vast sand.

Pine forests have disappeared,
The grassland — severely degraded,
The soil — gradually salinized;
Belonging to Horqin,
　In addition to the vast territory,
Only the heroes who create shelterbelts
　Are reluctant to leave.

They fearlessly stare into the future,
　　With their hands to continue to dream,
From spring and summer to autumn and winter,
　　Only expecting the future,
When the water and grass are abundant,
What is blowing is still the breeze.

⚘ ⚘ ⚘

148.

十二月十五夜　　　　　　　　　　袁枚

沉沉更鼓急，漸漸人聲絕。
吹燈窗更明，月照一天雪。

On the Night of December 15th　　Yuan Mei

The night watches are
sounding dimly from

afar, when gradually
human whispers die out.

The lamp blown out,
the window is brighter

— a skyful of snow
is lit by the moon.

沉浸在此刻　　　　　　　　　　林明理

1.
這義大利之脊
從小鎮蜿蜒到山谷
　從火山到大角峰
日日夜夜
　以挺拔姿態
加上米開朗基羅的大衛像
　引我遐思

2.
飛越山脈

一座聖母百花大教堂
在黎明的靜默中
　　似晴光下的鐘樓開啟
迴響著昔日的榮耀

3.
晨霧消散了
我從雲端上城堡
　　看呀看，一樣的牧羊人
或行走
　　或趕著到低地過冬
幾隻牧羊犬，不多也不少
　　保護賴以維生的羊群
跟數百年前一樣
　　未曾被打擾

4.
我所記得的梵蒂岡
　　像深林中一株野百合
又像誕生於傳說和烈火
　　莊嚴的聖鳥
它的目光澄亮
它的樣子更沉靜自由

　　　　　　　　　　　　　－2024.10.30

Immersed in the Moment　　　　Lin Ming-Li

1.
The ridge of Italy
Winding its way from a small town to a mountain valley
　　From volcano to Grand Horn Peak

Day and night
   With its upright posture
And Michelangelo's Davy image
   Which capture my imagination

2.
Flying over the mountain
   A cathedral of Our Lady of Flowers
In the silence of dawn
   Opens like a bell tower in the clear light
Echoing with the past glory

3.
The morning mist has lifted
I look up from the clouds over the castle
   And keep gazing, the same shepherd
Walking
   Or going in haste to lowland for the winter
A few sheepdogs, no more or no less
   Protective of the sheep for life
As undisturbed as they
   Have been hundreds of years ago

4.
The Vatican as I remember it
   Like a wild lily in the forest
And like a sacred bird born
   Of legend and fire
Its sight is bright
Its look is more free and serene

                            —October 30, 2024.

⚘ ⚘ ⚘

清詩明理思千載
古今抒情詩三百首
漢英對照

149.

吳中竹枝詞　　　　　　　　徐士鉉

陰晴不定是黃梅，暑氣薰蒸潤綠苔。
瓷甕竟裝天雨水，烹茶時候客初來。

A Bamboo Song　　　　　Xu Shixuan

In rainy season of broken
weather with yellow

plums, the heat is steaming
to nurture green moss.

The porcelain jar contains
water as rain from heaven,

when tea is prepared upon
the arriving of a visitor.

雨，落在愛河的冬夜　　　　林明理

雨，落在愛河的冬夜
數艘白色小船上
在這多雨的港都，彩燈覆蔭下
獨自發送著溫顏

剎時，母親之河
廣大而平實
在那兒牽著勞動者的手
像從前，端視著我

啊，雨，落在愛河的冬夜
一隻夜鴉低微地呻吟

在這昏黃的岸畔，群山靜聆中
何處安置我僅存的夢？

哭吧，我以感動之淚
接受雨，和恩典
聽吧，時間的小馬上
我是永恆的騎士，覓尋黎明的歌者

是的，收起遊蕩的翅膀
那生命的薔薇早已關上了門
不再憂鬱地望著我，只有躲在冷黑中的風
任遊子潤濕了瞳孔

Raindrops, Dropping on the Winter Night of Love
Lin Ming-Li

Raindrops, dropping on the winter night of love
On several white boats
In this rainy harbor, under the shade of colorful lights
Alone to send warmth

In an instant, the river of mother
Is wide and plain
Holding the hand of the laborer
As before, close looking at me

Oh raindrops, dropping on the winter night of love
A night owl is groaning low
On the yellow bank, among silent hills,
Where to place my last dream?

Weep, I receive rain
And grace with tears
Listen, on the little horse of time
I am an eternal knight, a singer in search of light

清詩明理思千載
古今抒情詩三百首
漢英對照

Yes, withdraw the wandering wings
The rose of life has closed the door
No longer look at me melancholy, only the wind in the cold black
Has moistened the eyes of the wanderer

🌷 🌷 🌷

150 ·

雨過 　　　　　　　　　　　　　　　　　　袁枚

雨過山洗容，雲來山入夢。
雲雨自往來，青山原不動。

After a Rain 　　　　　　　　　　　　　Yuan Mei

After a rain the
mountain is freshly

clean; with clouds
the mountain is dreamy.

The rain and clouds
come and go as they like,

the blue mountain always
remains and stays.

雨中的綠意 　　　　　　　　　　　　　　林明理

春在枝頭
雨輕盈地沾滿我的衣袖

雨呀如果你在海上
請跳到我的船兒
它是被風偷走的
我的翅膀
你可要小心輕航
用採擷來的紫丁香
朝遠遠的天邊飄去，飄去……
像一隻蝶
飛回
這夜的赭紅的溪水

我的心撥弄的詩琴
跟著徜徉在酒綠的河岸

任時間緩緩
停泊在那個雨意加深的午后
我的影子
在風裡追逐
是搖晃在雲層的隴頭雲
還是落葉是鳴蟲
低微地描繪
你的微笑和眼睛

春在枝頭
雨輕盈地沾滿我的衣袖

Green in the Rain   Lin Ming-Li

Spring on the branches
The rain lightly fills my sleeves

Oh rain, if you are at the sea
Please jump into my ship

清詩明理思千載
● 古今抒情詩三百首
　漢英對照,

It was stolen by the wind
My wings
Remember to sail carefully
With the plucked lilacs
To be floating, away to the distant horizon…
Like a butterfly
Flying back
To the red stream of the night

The poetic lute of my heart
Follows the banks of the wine-green river

Let time be slow
Mooring in that rainy afternoon
My shadow
Chasing in the wind
Is the clouds drifting in layers of clouds
Fallen leaves or chirping insects
To faintly describe
Your smile and eyes

Spring on the branches
The rain lightly fills my sleeves

附錄
Appendix

細讀張智中的一本書
Close Reading of a Book by Zhang Zhizhong

◎文／圖：林明理

Article and painting by Lin Ming-Li

　　長年以來致力於中國詩詞的翻譯與教學的張智中教授，已出版編、譯、著一百二十餘部，並獲翻譯與科研獎項等多種，是廣受海峽兩岸好評的翻譯家。智中是土生土長的河南博愛人，是農民的兒子，因而熱愛詩詞的他始終懷有鄉土情懷；目前是天津市南開大學外國語學院教授、博士研究生導師，已將漢詩英譯提高到英詩的高度，也保有一顆赤子之心的審美情愫。

　　日前閱讀了智中寄來的一本早期的著作《毛澤東詩詞英譯比較研究》。全書體現的主要特點有：一是詩歌形式和翻譯策略的創新性，既有不拘其形，散文筆法，也有詩意內容，讀者盡可以遐想。二是將修辭格與意象、文化因素結合，並採取多樣的詩詞翻譯版本進行比較研究，大量考據，是他在更廣泛翻譯研究上的一種嚴謹的學習態度與其力圖通過史料勾勒出翻譯詩詞美學的情感概括。三是詩詞翻譯傳神的體悟與為詩作添增了思想深度。在大量的翻譯詩中，也包孕智中對詩詞創作的追求，確是此書的一大特色。

　　印象中，在近年來中國大陸的英譯詩詞發展上，鮮少有人像張智中一樣，時刻努力以赴，在英譯古詩的審美心理結構上產生如此傳神的翻譯風格；並能夠超脫世俗，靜觀自在。我還記得有首《五古・詠指甲花》詩云：「百花皆競春，指甲

清詩明理思千載
● 古今抒情詩三百首
漢英對照，

獨靜眠。／春季葉始生，炎夏花正鮮。／葉小枝又弱，種類多且妍。／萬草被日出，惟婢傲火天。／淵明獨愛菊，敦頤好青蓮。／我獨愛指甲，取其志更堅。」揭示了毛澤東偏愛枝葉弱小，卻能頑強生長的鳳仙花（亦稱：指甲花），顯見他在少年時代就含有深邃的思想及藝術表現。

但最令我感動的是，文本的最後一頁，張智中為此書寫了一首詩：

晴川一片消遙游，芳草常青伴左右。
日出學海何處帆，烟波江上我不愁。

詩情濃郁，能彰顯張智中熱切求知、奮進的精神，也把持著與師長、同學在校園裡相守互勉的感懷，並多了點詩人為教育獻身的崇高感。

在我所認識的教師之中，智中是位對漢詩英譯與教學深深關注的學者。就像俄國大作家陀思妥耶夫斯基認為，意志力可以帶給我們能力、機智和知識。智中也是帶有堅強意志的詩人，他已通過生命的淬鍊，又以謙遜、博學的面貌呈現於廣大讀者面前。對我來說，他是一位可敬的友人，而其詩作也有一種自然之美，恰如日出的晨光，有著一種清新內斂的沉穩度，遂成為全書之中最獨特的音響。

2024.09.08 寫於清晨
——刊臺灣《更生日報》Keng Sheng Daily News（KSDN），副刊，2024 年 12 月 21 日，及畫作 3 幅。

Professor Zhang Zhizhong, who has been devoted to the translation and teaching of Chinese poetry for years, has published over 120 books, and has won a host of translation and research awards. He is widely praised by both sides of the Taiwan Straits. Zhizhong is a native of Henan Province, the son of farmers, so he loves poetry with local feelings. At present, he is a professor in the School of Foreign Studies of Nankai University, Tianjin, and is supervisor of doctoral students. He has raised the English translation of Chinese poetry to the height of English poetry, while retaining a childlike aesthetic feeling.

Recently I have finished reading a book entitled *A Comparative Study of the English Translations of Mao Zedong Poems* by Zhang. The main features of the book are as follows: First, it is innovative in poetic form and translation strategy, with both unrestrained forms, prose style and poetic content. Second, he combines figures of speech with images and cultural factors, and adopts a variety of translated versions of poems for comparative study. His extensive research is a rigorous learning attitude in broader translation studies and his attempt to outline the emotional summary of translated poetry aesthetics through historical materials. The third is the understanding of poetry translation and the depth of thought added to the poetry. In a large number of translated poems, there is also his pursuit of poetry creation, which is indeed a major feature of this book.

In my impression, it is rare thing, in the history of English translation of ancient Chinese poems in China, for Zhang Zhizhong to be constantly painstaking, so much so that he produces vivid and expressive translations in the light of C-E poetry translation aesthetics, while remaining detached from the unquiet world. I still remember a poem by Mao Zedong which entitled *Ode to Camphire Flowers*:

> A hundred flowers vie for the beauty of spring,
> when the camphire flower is asleep in quietude.
> In spring it begins to be alive with tender leaves;
> the height of summer sees the height of flowering.
> Small leaves on tender twigs, a variety of them
> with a variety of beauties. Myriads of grasses are
> bathed in sunshine — only the camphire flower
> is heat-proof. Tao Yuanming, a poet-recluse, loves
> chrysanthemums; Zhou Dunyi is a writer famous

for his *Love of Lotus Flowers*; as for me, I singularly love the camphire flower, which distinguishes itself for its will which is strong, stubborn, and unyielding.

The poem exhibits Mao Zedong's love of the camphire flower which is fragile and stubborn, as well as his profound thought expressed in artistic pieces in his childhood.

But what touches me most is a poem by him on the last page of the book:

In a stretch of boundless sunny land I roam in leisure:
green grass is lush here, and fair there. Sunrise, an
academic sail is sailing at the limitless sea — where?
Facing misty water and waves, I'm free from any worry.

The poem is rich in poetry, fully revealing Zhang Zhizhong's unslackening spirit in seeking knowledge and forging ahead, the feeling of mutual encouragement between teachers and students on the campus, as well as a sense of loftiness concerning the poet's dedication to education and translation.

Among all the teachers I know, Zhang Zhizhong is a scholar who is deeply concerned about the teaching and translation of classical Chinese poetry into English. As the great Russian writer Fyodor Dostoyevsky believed, the willpower can bring us power, wit and knowledge. Zhizhong is also a poet with a strong will. He has been through the tempering of life before presenting himself to the readers with a humble and knowledgeable appearance. To me, he is a respectable friend, and his poems have a natural beauty, like the morning light of sunrise, with a fresh, introspective calmness that produces a most unique sound.

Written in the morning of September 8, 2024.
Carried on the Supplement of *Keng Sheng Daily News* (KSDN)
in Taiwan, December 21, 2024.

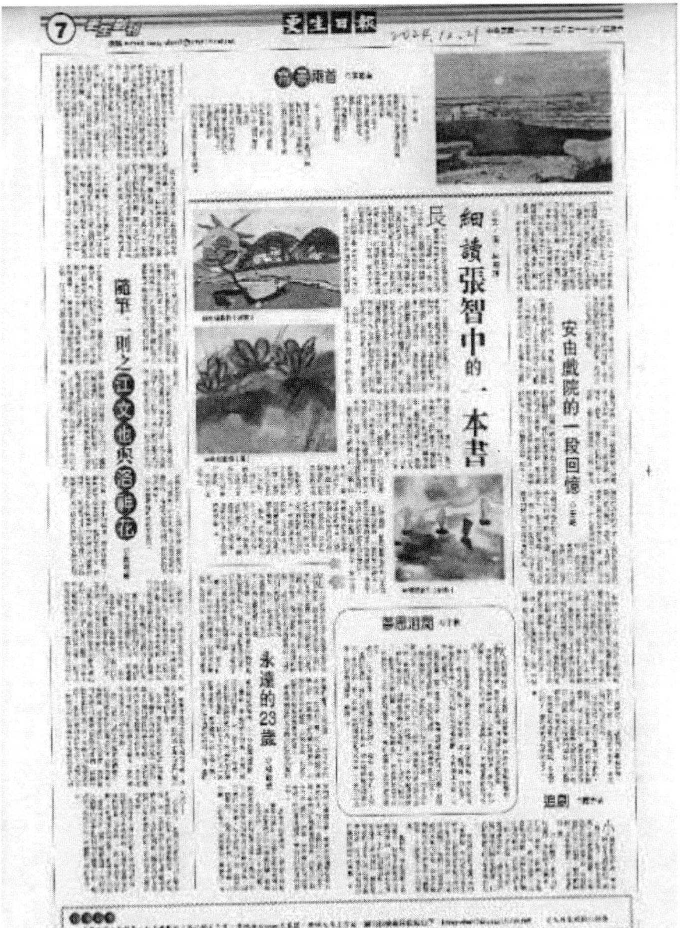
7
更生日報
細讀張智中的一本書
安由戲院的一段回憶
隨筆二則之江文也與洛神花
永遠的23歲
追劇

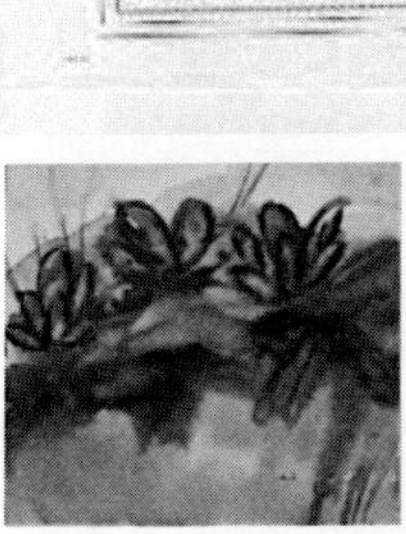

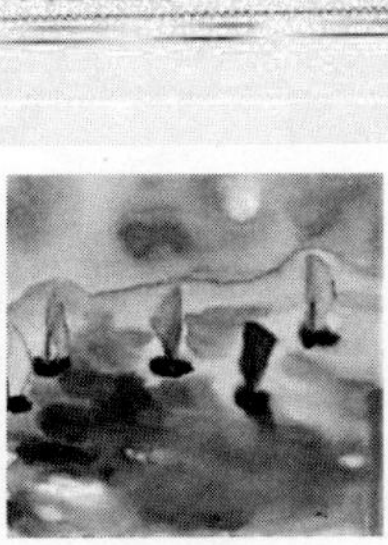

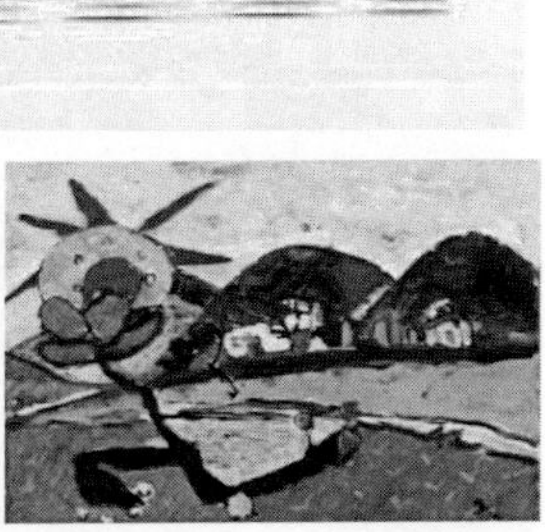

國家圖書館出版品預行編目資料

清詩明理思千載——古今抒情詩三百首（漢英對照）/
林明理　著、張智中　譯　－初版－
臺中市：天空數位圖書　2025.01
面：14.8*21 公分
ISBN：978-626-7576-08-3（平裝）
831.7
114000181

書　　　名：清詩明理思千載——古今抒情詩三百首（漢英對照）
發 行 人：蔡輝振
出 版 者：天空數位圖書有限公司
作　　者：林明理
譯　　者：張智中
美工設計：設計組
版面編輯：採編組
出版日期：2025 年 1 月（初版）
銀行名稱：合作金庫銀行南台中分行
銀行帳戶：天空數位圖書有限公司
銀行帳號：006—1070717811498
郵政帳戶：天空數位圖書有限公司
劃撥帳號：22670142
定　　價：新台幣 530 元整
電子書發明專利第　I　306564　號
※如有缺頁、破損等請寄回更換

版權所有請勿仿製

服務項目：個人著作、學位論文、學報期刊等出版印刷及DVD製作
影片拍攝、網站建置與代管、系統資料庫設計、個人企業形象包裝與行銷
影音教學與技能檢定系統建置、多媒體設計、電子書製作及客製化等
TEL　：(04)22623893
FAX　：(04)22623863　MOB：0900602919
E-mail：familysky@familysky.com.tw
Https://www.familysky.com.tw/
地　　址：台中市南區忠明南路 787 號 30 樓國王大樓
No.787-30, Zhongming S. Rd., South District, Taichung City 402, Taiwan (R.O.C.)